ANGEL

THE CAMBOY NETWORK
BOOK 3

LINDEN BELL

Copyright © 2024 by Linden Bell

Paperback ISBN: 978-1-7390763-5-1

All rights reserved.

No part of this book may be reproduced in any form or by any electronic or mechanical means, including information storage and retrieval systems, without written permission from the author, except for the use of brief quotations in a book review.

Cover Designer: Cate Ashwood

Editor: Helle Hansen

Content Warning: explicit sexual content, alcohol consumption (casual drinking during party), cum play, role-play while filming porn, shoe and foot fetish, mentions of homophobia and non-acceptance from friends and family.

 Created with Vellum

ANGEL

ANGEL

He was only supposed to be gay for pay.

ANGEL

I've never had sex before. And I've definitely never looked at a guy that way before. But with his brightly-colored hair and beautiful outfits, Rhys is hard to ignore--especially after I learn what he does for a living.

Signing up with The Camboy Network is way outside my comfort zone, but with Rhys guiding me the whole way, it doesn't feel all that scary. In fact, it feels like fate.

RHYS

I left home the minute I turned eighteen, so falling for a guy from the old neighborhood is the last thing I should do--especially since he's straight. But he's utterly adorable, so innocently kinky, and exactly my type.

We shouldn't fit together so well, but we do. No matter how hard I try to stay away, I can't. Our lives couldn't be more different on the outside, but maybe we're a lot more alike than we think.

Angel is a gay-awakening, opposites attract, size difference MM romance between a burly cinnamon roll construction worker and a flamboyant pole-dancing twink. Expect accidentally dirty text messages, completely unexpected kinks, and chivalrous courage that truly runs deep. Angel is the third book in The Camboy Network series, but can be read as a stand-alone.

CONTENTS

CHAPTER
ONE

RHYS

Stepping off the subway in Staten Island always feels like I've walked through the looking glass. On this side, I'm not Rhys Rawlings, pole dancer and camboy extraordinaire. Instead, I regress to Ricky Gallo, the scrawny, flamboyant gay boy from down the street.

I've even dressed the part. Jeans—ugh. And a t-shirt—double ugh. At least the jeans hug my ass like a second skin and my t-shirt sports a cute rainbow unicorn. Not that I expect anyone from the old neighborhood to appreciate the 'fit. The people I grew up with aren't the most... trendy.

I hightailed it out of here the first chance I got and I only come back when absolutely necessary. Like for Dad's sixtieth birthday party.

I was tempted not to come. It's not like anyone will really miss me anyway.

I don't remember the last time I had a real conversation with my dad, and my mom only calls when she needs something from me. My brother, Nico, and I get along pretty well, but he's always busy with his wife and kids. They have their own lives here that I'm not really a part of. And I haven't kept in touch with anyone else in the old neighborhood. There's never been any reason to.

It's about a twenty-minute walk from the subway station to the house where I grew up. Nico offered to come pick me up, but I need the extra time to psych myself up for the party.

I can hear it from a block away. Music floats over yards and rooftops. Voices mix with barks of laughter and parents shouting at kids. It sounds like the entire neighborhood's turned out for the big event. I wouldn't be surprised. The Gallos have been a part of this tight-knit community for generations.

I stop right before turning the corner onto my parents' street, gripping the strap of my crossbody bag tightly.

I can do this. I can totally do this. It's only for a couple hours. Just grin and bear it—like I'm performing on stage or on camera. Then I can escape back to Brooklyn and my real life.

I suck in a deep breath and turn the corner. The party sounds are about ten times louder. Cars line both sides of the small residential street, and people spill out the front door onto the driveway and lawn. I was wrong—they didn't just invite the entire neighborhood, they've invited the entire freaking city.

"Hey, little Ricky!" Someone shouts my name when I'm still three houses away.

I can't tell who it is, but I recognize the group of men standing in the middle of the driveway. They're my brother's friends, guys we both grew up with, all a few years older than me.

"Hey." I greet them with a wave, then brace myself as I'm dragged into their circle and passed around for hugs. It's not the way most people like me would've been greeted by people like them. But I'm lucky. Nico's always been protective of me, and so, by extension, have all of his friends. It's the only reason I didn't get bullied growing up —it helps having the entire football team watching your back.

Although, I've always wondered if they see me less as Nico's kid brother and more like a defenseless little pet. The way they toss me around and pat me on the head makes me think it's probably the latter.

"How you doing, Ricky?"

"Hey, welcome home, kid."

"Good to see ya, it's been a while."

"Good to see you guys, too." I can't help laughing at their enthusiasm.

They're good guys, even if I've never had a single thing in common with them. Even if they'd have a collective heart attack if they found out what I do for a living. I might not like coming home much, but I have to admit this warm greeting is nice.

I've worked my way through their makeshift obstacle course when someone says, "Nico and your parents are in the back."

"Thanks!" I venture inside. What are the chances I can sneak through the house and find my parents without getting stopped by some auntie or uncle? Absolutely zero.

"Ricky!"

"Look at you! Oh my lord, you're all grown up now!"

"Cute shirt!"

"Whatcha up to these days?"

"What the hell is he wearing?"

"You need to visit your ma and pa more often."

"Dina! Ricky's here!"

I'm shuffled along with random hands picking at my clothes, my hair, my cheeks. Arms pulling me into hugs and heavy slaps on the back.

Listen, I'm a pretty tactile person. I'm used to people getting handsy with me—I have to be, considering I'm a camboy and I moonlight as a pole dancer at a nightclub. But I don't get a quarter of this attention when I'm strutting around in my g-string at The Bronzed Rail.

By the time they spit me out on the other side of the living room, I need a minute to put myself back together.

Mom's in the kitchen, directing an army of neighborhood women. She turns when I stumble in and marches over to me.

"Did you eat yet?" she asks, as she pulls me into a short, but bone-crushing hug.

"Not yet," I manage to choke out.

"There's food in the backyard." Then she pulls back, holding me at arm's length, and I can feel her laser-like gaze scanning me from head to toe.

She narrows her eyes. "What did you do to your hair?"

I reach up to pat the messy bun that took me half an hour to get just right. It's probably actually messy now, rather than merely artfully tousled. "What about it?"

She plants her hands on her hips. "It's purple."

"Just barely," I mutter. It's a very dark purple. Dark enough that if you don't look too closely, it could pass as my natural black. She's lucky I didn't come with the bright pink I had last week.

Mom shakes her head disapprovingly. "Dyeing your hair will make it fall out faster."

Not the first time she's said that to me. Apparently, it's a little-known science fact that only applies to me. It certainly doesn't apply to her, since she's been dyeing her hair for decades to cover the gray, and yet, she still has a full head of the stuff. It also doesn't apply to Dad, who's never dyed his hair because, well, he doesn't have any.

"Okay, Mom. Sure." There's no point in arguing with her. Grin and bear it, remember?

She gives my shirt a skeptical look, and I brace myself for whatever disapproving comment she's about to throw at me next. But surprisingly, she just nods toward the back door. "Dad's out there. Go wish him a happy birthday."

She dismisses me then, turning back to her army of cooks. I slip out with a sigh.

One down, one to go.

It's not hard to find Dad in the backyard. His voice booms over the din of conversation as he holds court. I recognize the story he's telling. It's the one about him "being kidnapped" when he was a kid. Spoiler alert: he wasn't kidnapped. He wandered away from the playground and none of the adults noticed he was missing until hours later when a police officer brought him home.

But his hands are waving in the air and his facial expressions are more animated than the characters on a children's TV show. His audience is rapt, listening to him like he's a king sitting on a throne rather than an attention hog sitting on a lawn chair. Dad's never happy unless all eyes are on him, so it looks like the party is going well.

And I guess I know where I get my performance tendencies from.

I wander to the drinks table to survey the meager offerings. Beer—Coors and Coors Light. None of that artsy microbrewery stuff my roommate, Hayden, likes to drink. A bowl of punch for the kids and… ah, there we go! Wine coolers to the rescue.

I crack open a can and wait for Dad to finish his story. I've heard it so many times, I could probably recite it word for word. "They had no idea! Can ya believe it?!"

"Yeah, I can believe it," I mutter under my breath, then take a drink. I'm mid-swallow when an arm swings over my shoulders and drags me backward. Fruity alcohol goes spraying out of my mouth and a little goes up my nose. Ow.

"Oh shit, sorry, kiddo. You okay?" My super great, really amazing, totally-not-trying-to-kill-me big brother smacks me hard on the back.

I nod frantically. "Mmhmm, yep, all good," I squeak.

Nico laughs. "Didn't mean to scare you."

"You didn't. I just…" I wave my hand around, dismissively. "Never mind."

"I wasn't sure you'd come today," Nico says, voice lowered.

I shrug. "Mom didn't give me much choice."

Nico snorts. "Since when do you do what they tell you?"

I huff quietly. It's true. I might have a teeny tiny rebellious streak that makes me want to do exactly the opposite of whatever someone tells me to do. That whole reverse-psychology thing? Totally works on me.

"Anyway," Nico says, pulling me into a tight one-armed hug. "I'm glad you're here. I know Mom and Dad are too. Even if they don't say so."

I know he's right. My parents love me. They just don't understand me. Nico's always been the golden child. Smart, athletic, a real man's man. He married his high school sweetheart and they bought a house three blocks away.

But me? I've always been different. More interested in dolls than trucks. Wanted to play with makeup rather than sports. I grew my hair long in high school and started wearing "girls' clothing". My parents never forbade any of it, but they definitely disapproved.

"Have you said hi to Dad yet?" Nico asks.

"Not yet. Didn't want to interrupt his story."

Nico chuckles. "The one about getting kidnapped?"

I roll my eyes.

"Now might be a good time." He nods toward Dad.

Sure enough, Dad's standing with our old neighbor from across the street. The rest of his audience has dispersed.

I leave Nico by the drinks table and approach. Dad spots me as I draw closer and his friendly, life-of-the-party expression becomes shuttered. I sigh and force myself to smile.

"Hey, Dad. Happy birthday." I give him a hug, but unlike the one I shared with Mom or with Nico, this one is stiff and awkward. We barely get our arms around each other for a split second before we both back off again.

"Thanks, Son."

I bristle. Not because I'm not his son—I am. But because he says it like he's trying to remind me that I'm a boy, not a girl. And *I know* I'm a boy. Keeping my hair long and wearing makeup and dresses doesn't make me any less of a boy. It just makes me a boy who likes long hair, makeup, and dresses, damn it.

My smile might tighten around the edges, but like him, I'm a performer at heart, so the smile doesn't slip an inch.

"Having a good time?" I ask.

"Yeah, it was nice of everyone to come out."

I nod and silence fills the dead air between us. Neither of us know what to say to each other. We never have.

"You're gonna stay for the cake, right?" he asks, finally.

"Uh…" I scramble for an excuse, but he beats me to it.

"Your Ma spent all week baking it."

Which means that if I leave before the cake is unveiled, I'll be the disrespectful, ungrateful son who couldn't be bothered to have a slice of his mom's cake. Wonderful. I tamp down my irritation.

"Yeah, of course I'll stay."

"Good." Dad nods, then turns away. "Hey, Bobby!"

I've been dismissed. Thank fucking god. With my can of wine cooler, I manage to sneak back inside and up the stairs without anyone seeing me or stopping me. I don't let myself breathe until I'm back in my childhood bedroom, slumped down on the bed.

The room still looks the way it did when I was a teenager, and I'm not really sure why. The walls are plastered with posters of hot dudes—baseball players with their tight pants, Olympic divers in nothing but a speedo, a bunch of Australian firefighters posing with kittens. The bedspread is bright pink, with ruffles. The curtains are tied back with mini feather boas.

I would've expected Mom to strip the room down to

the studs and redecorate, but nope, everything is exactly as I left it when I moved out. Weird.

I grab my phone. There's a message from Hayden, who is my best friend in addition to being my roommate. It asks how things are going. And a second message from another good friend, Sebastian, asking me if I'm alright. I smile.

Moving away from home when I was eighteen was one of the scariest things I've ever done. I only moved from Staten Island to Brooklyn, but it felt like a world away. I didn't know what I was going to do with my life or how I would survive. I only knew I had to get out of this neighborhood.

Turns out, it was the best decision I've ever made.

CHAPTER
TWO

ANGEL

The guys are talking baseball, but I stopped paying attention the minute Ricky showed up. Or more like sauntered up. I haven't seen the guy since… I don't know. It's probably been years by now.

I was on the high school football team with his brother, Nico, so I used to see Ricky around all the time. But then I graduated and started working full-time, and he moved out to Brooklyn a couple years later. He doesn't come back often, I don't think. Or maybe our paths just haven't crossed.

He's wearing a pair of black jeans that look like they're painted onto his legs. His t-shirt is just as tight, showing off his lithe, toned body. And I swear I can see the outline of his nipples on either side of the rainbow unicorn on his chest. His hair is pulled back and up, leaving his long, elegant neck exposed. His boots have these super-thick soles, giving him a couple extra inches in height.

I think he's wearing makeup? His eyes look darker and more... I don't know, smoky or something?

He laughs as the guys say their hellos and his lips glisten when he smiles wide. I hang back. I don't know him as well as the other guys and they're all over him already. He doesn't need my paws getting into his personal space too.

But once he disappears into the house, the image of him stays with me. He looks so... happy? No, it's more than that. He looks confident, sure of himself, poised. He dazzles. Like a movie star who shines too bright for a simple suburban neighborhood like ours.

He was always like that, even when we were kids. He was never a part of the cool crowd, but as Nico's little brother, he didn't get picked on by the cool kids either. He wasn't a nerd, wasn't artsy. He didn't fit into any of the clearly defined groups that divided us as kids. He's always just been Ricky.

I've always found that brave. I admired it. He knew he wasn't like everyone else and he didn't bother hiding it. That's not an easy thing to do around here, where all the families know each other and gossip travels faster than wildfire. Where people aren't afraid of voicing their opinions, and judgment comes down hard and heavy without a second thought.

It's no wonder he left as soon as he was old enough. It's no wonder he rarely comes home. This place is too small for someone like him.

"Who wants another round?" Mario asks, holding up his empty beer bottle.

He's one of the guys I'm closest to in the group, and we

also work for the same construction company, building condos and office towers in Manhattan.

I snatch the bottle from him. "I'll grab it."

The guys pile their bottles in my arms, and I head inside to dump them in the kitchen. Just as I'm tossing the last one into a clear trash bag, someone steps in from the backyard, slips past me, and disappears up the stairs.

Was that Ricky?

I poke my head into the stairwell just in time to see the heel of a black boot vanish around the corner. My foot is on the first step before I can stop myself.

What am I doing? Am I trying to follow him upstairs? To do what? Say hello?

I don't even know Ricky that well. We're not really friends, barely acquaintances. I doubt he remembers me from when we were younger. Nico was a popular guy, and I've always stayed at the edge of the crowd.

Ricky's probably just grabbing something and coming right back down. There's no reason for me to go up there. And yet, my foot doesn't come off the bottom step.

A few moments pass and there are no sounds coming from the second floor. No footsteps or creaking floorboards. No Ricky jogging down the stairs.

My other foot lands on the second step.

Seriously. What am I doing? If I wanted to say hello, I should've done it earlier when we were in the driveway like a normal person. I'm being creepy. He probably wants to be alone. Maybe something happened, someone said something, and he needs a minute to himself. I know what that's like.

I take another step and the tread groans under my

weight. No one seems to notice, though—not from upstairs or from downstairs. I keep going.

This is ridiculous. He's going to think I'm stalking him. I'm a big dude, and people who don't know me think I'm intimidating. I don't want to scare him. But I don't stop.

I've never had a chance to come up here before. Back in high school, Nico's room was in the basement and the team hung out down there sometimes. But all the houses in the neighborhood were built at the same time and have pretty much the same layout.

The primary bedroom is at the end of the hall. Two more bedrooms on the left and a bathroom on the right. It's not difficult to figure out where Ricky is.

I stop short in the doorway of the second bedroom. Ricky's sitting on the bed, legs crossed at the knees, drink in one hand, cell phone in the other. He doesn't notice I'm there.

I clear my throat, not sure how else to let him know he's not alone.

He snaps his head around. The initial shock, tinged with a hint of fear, quickly morphs into a frown.

"Sorry!" I say, holding my hands up. "I didn't mean to intrude."

Except, I totally did. Why else did I come up here all by myself, uninvited and unannounced?

"That's okay," Ricky says. His voice is soft, lyrical, almost like he's singing. He cocks his head to the side. "You're… Angel, right?"

He remembers my name. My ears warm as they flush pink. Why does he remember my name? "Yeah, I'm friends with your brother."

Ricky nods. "The football team."

"Yeah." I lift a hand to my jaw, fingers scratching the short hairs of my beard. It's a nervous habit I have. Because suddenly, I'm super nervous. My tummy feels all strange and unsettled. My palms are a little clammy. I shift back and forth on my feet. Why did I come up here again?

Ricky studies me, examines me, cataloging everything from the top of my head to the soles of my feet. Then his lips twitch. "You just gonna stand there, big boy? Or you gonna come in?"

My ears burst into flames, and my tummy does a flip-flop thing that's never happened before. A part of me wants to dash back downstairs and race outside to where the guys are waiting for their beers.

But another part of me wants to stay. I don't know why. This is weird and strange and… my feet carry me forward of their own accord.

When Ricky pats the bed next to him, I sit down, feeling a little too bulky and rough for the frilly, pink covers under me. Ricky shifts, folding one knee on the mattress so he can sit sideways, facing my direction. I flatten my palms against my thighs, not sure what else I'm supposed to do with them.

His gaze is warm and weighty on the side of my face as he watches me. I can't bring myself to return it. Instead, I glance around the room.

It looks like a teenage girl lives here. But since Nico and Ricky don't have a sister, I assume the room belonged to Ricky when he was still living at home.

"This is, um, nice."

Out of the corner of my eye, I spy Ricky arching one elegant eyebrow. He looks like he's trying to suppress a smile. "You think so?"

Not really. "Yeah, um, it's very… pink."

He snickers and his smile widens, and in spite of the funny feelings he elicits in me, I turn to watch. His eyes are a deep brown, framed by long, dark lashes. There's a slight blush across the tops of his cheekbones. His lips are pink and shiny.

I've never seen a guy with makeup on before. Not unless they're an actor or something. The idea sounds odd to me—why would a guy want to wear makeup? But seeing Ricky made up like this, it actually looks really cool. His eyes are so dramatic. His lips look so plump and soft. I can't stop staring.

"My teenage self thanks you."

"Huh?" His what? Oh. The room. Right.

Ricky laughs and the sound skips along my skin, leaving a trail of goose bumps in its wake.

"Has anyone ever told you you're cute?"

The burn on my ears spreads to my cheeks. I duck my chin and scratch my jaw, trying to hide the flush. I don't know why I'm blushing so hard, or why my skin is tingling, or why my tummy feels all fluttery. Heck, I don't even know why I'm up here in the first place.

These feelings are so foreign, so unfamiliar. But I think I like them.

"So, um, how come you're not downstairs with everyone else?" I ask when a beat passes in silence.

Ricky's smile fades a bit, and I immediately regret asking.

I hurry to apologize. "Sorry, you don't have to answer if you don't want."

Ricky shakes his head and sighs. "No, it's fine. To be honest, I wish I could've skipped the party altogether."

My brow furrows in confusion as my gut objects to the suggestion. "But it's your dad's sixtieth birthday," I say, as if that's the reason why I think he needs to be here, and not because I'm kind of enjoying sitting on this bed with him.

"Yeah, I know. It's just..." He shrugs and picks at a loose thread on his jeans. There are traces of color on his fingernails, like he tried to remove nail polish but couldn't get it all off. "Things are always weird with my parents."

I shift, angling myself toward him a little more. I don't like how subdued he's suddenly become. I want to see that smile of his again. "What do you mean?"

He doesn't answer for a moment, instead peeking up at me through his lashes. My breath hitches in my chest, and the fluttering in my stomach intensifies. Why is he looking at me like that? Why does it make me feel so funny? Why do I like it so much?

Ricky drops his gaze and I remind myself to draw in a lungful of air. My heart is hammering against my ribs. My hands are curled into fists on my thighs.

"I look like this." He uses his free hand to gesture to himself, like he's presenting himself to me.

I take in the stray strands of hair framing his face, the little pout of his bottom lip, the proud way he holds himself tall.

"My parents don't understand why and I don't know how to explain it to them. So we all just pretend there's nothing wrong, even though we all know there definitely is." He drops his hand in his lap and his shoulders slump a bit in defeat. "It's fine."

Except it doesn't sound fine at all. It sounds kind of sad.

I don't know what to say. "Sorry" is so empty and meaningless that it'd almost be offensive if I said it. Obviously, I have no idea what it's like to be in his shoes. I've always blended in more than I stood out. But there's something about the way he said "fine" that reaches into me and tugs—hard.

Ricky waves his hand in the air, as if to shoo away the sadness that's creeped in around us. "Anyway, enough about me and my daddy issues. What about you? Why are you up here?" He gives me a light poke in the arm.

The spot tingles, even though the touch was barely there. I curl my fists a little tighter so I don't reach up to trace it with my fingers.

Why am *I* up here? Heck if I know. "I, um, it was, uh, I just needed a break from… you know."

Ricky's eyes dance with laughter as I stammer my way through my incoherent non-answer. My ears are burning so hot, I'm gonna need to dunk my head in a bucket of cold water. Ugh, what's happening to me? I drop my face into my hand, trying to hide the unexpected, inexplainable reactions I'm having.

"God, you're adorable," he says softly. "A giant teddy bear."

The comment makes me blush harder. Whyyy? This is so embarrassing.

Delicate yet strong fingers land on my wrist, and Ricky gently pulls my hand away. "It's okay. You don't have to be shy around me. This is a no-judgment zone."

I believe him.

With my friends and family in the neighborhood, they'll invite me into their house if I show up out of the blue. They'll drop everything to help me with anything.

But being a part of the community comes with certain requirements. It comes with a price.

I've always paid it, but Ricky hasn't.

He's an outsider. He's not bound by expectations or rules. He doesn't fit into a box and doesn't care what other people think. He doesn't have any strings attached.

Not like me.

That must be freeing.

CHAPTER
THREE

RHYS

I remember Angel from back in the day. Well, sort of. I remember his name and how much it doesn't match what he looks like. If anything, he's the opposite of angelic.

The thick, dark hair on his head matches his full, lush beard, which matches the soft carpet of fur on his fore-arms. I'd bet my favorite pair of heels that his chest and stomach and legs are covered the same way too. He's wider than he is tall, with broad shoulders and a belly I really want to tickle. His hands are meaty and rough, decorated with scars from nicks and cuts.

I can't help cradling one of them in my own. His palm is nearly the size of my entire hand, and his pinky is just as thick as my thumb. There's a smattering of hair across the back of his knuckles.

I should let go, but god, I really don't want to. He's so fucking adorable with his blushing and stammering. This big guy should be the most intimidating person at the party, but he's just a squishy teddy bear. Exactly my type of bear.

Ngh. I respectfully set his hand on his thigh again... with one last pet on the back—sue me, I'm only human.

"What do you do for work, Angel?" It has to be something with his hands. *Please* let it be something with his hands.

"Construction worker."

Swoon. Can a guy be more perfect? If only he were gay. I'd also take bi or pan—I'm not picky. But that's beyond unlikely. Angel pings negative on my always-reliable gaydar.

"How about you?"

Uh...

Angel's expression is one of genuine curiosity, like he really wants to know and isn't just asking to be polite. Whenever people in the old neighborhood ask me that question, I usually tell them I'm a chorus dancer in some Off-Off-Broadway shows. It's enough to satisfy them and shut them up.

Except I don't want to give Angel a brush-off like that. I want to tell him the truth. Ha—that's not something I would've thought was possible in the old neighborhood. But then, I totally didn't expect to encounter Angel either —not like this.

"Are you sure you want to know?" I have to prepare the guy. It's the kind thing to do. "Fair warning. It's gay."

Angel blinks like the word doesn't mean anything to him. Then a series of emotions play over his features like there's a projector connecting his brain to his face. Confusion, understanding, shock, fear, worry, resolution. It takes no more than a couple seconds, but I feel like I've watched a full-length movie.

"I can handle gay," he says, with a tad more determination than necessary, almost like he's trying to convince himself it's true.

I hesitate. The last thing I want is to chase the guy away with my super not-straight career choices.

Wait. What? Why do I care if I chase him away? It's not like we're *friends* or anything. I probably won't see him again for another couple years, and even then, only in passing. If he reacts badly, I never have to interact with him again. I'll just zip out of the house, Mom's cake be damned.

I straighten. "I'm a dancer."

He brightens like he's pleasantly surprised.

"You know, a *dancer*." I lace the word with enough innuendo that it's unmistakable what I mean.

His entire thought process flashes across his face again, and I can tell the instant understanding dawns.

"You're a…" He swallows like he's psyching himself up to say the next word. "A stripper?" he stage-whispers to me, as if there's anyone else in the room who might overhear us.

Oh, my sweet, sweet Angel-bear. His ears are so red, I might burn my fingers if I touch them. His eyes are wide and his jaw hangs open. For a moment I'm afraid I might have shocked him to death.

I take pity on him. "Well, not exactly. I'm a pole dancer, which sometimes involves stripping, but not always."

"Pole dancing."

I don't know whether I want to cringe or laugh. I definitely want to pull the guy into a hug, but something tells me that would make things worse.

"Yeah, you know, metal pole that goes from floor to ceiling? I spin around it?" I twirl a finger in a circle to help paint the picture.

His eyes go a little unfocused. He's probably trying to imagine me wrapped around a pole. When he speaks, there's so much awe and wonder in his voice that it takes my breath away. "You know how to do that?"

I nod. "Mmhmm."

My hand goes to my phone before I can think better of it. Should I? No, I shouldn't. Talking about being a pole dancer is one thing. Angel might be okay with it as a concept. But seeing it? With my sparkly thong and plat-form boots? With my legs spread wide in midair? It might push the poor guy too far.

And yet, I hold up my phone. "Wanna see?"

His eyes grow even wider. "You have pictures?"

I quirk my lips as I unlock my phone. "A video."

His gaze drops to the screen of my phone, and I rearrange myself so we're sitting side by side. He scoots in close enough for his leg to press against mine.

Mmm. So thick. So muscular. I bet he could crush me so good with those thighs.

Focus.

I make sure the sound is turned down low before hitting play. Angel angles himself so one arm is behind my back and he's peering over my shoulder. He cups his other hand underneath mine so we're holding my phone together.

His hand is warm—no, hot—and rough. It would rasp

across my skin if he touched me. It would leave me feverish and tingling.

He smells like fresh sawdust. Like he's been working in the carpentry shop and the clean scent of newly cut wood still lingers on his skin. I breathe in, nice and deep, trying not to be too obvious about smelling him.

He's transfixed as he watches the video, eyes twinkling and lips curled in a slight smile. His tongue sneaks out and swipes over his bottom lip. His Adam's apple bobs as he swallows. He shifts, like his clothes don't fit as well as they did a moment ago.

Ngh, it's not fair. Why does he have to be so perfect in every fucking way?

"Do you have any more?"

"Huh?" I'm so engrossed in studying Angel I haven't noticed that the video ended.

With one hand still holding mine in place, Angel brings his other arm between us to swipe at the screen. I'm too slow to stop him, and the pole dancing video slides off the screen. The next video autoplays.

It's one of me and Hayden from a while back. We're both naked, lying on our sides, him behind me. My leg is drawn forward so the camera has a perfect view of Hayden's dick pumping in and out of my ass. I'm moaning—loudly. Hayden grunts each time he bottoms out. The camera zooms in for a close-up shot of Hayden's cock stretching me wide. The skin around my hole is shiny from the lube.

Hayden isn't just my best friend and roommate. He's also a camboy and we've done a number of videos together. Our fans love the best-friends-with-benefits storyline we've got going. This is one of our more popular ones.

Fuck, fuck, fuck.

I'm stunned—or maybe embarrassed—into inaction, and it's several long seconds before I react. Except, instead of pausing the video and locking my phone's screen, I somehow hit the volume button and my phone moans louder. The sound of skin slapping against skin fills the room.

"Fuck, fuck, shit. Fuck. Sorry!" I stab my finger against the screen until the damn thing turns off, and I fling it into my bag.

Neither Angel nor I say anything. The sounds of the party downstairs float up to us.

I'm a hundred percent not ashamed of my work as a camboy. It's what pays the bills. It's how I met Hayden and our other friends, Sebastian and Noel. It's how I was able to afford pole dancing classes and how I pay for the fancy outfits I wear on stage. I like being a camboy. I'm good at it. But I'm not about to go announcing it to someone from my old neighborhood.

I clear my throat. "Sorry about that."

Angel's still sitting beside me. His leg is still pressed against mine. I shift away from him, giving him a bit of space from the effeminate, gay, pole-dancing camboy. It's a lot for anyone to take in, never mind a guy like Angel from a community like this.

He clears his throat too, but even then, his voice is a little hoarse when he speaks. "Um, was that a, um, sex tape?" He mumbles the last two words.

I wince. Technically, yes, it is a recording of me having sex. But that's not what Angel means.

"Sorry, I shouldn't pry. You don't have to answer that." It's not just his ears that are red now. His entire face is.

Shit. I've embarrassed him. And not in a cute way like before. He's uncomfortable. He looks like he's about to bolt.

"It's not really a sex tape," I say evenly, trying not to spook him. "It's a video, yes. Of me having sex with Hayden—he's my friend. We cam. You know, like OnlyFans?"

Angel cocks his head to the side as a flicker of recognition flits across his face. "OnlyFans?"

"Have you heard of it?" I wouldn't be surprised if he hadn't. Angel gives off more of a dirty-magazine-hidden-under-the-bed vibe than subscription-to-an-adult-only-content-streaming-site.

"It's... porn?" He doesn't so much *say* that last word as mouth it silently.

A smile tugs at my lips, despite the awkwardness of the situation. He can't say the word "porn" out loud. He's so goddamn precious.

I nod. "It's called camming. We're camboys."

"But it's... *porn*." Again with the mouthing.

"Yes," I say, careful to keep my voice low. "It's porn."

Angel blinks, his gaze drifting off into space. He looks dazed. Like I just told him that the world is going to end in forty-eight hours. I let him sit and absorb the news. Not only am I a pole dancer, I'm also a camboy. Yes, I have gay sex on camera and other people pay to watch.

"Does it... pay well?"

My eyebrows shoot up. Shit. That's the last thing I expected him to say. "Why do you ask? You thinking about starting your own page?" I'm teasing, obviously.

Though I probably shouldn't, considering. I've put Angel through a lot already in the short time we've been chatting.

But then his ears flush red again and he fidgets while rubbing his palms over the tops of his thighs. He's not saying no. Most people would immediately—and loudly— say no.

"Angel?"

"No! I mean…" He shifts around, making the bed dip, and I slide a little toward him. "No."

The second "no" sounded a whole hell of a lot less certain than the first. It sounded almost… reluctant? Holy fucking shit. It's my turn to blink in astonished silence. Maybe sweet, wholesome Angel isn't quite as sweet and wholesome as I thought.

"It's just… interesting," he says, as he scratches his jaw.

Interesting is definitely one way to describe it.

"But I'm not—I'm not gay." He shakes his head with a furrow in his brow, then his head snaps up like he only just remembered he isn't alone. "Not that there's anything wrong with being gay. I don't have anything against gay people. It's just, I'm not."

Oookay. I feel like I've missed about three-quarters of the conversation he's having with himself. This whole situation has gone totally off the rails, and I don't even know how it happened.

"I don't think you're gay," I say gently, as much as it pains me.

"I'm not. I've had girlfriends."

"That's…" *Great? Wonderful? Congratulations?*

"I…"

Oh god. Is he about to stroke out? Have an episode of some kind? Do I need to run down and call for help?

"Angel?"

He blinks, staring into space. "You don't... do you... do you have to be gay to, you know, do gay porn?"

What. The. Actual. Fuck?

CHAPTER
FOUR

ANGEL

Wait. What just came out of my mouth? It wasn't what I think it was, was it?

I sneak a sideways glance at Ricky, whose jaw is on the floor.

Shoot. I did ask him about gay porn. *Why* did I ask him about doing gay porn?

My brain kind of short-circuited when that video popped up on his phone.

I mean, I've watched porn before. Pshh, who hasn't? But it's always been straight porn. Girls with big boobs that bounce up and down while the guy does his thing. It's nothing mind-blowing, but it does the job.

This video though. The sounds. All that skin. The close-up shot of the guy's *thing* going into Ricky's *thing*. Oh god.

I keep seeing it like the image has been burned into the backs of my eyelids.

But I'm not gay. I'm not. I've had girlfriends before. I was attracted to them. I've never, you know, gone all the way, but only because I didn't want to force myself on them. I'm a respectful guy.

I've never thought about other guys, never looked at other guys. I had tons of opportunities to stare when I was on the football team, but I never did. Not once. Not even a little tempted. So, no, I'm not gay and I'm not doing gay porn.

No, wait, I'm not doing *any* porn, dang it.

So where the heck did that question come from?

Ricky snaps his mouth shut, but his eyes are still impossibly wide. "I, uh, um, do you have to be gay to do gay porn?" His mouth opens and closes a few times before he manages to answer. "I guess not?"

"A hole's a hole, right?" A slightly hysterical laugh escapes me before I clap my hand over my mouth. Oh good lord, what is happening to me? "Sorry! I'm so sorry. Don't answer that. You probably think I'm a perv."

First, I follow the guy upstairs and corner him in his childhood bedroom. Then I'm ogling a video of him dancing practically naked around a pole. Then that *other* video. Now I'm asking him inappropriate questions about gay porn. Something is seriously wrong with me.

I drag my hand over my face and start to stand. I need to leave. I shouldn't have come up here in the first place.

But he stops me with a hand on my arm. It's so small, but not dainty. There's real strength in those fingers and calluses on his palms. It has to be from the pole dancing, from holding himself up in midair. Ricky might be petite, but definitely not weak.

"I don't think you're a perv."

There's a gentleness in his voice that makes me brave enough to glance at him again. He's smiling, warm and kind, and there's that fluttering feeling in my stomach again.

"And actually," he continues with a hint of laughter. "There's a whole subset of gay porn called gay for pay."

"Gay for pay?" The words feel weird on my tongue. Like they're not even English.

"Yeah, you know, straight guys doing gay porn to make money."

Straight guys. Doing gay porn.

My heart thuds heavily against my ribs. *Straight* guys doing *gay* porn.

Straight guys—like me. Doing gay porn like what I saw in the video. The curve of Ricky's bent leg, the roundness of his bum. His skin shimmering and shining. I gulp.

And his face. He looked so… blissed-out, like he was high from the sex. His fingers were intertwined with the other guy's, like they were in it together, like they were connected more than just physically.

"Is that something you'd be interested in?" Ricky asks. His expression is carefully schooled. It's a perfect balance between sensitive and curious, encouraging but not overly aggressive. There's no hint at which answer he wants me to give.

I can't answer. I mean, I know how I *should* answer. I should say no. No chance. No way. Absolutely not. I have no reason to want to, no reason why I would need to. Not straight porn, and certainly not gay porn.

But my jaw won't move, my tongue won't make the right shapes. My heart beats harder, faster. Why can't I just say no?

Ricky's lips quirk and his eyes fill with compassion and understanding. "If you are, I might know someone you can talk to. *If* you are. No pressure or anything. Just putting it out there."

Is he serious? He can't be serious. I would *never* consider doing anything like that.

My heartbeat roars in my ears. My throat feels tight and my stomach churns dangerously. I grip my knees so tightly, I might give myself bruises.

Ricky holds out his hand, palm up. "Give me your phone?"

I stare at his hand, not fully grasping what he's asking me for. He wants my phone? Why does he want my phone?

Then suddenly my phone is out of my pocket and in his palm, and I have no idea how it got there.

Ricky's thumbs fly across the screen, and a second later, his bag buzzes. "There. Now you have my number. If you ever want to…" He seems to lose his train of thought. Then he smiles, almost sheepishly. "You know, whatever, you know how to reach me."

He holds out my phone, and when I take it I accidentally close my whole hand around his. He doesn't pull away and neither do I. We sit there, sort of holding hands, staring into each other's eyes.

The world spins like I'm standing at the top of a skyscraper, staring down at the street below. The wind blows through the steel frame of the building, cold and biting. The soles of my feet tingle. If I step off the edge, I could fly.

I'm snapped back to reality when Ricky slides his hand out from under mine. Then quickly, faster than I can react, he darts in and plants a kiss on my cheek. Then he's on his feet, saying goodbye, and disappearing down the stairs.

My cheek is on fire.

It only lasted a second, but I can still feel the soft press of his lips. I can still smell the whiff of his cologne—or is it perfume? I breathe deep, dragging in any lingering trace of it.

I glance at my phone. The screen is still on, showing a new text message thread. But the contact name doesn't say Ricky. It says Rhys Rawlings.

By the time I get downstairs, he's gone, and no one seems to have noticed him leave.

———

Later that night, after I've said goodnight to Mama, my sister Sabrina, and her infant son Jonah, I head upstairs to our duplex's second apartment. I moved up here after I got my construction job and started earning enough to cover the extra rent Mama charged the other tenants.

For a while, it was just the two of us—Mama down stairs in the apartment me and Sabrina grew up in, and me upstairs by myself. Three months ago, Sabrina moved back in with her newborn son after her douchebag boyfriend walked out on them. And now we have a screaming baby in the house.

I love my nephew, I really do. The kid is cute as heck when he's quiet. But look at him the wrong way and he'll burst your eardrums. The little dude's got lungs like an opera singer, and he seems to think the middle of the night is the perfect time to exercise his vocal cords. When he's wailing, it sounds like he's right next to my bed in the upstairs apartment.

We're all suffering.

Upstairs, I kick off my shoes and drop onto the couch, head falling back to stare up at the ceiling. If I was smart, I'd try to get some sleep now, when it's still quiet. But my mind is still racing from my conversation with Ricky earlier.

Maybe I hallucinated the whole thing. Following Ricky upstairs, sitting on that frilly, pink bed, accidentally seeing the sex video, asking insane questions about gay porn. There's no way any of that was real, right?

And yet, my cheek is still warm from the kiss Ricky— or maybe Rhys—planted on me. My hand floats up to the spot. It doesn't feel any different under my fingertips. There's no cut or burn or anything. But the ghost of that kiss lingers, a very real wisp that I can't quite grasp.

I sit up and shake my head. What am I doing? Why am I still thinking about Ricky? He left before the party ended and he won't be back in the neighborhood for months, if not years. I won't see him, won't talk to him, won't have anything to do with him, maybe forever. That conversation was a onetime freak accident.

Heck, maybe I was possessed or something because I definitely wasn't acting like myself. I don't go out of my way to chat with people I'm not close to. I don't talk about naughty things like stripping and porn. I definitely have no desire to actually do porn myself—gay or straight.

Except, maybe I'm still possessed, because suddenly I'm opening my laptop and searching for Ricky Gallo.

There's an old, defunct Facebook profile with mentions of our high school. But that's it. No other social media accounts. No clues pointing to what he's doing with his life now. It's like Ricky Gallo fell off the face of the planet after he turned eighteen.

I should stop. I should close my laptop and go to bed. I did the search and didn't find anything. There's no point in continuing. Nothing good can come of this.

I type in Rhys Rawlings. And strike gold.

Not only is there an Instagram account, but there's also a website called The Camboy Network, another website for a nightclub called The Bronzed Rail, and even a Wikipedia page. Ricky has his own Wikipedia page?! Jeez.

I'm a little afraid to click on any of the links. They feel like doors I won't be able to close after they're open. I won't be able to unsee things, unknow things. Just like I can't unsee that video or unknow what Ricky looks like naked.

But there's a tiny, minuscule, microscopic part of me that maybe, kinda, sorta wants to?

I take a breath and squeeze my eyes shut. I shouldn't. I shouldn't. I shouldn't.

My finger presses down on the trackpad with a distinctive click. Oh no.

I peek, just one eye at first. I squeeze it shut again. There are pictures… pictures with a lot of skin… way more skin than I'm usually comfortable with. And yet…

I squint at the screen, as if it's too much to look at directly. Air rushes out of my lungs and my eyes fly open as if the photos have punched me in the gut. I struggle to breathe, but the clear and unobstructed view isn't doing anything to lower my heart rate or settle the churning in my stomach.

Dear lord. The pictures. Ricky—or Rhys—isn't entirely naked in any of them, but he's not wearing much. Sometimes only a scrap of fabric that passes for underwear. Sometimes one of those corset things or a crop top.

Sometimes he's wrapped around a pole, legs spread wide, with dangerous-looking boots on his feet. Sometimes he's with another guy, or several other guys. They're all wearing just as little as he is, piled on top of one another. Hugging. *Touching.*

My gaze zeroes in on the places where skin meets skin. Thighs. Arms. Chests. Backs. Acres of skin that looks so soft and supple.

My eyes flick up to his face. His eyes are dark and sultry, outlined in makeup. His lips hold just a hint of a smile. His hair falls in waves over his shoulders. It's purple, red, blue, pink, green, orange, a different color in every picture.

I can't help staring at the angle of his jaw or the length of his neck. There's something so…

I try to draw in a strangled breath. Oh god, what's happening to me? My chest feels like it's about to explode.

I push my laptop away and lean forward, hands braced on my knees, and force myself to breathe. I feel funny all over. So hot that my brow is damp. Everything tingles and my clothes feel too tight and rough on my skin.

And I'm hard, I realize, as I cup myself. Oh my word, I've gotten an erection from staring at pictures of a naked Ricky—Rhys. Who is a guy. A man. How— What— I don't—

No, I shouldn't be turned on by a man. I'm not gay. I've had girlfriends. I like women.

I close my eyes and try to conjure up an image of a naked woman. Boobs. Curves. Shapely legs. Long, silky hair. She giggles and tosses her hair over her bare, elegantly rounded shoulder. But when she peers back at me, it isn't a woman at all—it's Rhys.

My eyes fly open. I can still see him. The sparkle in his eyes. The tease of his smile. I squeeze myself through my jeans. The friction eases some of the pressure, but it's not enough. I need… more, or less, I don't know.

I don't remember ever feeling like this before. Aroused when I don't want to be. Achingly hard after only a few pictures. I don't usually react this way. I'm not usually so responsive.

Dang it. I need to come. There's no other way to get rid of this erection. I'm too worked up for it to go away on its own.

I close my eyes and try to imagine a woman again, but all my imagination gives me is Rhys. Rhys in the pink, sparkly thong. Rhys leaning against a bronze-colored pole, round bum sticking out. Rhys sprawled on some other guy's lap, legs spread open, bulge on display.

I lean back, undoing my jeans with unsteady fingers. I stick my hand into my boxers and grip myself tight. I'm leaking enough pre-cum to slick up my palm—thank goodness, because I don't know if I even have lube in the apartment.

The slide of my hand over my dick feels so good that my whole body shudders. But it's still not enough. I need more.

I know where I can find more.

I sneak a glance at my laptop, my ears heating as if the stupid computer is judging me. Am I really going to look at porn? Of a guy I know? Gay porn? Even when I'm not gay?

My dick twitches in my hand and another I shudder again.

I don't care anymore. It's not like anyone will know. I'll

delete my browser history and it'll be like it never happened.

I lift my hips off the couch and push my jeans and boxers down around my thighs. My laptop sits next to me, showing a series of thumbnails. I don't look at them too closely, just click on a random one.

It starts playing and I forget to breathe. Rhys spins around a pole, rolling his body, arching it. He spreads his legs wide and holds himself there while the camera zooms in on the dark shadow between his ass cheeks. He goes to his knees. Writhes around on the floor.

Then someone else comes onto the stage—the same guy from the video I saw on Rhys's phone. He's fully clothed, while Rhys is only in a thong.

The other guy pulls out his dick and Rhys greedily sucks it down. He takes it all the way, eyes fluttering, spit leaking out the sides of his mouth. The guy fists Rhys's hair and thrusts into his mouth. Rhys's jaw hangs open as he lets the other guy use him.

I jerk myself harder and faster than I've done in a long time. I'm so close. So close.

The scene switches. Rhys is on all fours with the other guy taking him from behind. The narrow strip of fabric of his thong is pulled to the side, framing Rhys's ass cheek. It's so round, so plump. What would it feel like under my palm? Bouncing against my hips?

Oh shit, crap. My balls pull up tight.

The camera moves in for a close-up view of the guy's dick sliding in and out of Rhys's hole. It just… disappears. There one second, gone the next, then there again. But it's not really gone, is it? It's inside Rhys's body. It's inside Rhys.

"Shit. Shit." My hand flies over my dick. I reach down with my other one to tug on my balls.

Inside Rhys. I could be inside Rhys. I *want* to be inside Rhys.

I come, arching off the couch as I spray myself. Ropes and ropes of cum shoot out of me, landing on my hand, my shirt. I don't remember ever coming so hard before. I didn't know it could take over my entire body like that.

Maybe it's because I haven't jerked off in a while, so all the cum has built up in my balls. But I don't think that's it. I think it's because of Rhys.

CHAPTER
FIVE

RHYS

"No, brunch is only for us. No boyfriends allowed."

Noel pouts at Sebastian. Well, I think he's trying for a scowl, but it definitely looks more like a pout.

Ever since Noel's boyfriend, Bellamy, moved to the city, the two of them have been attached at the hip. He even wants to bring Bellamy to our standing monthly brunch dates.

But these brunch dates are sacred, damn it. It's been the four of us for years: Sebastian, the leader; Noel, the bad boy; Hayden, the golden retriever; and me, the sassy one.

We're the original members of The Camboy Network, this thing Sebastian put together to help content creators pool resources. It's grown since then, evolving into a studio and production company. But the four of us have been friends and camming collaborators since long before any of that happened. Long before Noel started dating Bellamy, and even before Sebastian started dating his boyfriend, Christian.

"But Bellamy doesn't have any friends here." Noel protests.

Sebastian levels a stern look at him. "If I can live without Christian for a couple hours on a Sunday, then you can live without Bellamy for just as long."

Noel's scowl deepens, but that only makes him look poutier. I'm almost tempted to reach over and pinch his cheek. But I don't have a death wish.

Noel is secretly a squishy marshmallow on the inside, but his outside is genuinely prickly.

Sebastian turns away from him, discussion about boyfriends at brunch obviously closed, and redirects his attention to me. "So, Rhys, how was your dad's birthday party?"

I whine, slumping in my chair. How was it? Exactly how I thought it would be and entirely unexpected at the same time. "I don't know. Fine, I guess?"

Hayden shoots me a sympathetic look. We already debriefed when I got home that day—when I snuck out of the party after running away from Angel. I still can't quite believe that whole conversation happened. Like, wha…?

"Were your parents bad?" Sebastian's brow furrows in concern, and I can already tell that his mind is whirring. Sebastian is the problem-solver of the group. He's never faced a challenge he couldn't find a solution to.

"They were fine," I say, waving my hand dismissively. They will be what they are. There's no changing that. "It's…"

I sneak a glance at Hayden who gives me an encouraging nod. I told him all about Angel and we engaged in the requisite internet stalking. A lot of his photos are old or he's standing at the back of a group. They don't do justice to the yummy teddy bear I sat next to on my childhood bed.

I take a deep breath so I can let it all out in a dramatic sigh. "There was a guy."

Sebastian's eyes light up. Even Noel cocks an eyebrow in interest.

"A guy?!" Sebastian leans forward, pushing his empty plate out of the way so he can plant his elbows on the table. "Who is he? What's his name? How do you know him? Does he know about what you do?"

Hayden snickers at the barrage of questions Sebastian throws at me.

I lift my hands, as if I can physically fend them off. "Whoa. Chill. It's not like that. Angel is straight. I think."

That word comes out a little strangled.

He said he wasn't gay. My gaydar was a flat line almost the entire time we spoke. Okay, there were those couple moments when the video of me and Hayden popped up where the needle wiggled, but that's clearly within the margin of error. And listen, I'm the last person to make assumptions about someone based on their appearance, but he doesn't *look* gay at all. He looks completely, entirely, one-hundred-percent straight.

Straight and narrow, in fact, if that little gold crucifix he wears around his neck is any indication. It must have been tucked under his shirt at the party, because I didn't notice it. But it was in almost every picture Hayden and I found online.

Everyone in the old neighborhood is Catholic. Some, like my family, are the Christmas and Easter types. But there are definitely pockets of more devout families. Angel's must be one of them.

But what kind of dutiful, straight, Christian boy asks about doing gay porn? About gay for pay?

And the way his ears went red-hot. How still he got when that damn video started playing. Jesus. It was a good thing my jeans were so tight, or else the bulge between my legs would've been obscene.

Sebastian's head is cocked to the side. "You think? Meaning he might not be straight?"

I wince. I probably shouldn't be talking about Angel's sexuality behind his back, right? And it's not like I'm going to see the guy again, so who cares if he's straight or gay or whatever?

Hayden reaches over and rubs my arm in a comforting gesture. I lean into the touch.

"He asked whether a straight guy can do gay porn," I say.

Noel chokes on the Bellini he's sipping. "Jesus fuck. You can't spring something like that on us without warning."

Sebastian sits bolt upright, eyes shining with a million ideas. "He did? Does that mean he's interested? What does he look like? Would he want to film with you? Or maybe he'd be more comfortable with someone he doesn't know?"

"Slow down!" I wave my hands to shoo Sebastian's questions away. "I didn't say *he* wanted to do gay porn. The conversation was just hypothetical."

Hayden leans toward Sebastian and in a not-so-quiet voice whispers, "He's friends with Rhys's older brother. They all grew up together. He's a total teddy bear. Furry all over and super cute. Even works in construction."

"Denny!" I give Hayden a harmless slap on the arm.

The last thing Sebastian needs is encouragement. Angel is *not* performing in a video for The Camboy Network. He's just not.

"A bear, huh?" Sebastian's got his phone in his hands, typing away with a look of extreme concentration on his face. "Definitely pairing him with someone small, even if you don't want to do it, Rhys."

"Sebby! Stahp! You can't just cast the guy against his will." I reach across the table and try to snatch Sebastian's phone out of his hand, but he's too fast for me.

Pulling it to his chest, he looks at me like I'm the one getting ahead of myself.

"Relax! It's just an idea. If *your Angel* doesn't want to do it, then I can look for someone who resembles him."

I frown at Sebastian. "He's not *my Angel*." Although the way those two words roll off my tongue does send a tingle of excitement up my spine.

Three sets of eyes stare at me with skepticism.

"What? He's not!" I exclaim. "Before the party, I hadn't spoken to the guy in years and I'm probably not going to again!"

My phone buzzes.

It's sitting face down on the table, so I can't see who messaged me. Normally, none of us would notice something so quiet, and yet, we all turn to the device like it's blaring an alarm.

"Are you going to get that?" Noel asks.

"Get what?" I hike up a shoulder, hoping they'll buy my fake indifference.

"Your phone." Sebastian pointedly glances from my face down to said phone.

"It's just a text." I flick my hand, dismissing their insinuation. "No big deal."

"But what if it's him?" Hayden asks.

I can't believe what they're trying to imply. There's no way Angel would text me at the exact moment I'm claiming I won't speak to him again. I play dumb. "Who?"

Hayden turns his sad, puppy-dog eyes on me. "You know who."

Meanwhile, Noel doesn't bother with niceties. He scoffs and grabs my phone.

"Hey!"

He scowls at the screen, then his lips twitch. That's not a good sign.

"Give it back!"

Noel holds the phone out of my reach, then furrows his brow in confusion. "Who's Teddy Bear?"

Oh, fuck. "I said, give it back!"

Sebastian takes the phone from Noel, scans the screen, and cocks his head to the side. "Teddy Bear? Wait, that's not what you saved his number under, is it?"

With a growl, I push my chair back and stand up, stretching over the table to pluck the phone out of Sebastian's hand. "Give me that!"

When I plop into my chair again, I hold the phone close to my chest. My heart rate picks up and I get a little flutter in my stomach. It's the same feeling I get right before I go on stage to perform at The Bronzed Rail. Stage fright mixed with a dash of adrenaline. Anticipation heightened by uncertainty.

I peek at my phone. There's a notification on the screen.

TEDDY BEAR

> Hey, how you doing?

I swipe at the notification and my phone unlocks to the messaging app. There's the single message I sent myself last week at my dad's birthday party. Then the one from him just now. That's it. No follow-up text. No bouncing dots teasing at more. Just "Hey, how you doing?"

God, that's such a straight dudebro thing to do. Coming from anyone else, I'd roll my eyes and drop my phone back on the table—it's not worthy of an immediate response.

But Angel is different. He's…

There's an audible gasp from across the table. "Aw, look at that smile!"

I slap my phone against my chest to hide the screen, then scrunch my face into a scowl.

Sebastian's grinning like I'm his kid and he's a proud mama on prom night. Hayden's wearing an equally enamored expression, and Noel's smirk is almost endearing.

I try to maintain my scowl, but it's no use. Angel is too cute to resist. I huff, setting my phone face down on the table with a little more force than necessary. "Ugh, shut up!" I whine.

Noel shakes his head like I'm being ridiculous.

"Aren't you going to reply?" Sebastian asks, eyes glued to the pink and purple cover on my phone. "He asked how you're doing."

"You can't just leave him on read," Hayden adds.

"I'm not! I'm just…" I scramble for an excuse. "Don't you know it's rude to text while at the table?"

"Since when has that ever stopped you?" Noel snorts.

I throw him a glare that actually has a bit of heat behind it, but that only makes Noel smirk.

"You should respond." Sebastian waves at my phone. "See what he wants."

I slap my hand on top of my phone, in case any of the boys try to steal it again. "He's just saying hello."

"Or he might want to know more about performing," Sebastian shoots back.

"Why the hell would he want to do that?"

"Because he's already asked you once. Maybe he has more questions."

"You did offer to put him in touch with Sebastian," Hayden jumps in. Totally unhelpful.

Sebastian sits up a little straighter, his eyes widening in victory. "You did? That's amazing! I'd *love* to chat with Angel Teddy Bear about doing gay porn."

I glower at Hayden—whose side is he on, anyway?

He shrugs. "You won't know until you talk to him."

I heave a sigh. "I hate all of you."

Sebastian and Hayden beam at me. Noel dips his head sideways in indifference.

Fuck.

I pick up my phone and stare at that simple four-word message again.

TEDDY BEAR

Hey, how you doing?

It gives nothing away. I can't tell if he's working up to the porn questions or if he's bored and messing around on his phone. Hell, maybe he meant to send the message to someone else entirely. We've barely been acquaintances since we were kids, so why would he suddenly want to be friendly?

Ugh. I'm way overthinking this. Angel is cute and totally my type, but I need to remember he's straight. There's no reason for me to act like a silly teenager with a crush on my older brother's friend.

I tap on the screen to pull up the keyboard.

RHYS

Great! *winky face emoji* Having brunch with the boys.

I attach a selfie I took earlier for social media. Hayden, Sebastian, and Noel are all in the background with Bellinis in hand.

RHYS

What are you up to today? *grinning emoji*

Three dots appear immediately and I brace myself for an apology message. *Oh, sorry, messaged the wrong person. Have a good life.* But when it comes through, it is the absolute last thing I would ever expect.

TEDDY BEAR

Doing yard work.

Followed by a selfie of Angel wearing a thin, white tank top that does nothing to hide his wide, furry chest. He's got a pair of sunglasses perched on his head, and he's squinting a bit, like the sun is in his eyes. His cheeks are pink from all that sun exposure and his lips are rosy, like he's been licking them. The camera's angled to show him holding the handle of a lawn mower, arms thick and powerful, standing on a patch of lush, green grass.

My jaw drops. My cock plumps. Fuck me. Right now. As hard as he possibly can.

"What is it?" Sebastian tries to peer across the table at my screen.

Beside me, Hayden leans over and gasps. "Holy shit."

He seizes my phone, tapping on the screen to enlarge the picture.

"What is it?" Sebastian asks again, coming right out of his seat to peek over Hayden's shoulder. "Oh shit! You weren't kidding when you said he's a bear. Look at that beard. All that body hair. I wonder if it's as soft as it looks."

My fingers lift to my mouth at the memory of the parting kiss I planted on Angel's cheek. It was an impulsive thing to do, and I never would've done it with anyone else from the old neighborhood.

But he had his hand cradling mine, rough and warm. The browns of his irises held a touch of yearning. He listened to my woe-is-me story about my parents and actually seemed to understand.

I moved before I knew what I was doing, and my lips touched his cheek before I could stop myself. I can still imagine it now. The softness of his skin, his beard. The clean, manly scent of fresh sawdust. I carried that scent with me all the way home that afternoon. My lips tingled well into the next day.

"Rhys!"

I'm jolted back to the present by Hayden's voice. "What?"

"Daydreaming?" Noel asks with a smug smile.

I open my mouth to deny it, but what's the point? They've seen Angel's picture. They know my type. They'll never believe me if I say I'm not attracted to Angel that way.

"Shut up."

Sebastian drops back into his own chair. "He's totally going to ask you to talk to me."

"How do you know?" Hayden asks as he hands my phone back.

Sebastian smiles like he's got a devious plan in the works. "Because completely straight guys who have no interest in gay porn don't send selfies like that to guys like Rhys."

CHAPTER
SIX

ANGEL

My phone vibrates in my pocket, sending my pulse skyrocketing. Is it him? Did he message me back? Leaving the lawn mower idling, I pull out my phone.

> **RHYS**
>
> Great! *winky face emoji* Having brunch with the boys.

I recognize the photo. It's the same one he posted on social media earlier today. The one where his long, purple hair falls in waves around his shoulders, and his eyes smolder as he peers into the camera through his lashes.

> **RHYS**
>
> What are you up to today? *grinning emoji*

Trying not to think about you and failing miserably. It's what I've been trying to do for the last week, but no matter how hard I try to forget about our conversation, I can't. It replays in my mind whenever I have a moment of quiet.

There's a whole subset of gay porn called gay for pay. Is that something you'd be interested in? I know someone you can talk to.

And then the videos. Oh heavens above, the videos. I've never jerked off so much in my life, not even when I was a horny teenager with raging hormones. After that first night, I've been going back to that website, looking for more videos of Rhys.

Then I found him on social media and created new accounts just so I could follow him. His social media photos are a lot tamer than that website, but somehow more intriguing. They're a glimpse into his life—how he spends his days, the people he surrounds himself with, the places he likes to be. It feels like a world away from here, even though he's only a thirty-minute drive away.

I push my sunglasses to the top of my head, then hold my phone out. I'm nowhere near as good at taking selfies as Rhys is, but the one I snap doesn't look terrible.

ANGEL

Doing yard work.

Instead of standing there, staring at the screen while waiting for Rhys to respond, I make a point of stuffing my phone into my pocket again. I've got a lawn to mow and a garden to weed. If I stay busy with yard work, then I won't be obsessing over why I messaged Rhys today.

Because I've got absolutely no clue. Why today? Why not yesterday? Why not tomorrow? Why did I message him at all? We're not friends. He didn't say anything about wanting to be friends. He only gave me his number in case I wanted to ask more about the whole gay-for-pay thing.

Which I don't.

Right?

Dang it. I don't.

My phone vibrates again. I should ignore it. I can check it later, when I'm done with mowing the lawn. Maybe I'll leave it inside so it doesn't distract me.

Crap.

I stop the lawn mower and pull my phone out again.

RHYS

eyes emoji *fire emoji* *sweating emoji*

I stare at the message. Is that— Does he— Is he asking me if it's hot outside?

ANGEL

It's not too hot. There's a nice breeze.

Three dots immediately appear at the bottom of the screen. Then disappear. Then reappear again.

RHYS

teary-eyed smiling emoji *halo emoji*
Make sure you stay hydrated. *winky face emoji*

A smile blossoms on my face as warmth spreads through my chest. Rhys is such a thoughtful person.

ANGEL

I will. Thanks!

The smile stays with me through mowing the rest of the lawn and weeding the garden. Even after I've showered and had Sunday dinner with Mama and Sabrina and Jonah, my lips keep wanting to curl upward. It's only once I'm ready for bed and settled under the sheets that the heat travels a little lower in my body.

I pull up that website again. The Camboy Network. I squint at the pictures of the guys on the page. They're the same guys that Rhys was at brunch with today. So when he says "the boys", he means the guys he films porn with?

My dick fills so fast my head spins a little.

So Rhys is friends with the people he works with. He hangs out with them even when they're not working. What's the big deal? Unless it was some kind of business meeting? Were they talking about the videos they want to make in the future? Did Rhys mention my questions about a straight guy doing gay porn?

"Ow," I mutter, as I press the heel of my hand against my dick. It's so hard it hurts. Jeez, am I getting turned on by the idea of a business meeting? What the heck is wrong with me?

Except, it's not the business meeting, is it? It's the prospect of Rhys telling his gay-porn friends about me. About how interested I was that day when he explained what gay for pay is. About how they should invite me to shoot a video with them.

I fumble for the bottle of lube I picked up the day after the party. It's already half empty.

I stick my lube-slick hand into my boxers, then hiss as I wrap my fingers around my dick.

"He's straight?" one of Rhys's friends asks.

"Yeah, but Angel's totally cool," Rhys says. "You guys'll love him."

"But he has no experience."

"I'll show him the ropes," Rhys offers. "We'll do a couple practice sessions before going in front of the camera."

The scene changes.

Rhys is on his knees in front of me. My jeans are halfway down my thighs. His fingers, tipped in bright blue, are wrapped around the base of my dick. His lips, glistening and cherry red, are stretched thin as he sucks the head. His lashes flutter, his cheeks hollow, and he moans. Then he flicks his gaze up to mine. Framed in dark makeup, the browns of his eyes are deep pools that drag me down into their depths. I'm drowning. I can't breathe.

The orgasm hits me hard and fast, racing through me and leaving me feeling a little drunk. I lie there for a moment as I catch my breath, the image of Rhys on his knees melting away. Then I force myself to get up and clean the cum off before it dries on my belly.

When I get back to bed, the screen on my phone is on and there's a message from Rhys. My ears go hot, even though there's no one here to witness my embarrassment. There's no way he could know I was just jerking off. And definitely no way he'd know I was fantasizing about him. Rhys can't read minds. Mind reading isn't a thing!

With my heart pounding in my chest, I cautiously pick up my phone and read the message.

RHYS

> How did the garden turn out? *flower emoji*

My bed squeaks in protest when I collapse onto it. He's asking about the garden. Because I told him I was gardening, dummy. But he remembered and he cares enough to ask. My tummy flip-flops at the thought.

ANGEL

It's a vegetable garden. *tomato emoji* *cucumber emoji* *carrot emoji* *eggplant emoji*

RHYS

hand over laughing face emoji No peaches?

No, peaches come from trees. I'd love to have a peach tree in the backyard though.

laughing emoji That would be pretty cool.

I get more comfortable on the bed, turning onto my side and grabbing a pillow to hug against my chest.

The dots bounce at the bottom of the screen and I hold my breath, waiting to see what Rhys has to say next.

RHYS

My friends saw the picture you sent me, btw. I tried to stop them, but they stole my phone.

They think you're cute! *grinning emoji*

Rhys's friends think I'm cute. The same friends he does gay porn with. What does that mean? Did he actually tell them about me? About our conversation at his dad's birthday party? My stomach twists around itself and my palms get all clammy.

RHYS

Sorry. I hope that's okay. *sad emoji*

Oh, no! I don't want Rhys to feel bad. He hasn't done

anything wrong. My thumbs feel too big and clumsy as I hurry to type out a response.

ANGEL

> Yeah, it's okay. I don't mind. Tell them I said thank you.

RHYS

> *grinning emoji* So polite.

> These are the friends you work with?

I cringe the second I hit send. Why did I ask that? What does it matter? Will he even know what I mean by "work"? I'm trying to delete the message when Rhys's reply comes through.

RHYS

> Yeah, the guys I do porn with. *winky face emoji*

My ears burn and I bury my face into the pillow. Why am I having this conversation? I should tell Rhys that I'm going to bed because I have to get up early for work tomorrow. I should stay far away from any talk about porn, especially gay porn.

I lift my face from the pillow, just enough for me to see the screen.

ANGEL

> I recognize them.

Shit. Shit. Crap. Dang it. *Why* am I doing this?

RHYS

> You do?? *eyes emoji*

Dare I ask from where?

ANGEL

From the videos...

shocked emoji Do you mean The Camboy Network videos??

Maybe...

I smother myself with the pillow again. I can't *believe* I'm admitting this to anyone. Although, I guess if I had to, Rhys would be the only person I could tell. Even then. *Why?!*

My phone buzzes. Three times, four times, five times, in quick succession.

RHYS

Angel! Oh my!

Maybe you're not quite as angelic as I thought!

Which ones did you watch?

Did you watch any of mine?

What did you think?

Despite myself, despite the mortifying embarrassment, a smile curls my lips. He doesn't think I'm a bad person for watching those videos. He isn't angry or offended. In fact, he sounds almost... excited? Like he's happy that I watched them?

RHYS

Come on! Don't leave me hanging!
praying hands emoji

I stifle a giggle that wants to bubble up from my chest. I'm a grown man—I don't giggle.

ANGEL

I've seen a few. I like the one where you're dancing the best.

RHYS

The pole dancing one? I'm wearing a thong and then Hayden fucks me on stage while he's fully dressed?

Jeez, how can he say those things out loud like that? Or type them. Whatever. Just put those words out there like... like... like it's normal?

ANGEL

Yeah, that one.

RHYS

smirk emoji *kissy face emoji*

I like that one too.

The dots go bouncing again, stopping for a moment before starting back up. Every time there's a pause, I rack my brain, trying to think of something else to say, something witty or smart or charming. But I keep coming up blank. Then the dots pop up again. What is Rhys typing? It must be something big. Why else would it take him so long?

I bite the pillow and force myself to breathe so I don't

pass out. My heart feels like it's lodged in my throat. It takes *forever* before Rhys's message comes through.

RHYS

> So… Sebastian is one of the guys from brunch today. You might've seen him on The Camboy Network too. He's the guy I was telling you about. The one you can talk to if you're curious about the gay-for-pay stuff.

My lungs stop working as I read and reread the message half a dozen times.

Sebastian is the guy with the brown hair and the friendly smile. He does a lot of videos with an older man who has both arms covered in tattoos. Yeah, I recognize him. I definitely recognize him.

RHYS

> Not that you have to! *squinty eyes, tongue out emoji*

> Just pointing him out to you, you know, just in case.

I swallow, but my heart still feels like it's wedged in my throat.

Just in case, Rhys said.

Just in case I want to go gay for pay.

CHAPTER
SEVEN

RHYS

A part of me feels terrible for bringing it up again. But another part of me—the devilish counterpart to Angel's... well, angel—is having a fucking field day.

I cannot believe Angel's been watching videos on The Camboy Network website. There's only one reason why he would be doing that, right? Well, maybe two reasons. But both of them are like, whoa, what the actual fuck?!

Either Angel's seriously considering the whole gay-for-pay thing and is conducting some "research", or Angel is not as straight as he claims to be.

Please. No straight boy takes the initiative to dig up our website and watch not just one, but several videos. No straight boy has *a favorite video*.

Hayden pokes me with his toes. "Are you messaging Teddy Bear?"

I poke him back. We're on opposites ends of the couch. Hayden's laid out on his side, watching TV, and I'm curled up in a ball with my phone an inch from my face.

"Maybe."

"You definitely are. You're smiling so hard, I'm surprised your face hasn't broken."

"Shut up. I'm not smiling." Except I totally am. If I wasn't having this conversation with Angel in real time, I wouldn't believe it was real. He doesn't know what a peach emoji means. Or an eggplant emoji for that matter. It's so sweet I think I'm developing cavities.

TEDDY BEAR

Thanks.

I wait a moment for another message to come through, but there's nothing. Fuck. Did I push too hard? Come on too strong? Maybe I shouldn't have brought it up at all. I was trying for a teasing tone, but that doesn't always come across very well over texts.

Shit. Fuck. I'm typing an apology when another message finally pops up.

TEDDY BEAR

I'm still not sure how I feel about all that.

My thumbs hover above my screen.

He's not sure how he feels. Which isn't an outright rejection. Which means there's a chance he might actually be interested.

Oh my god, can I talk him into it? *Should* I talk him into it? I can be very persuasive, but being an enabler doesn't feel quite right when it comes to porn. It's something a person needs to decide for themselves because once it's on the internet, it'll be impossible to take down. There's no going back.

RHYS

> Did you want to talk about it?

My message appears in the thread, then three seconds later, my phone starts ringing. I almost drop the thing—no one but Mom ever calls me. That's such a weird, old-person thing to do.

But it's not Mom. It's Angel. Why the fuck is he calling me?

Oh shit. Did he think my message was an invitation to *actually* talk? Like, with our mouths?

I jump to my feet, holding my phone away from me like it's a bomb I don't know what to do with.

Hayden's gaze flits to me, otherwise he doesn't move a muscle. "Everything okay?"

"Uh... I don't know?"

"You going to answer the call?"

"It's a video call."

Hayden bites back a smile. "Pretty sure they work the same way."

"But I look— I'm not— Ugh!" I dart around the coffee table and into my room, slamming the door shut behind me. I'm not ready to be seen on camera. My hair is in the world's messiest bun—an actual messy bun, not an artfully messy one. I've already washed my makeup off. I'm wearing nothing but a pair of silk sleep shorts and the matching silk robe. "Fuck!"

I cover the phone's camera with my hand, then swipe to answer. "Hey! Hi! Hold on a sec! Lemme just..."

Ring light plugged in and switched on. Pointed at an angle to create mood lighting. Bedcovers tugged sort of into place. I scoot all the way back so I'm leaning against the wall. The elastic in my hair comes out and I fluff up the strands with my fingers. When I finally uncover the camera, I look… not terrible.

"Hi, hello, sorry about that." I finally take in the image on my screen and have to stifle a gasp.

Jesus fucking Christ. I might look like I'm about to slide into bed, but Angel is *already in bed*. Lying on his side, pillow tucked under his head. Warm, yellow light casts shadows across his face, but the camera clearly captures the angle of his collarbone and his very naked shoulder. The gold chain of his necklace rests on his skin.

Oh, fuck me, right fucking now, please.

"Hey, um, I hope it's okay that I called. Is this a bad time? I can call back later. Or not call. Or whatever."

"Yes! No!" I wince. "I mean, no, it's not a bad time, and yes, it's totally cool that you called. What's up?!"

What is up is my cock, growing from sleepy to chubby to plump in zero point five seconds. I grab my pillow and press it into my lap. Angel can't possibly see the tent in my shorts, but I've suddenly been hit with a bout of bashfulness.

Angel is so sweet and I am so very not. I'm super comfortable in my own body and clearly sex positive, but when faced with Angel's obvious innocence, I kinda feel like I'm corrupting him.

Which is ridiculous, of course. Hello, he was just telling me about which gay porn videos he likes to watch. But still! He's just so… ngh!

"You… you asked if I wanted to talk about… you know." His voice is all low and rumbly, exactly how I imagine a bear would sound if the animal could speak. I swear I can feel it vibrate all the way through the call and into my chest.

"Ye—" I clear my throat. "Yeah, for sure. Did you have questions? What were you thinking? Sebastian's the best person to talk to, but I'll try to answer the best I can."

Great. Now I'm rambling.

"I just…" Angel blinks his incredibly long, dark lashes. When he speaks, it's barely a whisper and I have to bring the phone closer to hear him. "Can you… can you tell me how you got into… you know. And um, why?"

He can't bring himself to say the word "porn". I fight back a doting sigh.

"Of course I can." I shift to get more comfortable and prop my arm up on a pillow so the camera is angled just right. "It's not a very interesting story. I moved out of my parents' house when I was eighteen and I needed money. Camming was an easy option. You don't really need any skills to get started. There's no manager you have to convince to hire you."

There's the slightest furrow in Angel's brow, and his lips are pressed together in concentration. He's really listening to my answer, like he really wants to know.

"I was good at it and it was fun. I built up a following really quickly, then I met my friends—Hayden and Sebastian and Noel. We work together a lot, especially since Sebastian started The Camboy Network. And now it's kind of, like, a career?"

I hate that my voice goes up at the end, as if I have doubts. Because I don't. Camming *is* my career. Sex work is work, damn it. We've all put a lot into making The Camboy Network successful and our efforts are totally paying off.

"But that's not the only thing you do, right? You also dance?" Angel asks. There's no derision in his voice, no hint of accusation. He's genuinely interested in my life. He actually wants to understand.

No one's ever done that before—taken an interest in what I do for a living. My family makes a point of not asking, and all my friends are already in the industry. I've never had a chance to explain why I do what I do.

My stomach flutters with butterflies at the chance to brag about myself a bit. And the intensely focused look in Angel's eyes makes me warm all over. I can't help sounding a little giddy when I speak.

"Yup! The camming pays for the dancing. Especially at the beginning when I was taking a lot of classes. I get paid for pole dancing now, but nowhere near enough to live off of. If it wasn't for the camming, I wouldn't have the time to dance."

Angel's quiet for a moment, gaze drifting off to the side. It looks like there's a lot going through his head and I don't want to rush him into talking if he's not ready. Then suddenly, he buries his face into the pillow and mumbles something I can't understand.

"Uh, I didn't catch that."

He pops open one eye and shifts just enough to unmuffle his lips. "I can't stop thinking about it?"

I press my lips together and take a slow, calming breath. Jesus Christ Almighty, how is he so goddamn adorable?! I want to reach through the screen and pinch his cheeks. I want to see if his ears have gone pink like they did that day at the party. I shift to press the pillow more firmly against my aching erection.

"Um, what part can't you stop thinking about?"

Angel buries his face again and stays like that for so long I'm worried he's going to suffocate.

"It's okay if you don't want to share," I say, trying to coax him out of the pillow.

Angel lets out a huff and a grumble, then the camera goes all blurry. The sound of a mattress squeaking comes through the line, then Angel comes back into view. He's sitting up now, leaning against the headboard, wide, hairy chest on full display.

My cock is rock hard. Holy hell, that chest. With the low lighting, it's not super clear, but I can make out the rounded pecs and the swell of his belly. All covered in dark hair with two distinct nipples peeking through.

My mouth waters. It fucking waters and I have to gulp down my own saliva before it leaks out the side of my mouth.

"It isn't any one thing, I don't think," Angel says, and I quickly blink away the fog of lust to make sure I don't miss anything. "It's... everything. All of it. Together."

He's not looking at the camera as he speaks. Instead, his gaze is focused somewhere off to the side, and his brows are drawn together, and his lips are twisted up. He's not merely concentrating. He looks frustrated.

"Does that make any sense?" He shifts his gaze to the camera, and even though the lighting is bad and the angle isn't great and his face is about half the size of my phone's screen, it feels like he's looking straight into my soul.

I don't know how to describe the look in his eyes, but it's intense and potent. It catches me in its snare and I don't want it to let me go. There are hidden depths to this man, places in him that I doubt he's ever explored himself. Places he probably doesn't even know exist. He might be a cuddly teddy bear on the surface, but his soul is old and profound.

Has he always been like this? Even back when we were kids? I had no reason to be friends with him back then, but now I wish I'd taken the time to get to know him. Maybe I would've discovered this buried treasure years before now.

"I…" *have no idea what you're asking because I'm too distracted by your hairy chest and soulful eyes.*

He drops his gaze again and I suck in a lungful of air. I hadn't realized I stopped breathing. I blink and shake my head. I feel like I'm coming out of some sort of hypnotic daze.

"Um, I think it'd be good for you to talk to Sebastian," I finally say, then hurry to add, "It doesn't mean you're committing to anything. But Sebastian's a cool guy and he's really smart. He always has an answer for everything."

There's that look of intense concentration again, as if the offer requires serious consideration before he signs his life away.

"I can be there, if you want. We can chat about camming or about being gay or about whatever you want! You can come over to our place and we can have drinks or order in or just hang out. It'll be low-key."

God, I need to stop rambling.

But there's a quirk at the corner of Angel's mouth, and the solemn look in his eyes lightens.

"What do you say?" I ask again, wanting him to say "yes" way more than I should.

When he finally nods, it feels like fireworks go off in my stomach. I almost want to jump up and down on the bed.

"Yeah?" I ask, needing verbal confirmation.

"Yeah, I'll meet with you and Sebastian."

CHAPTER
EIGHT

ANGEL

I've lost my mind. It's the only explanation for why I'm in Brooklyn, loitering outside Rhys's apartment building.

I've been telling myself that this isn't a meeting, it's just hanging out with some guys. Drinking beer and eating pizza, shooting the shit, and stuff like that.

So maybe we talk about porn. Guys talk about porn all the time. No big deal.

Except my palms are sweaty and my stomach is queasy and I can't seem to catch my breath. I lean against the side of the building, pressing my palms into the rough brick behind me.

I'm calm. I'm cool. Everything is fine. Nothing's wrong.

When the urge to hurl passes, I find the right button on the building's intercom. My hand shakes a bit as I press it and a part of me hopes that this is the wrong building, or I've gotten the date wrong. *Anything* that will work as an excuse for me to turn around and go back home.

But nope. Rhys's voice comes through the intercom, bright and cheery.

"Hello?"

"Hey, hi, it's… uh, this is Angel. We spoke on the phone the other day?" I squeeze my eyes shut and my ears get a bit warm. Ugh, why do I sound like I'm a plumber coming over to check his pipes?

Rhys laughs as he speaks. "Yup, I remember! Come on up. We're on the third floor."

The buzzer sounds and I push through the front door. My feet are heavy as I take the stairs and my palm sticks to the handrail when I steady myself. It takes way too long and not nearly long enough to get up to the third floor.

When I get there, there's a door already propped open and voices float out into the hallway. I stall out on the landing, catching my breath while the sound of my heartbeat pulses in my ears.

I can still turn back. I can disappear down the stairs and out the front door. I can ignore Rhys's messages or delete his number from my phone entirely. I can pretend the last couple weeks haven't happened at all.

The door opens and Rhys appears with a big smile on his face.

I forget to breathe.

His hair is still purple, but lighter than the last time I saw it. It flows around his shoulders in waves. The collar of his shirt hangs off one shoulder and the hem is cropped above his belly button, revealing a flat and toned midriff. His shorts are… very short, leaving his long, shapely legs completely bare.

When my eyes finally reach his face again, Rhys's smile

has turned sly. Like he knows I'm checking him out. Like he knows I like what I see.

But was I? Do I? The answer should be no, right? Because I'm not gay. I'm not supposed to be gay. I gulp.

"Hey, Angel," Rhys says, and his voice has me stepping forward, drawing me in.

He doesn't back away as I approach. Instead, his chin lifts so he can peer up at me. The movement changes the angle of his long, elegant neck. He blinks once, and his long lashes fan down to pink cheeks before lifting again. His lips part slightly and his breath hitches so quietly I wouldn't have noticed if I wasn't standing so close.

Someone clears their throat loudly, breaking through this strange trance we've found ourselves in. "You want to let the guy in?"

Rhys rolls his eyes and shakes his head, but he steps back, holding the door for me. It opens onto a long, narrow hallway that isn't wide enough for us to stand side by side. So I take the door from Rhys, locking it behind me, before following him into the apartment.

His hips sway as he walks. His shorts barely cover the rounded globes of his bum. I don't mean to stare, but it's just... it's right in front of me and it's so round and it's swaying.

"Boys, this is Angel. Angel, this is Hayden and Sebastian."

I tear my gaze away from Rhys's butt to find two other guys in the living room. I recognize both of them. Hayden's got reddish-blond hair with eyes so green, they almost look fake. Sebastian's got brown hair, brown eyes, and tanned skin that makes him look like the boy next door.

They're both smiling knowingly at me.

Crap. They caught me staring at Rhys's ass. My ears go red-hot and I completely lose my ability to form words.

Sebastian's eyes widen a fraction before he jumps into action. "Hey, Angel! Great to meet you!" He holds his hand out for a handshake and I wipe my palm on my jeans before I take it.

"Hi, how you doing?"

"What do you want to drink?" Hayden asks, pointing over his shoulder with his thumb. "We've got beer and cider. Or I just mixed up some strawberry daiquiris for these two."

Sebastian picks up a glass of bright pink slushy from the coffee table to show me. "It's really good. Hayden's a wiz at anything kitchen-related."

I reach up to give my jaw a quick scratch. "Uh, beer is fine. Thanks."

"Coming right up!"

Rhys stands off to the side with his own glass of pink slushy. He plays with the straw before bringing it to his lips for a sip. His eyes lock with mine as he sucks, and the heat from my ears spreads across my cheeks.

"Here you go!" Hayden holds out a dark brown bottle.

I take it, clutching at the cold, solid glass. The alcohol goes down smooth and settles in my stomach. It douses some of the heat burning inside me and before I know it, I've finished half the bottle. Oops.

"Grab a seat!" Hayden directs me over to an armchair. "I'm going to order some pizzas. Any requests?"

I shake my head. "N-no. I'll eat anything. Thanks."

I sneak a glance at Rhys who's taken the end of the couch farthest away from me. He's all curled up, with his legs folded under him and an elbow resting on the back of the couch. His fingers are threaded through his hair and the strawberry daiquiri is balanced on his knee.

Sebastian sits down closer to me. "So, you and Rhys grew up together?"

It takes me a second to realize Sebastian's talking to me. "Oh, uh, yeah, well, sort of. I grew up with Nico."

"My brother," Rhys adds for clarification.

"What was Rhys like as a kid?" Sebastian asks with a twinkle in his eye.

Rhys's foot shoots out from under him and his toes dig into Sebastian's side. Sebastian yelps and squirms away with a laugh.

"What? It's a legitimate question!" he exclaims.

"No, it's not. I was born this fabulous!" Rhys flicks his hair over his shoulder and strikes a pose.

"Pizzas ordered!" Hayden scoots around the coffee table and grabs Rhys's ankle. He lifts it out of the way so he can sit down between Rhys and Sebastian and wriggles around until he's snuggled in.

They look cozy, all three of them squished onto the couch like that. And I'm in this armchair all by myself. Not that I want to join them or anything. It's just...

My gaze drifts to Rhys again and he's watching me. I don't know how to interpret the look in those deep, dark eyes. There's a wariness in them, maybe a touch of shyness? Which makes no sense because Rhys is the exact opposite of shy.

"What are we talking about?"

"Angel was just telling us about baby Rhys."

"No, he wasn't," Rhys objects without taking his eyes off me.

Is that what he's worried about? Me telling his friends about what he was like as a kid? A smile grows on my lips.

"He was cute," I say, the words leaving my lips before I've consciously thought them. Images, memories of Rhys as a teenager rise to the surface, and I have no idea where they're from. "He never dressed like the rest of us."

Rhys sighs dramatically and rolls his eyes. "It's not my fault no one in the old neighborhood has any fashion sense."

My smile grows wider at his reaction. "His hair was long already."

He twists a lock between his fingers. "You do not want to see me with short hair." He shudders, like the idea gives him the creeps.

"You always knew when he walked into a room. Everyone would go quiet."

Rhys's expression goes wary again. "They would stare at me," he says quietly.

"They couldn't look away."

Just like I can't look away now. There's something about Rhys—even barefoot, in shorts and a crop top, curled up on the couch—that's irresistible, that demands attention. A star that shines so bright, it can't be ignored.

Rhys breaks eye contact first, dropping his gaze and taking a large slurp of his daiquiri. I shift in my seat before taking another gulp of my beer.

I don't understand the effect Rhys has on me. It feels like magic or witchcraft, and the scariest part is, I'm not running for the hills. I don't want to run away from it. I want to run toward it.

"So..." Sebastian's voice cuts through the silence. "Rhys says you work in construction? What's that like?"

I shift again and rub my palm along the top of my thigh. "Yeah, I, uh, like working with my hands."

Sebastian nods. "Mmhmm, and what types of projects do you work on? Home renos and stuff like that?"

"Uh, no, commercial projects. We're doing an office building in Midtown right now."

"Construction workers are hot," Hayden says, to no one in particular.

"They are," Sebastian agrees. "Tons of videos with construction workers."

"You've run the numbers?" Rhys asks, eyes narrowed.

Sebastian scoffs lightly. "Of course I've run the numbers. Who do you think I am?"

"He means numbers for videos," Hayden explains to me. "Like number of downloads and views, number of subscribers, things like that. To see if they're profitable. Sebastian's very business-minded."

"And I can confidently say that videos with construction workers do *very well*." The emphasis he places on those two words makes my tummy feel unsettled and fluttery. "Especially *straight* construction workers."

I drain the last of my beer, but instead of cooling me off, the alcohol sits like a warm pool in my stomach. My ears burn and I can't help tugging at my collar.

"Sebby!" Rhys scolds him in a hushed voice.

"What? I thought you said that's what we're meeting about." Sebastian sounds confused.

"Yeah, but you don't have to..." Rhys waves his hands around. "You know."

Sebastian glances at Hayden, who shrugs. Apparently neither of them knows.

"Don't pressure him!" Rhys's eyes flash in defiance as

he tries to speak without moving his lips, as if I won't be able to hear him that way.

Rhys is being so protective and it loosens something inside me that's always been wound up tight. I'm usually the protective one, using my size to block players on the football field or help Mama around the house, or even just stand there intimidatingly when Sabrina's trying to get rid of a guy she doesn't like. People don't really rush to my defense, they don't bother standing up for me.

"That's okay," I say quietly, suddenly feeling a little choked up.

"Are you sure?" Rhys asks me, so full of concern.

I nod, despite the queasiness that's making the alcohol slosh uncomfortably in my stomach. I appreciate Rhys trying to protect me, but Sebastian's right. I'm the one who brought up the idea with Rhys in the first place. I agreed to come here today. As insane as this whole thing is, it would be cowardly of me to leave without having this conversation.

"Yeah, I, uh…" I gulp, then clear my throat. "It's okay."

Silence stretches several long moments before Sebastian speaks. When he does, his voice is gentle and calm. "How about I tell you about what we do at The Camboy Network?"

I nod, glad to be able to listen rather than speak.

Sebastian sits up straighter, and his face lights up. "It's basically a film studio these days. We specialize in gay adult content. I do most of the producing, directing, and editing. And Rhys and Hayden and the others perform."

Sebastian pauses and I nod to show him I'm following. Even though I'm not, not a hundred percent. But I think I've got the gist and the prospect makes me feel all sorts of things I don't understand. Jittery and cramped, but also hot and a little tingly. I'm uncomfortable, but the only thing I can think of to ease the discomfort is... to take all my clothes off. It makes absolutely no freaking sense.

"If you wanted to work on a project with us, we'd pay you a standard daily rate. If the video does well and if you enjoy performing, we could talk about doing a series of videos."

I nod again, although, at this point, I don't know what it means anymore. Am I just saying I get what he's saying? Or am I agreeing to something more?

"If you don't mind me asking..." Sebastian shoots a sideways glance at Rhys, whose expression is serious and guarded. "Have you been with a guy before?"

I curl my hands into fists on my thighs. My ears burn red-hot and my tongue feels too big for my mouth. I shake my head, not trusting myself to speak.

"So... why would you want to do gay porn?"

All of a sudden, I forget how swallowing works, or how saliva works, or how my throat works, and I start choking on my own spit.

All three stare in alarm for a moment before jumping into action. Hayden races to the kitchen and Rhys rushes to my side. Perching on the arm of my chair, he holds my shoulder with one hand and rubs my back with the other. The steady rhythm and firm pressure calms the weird spasm that's overtaken me. It feels so nice.

"Sebby!" Rhys growls at Sebastian over my head.

"What? I didn't do anything! I just asked a question!"

Hayden returns with a glass of water in his hand. "Here you go."

I take the glass and sip—carefully—as my coughing fit

fades. My throat feels a little raw, like there's still something in it.

"You don't have to answer the question," Rhys says to me, his hand still roaming over my back. "You don't owe us an answer."

He's probably right. I don't owe them an answer. But I owe *myself* one, don't I? Shouldn't I know why I'm so interested in this? Shouldn't I know why I'm here?

"Is it for the money?" Sebastian prompts.

"Sebby!" Rhys hisses, again.

"It's why most people get into porn. There's nothing wrong with needing a bit of extra cash."

Money. Could that be it? I mean, I could definitely use it. With Sabrina and Jonah living with Mama now, there are two extra mouths to feed, plus all the baby stuff that Jonah needs. I'm still paying the mortgage on Mama's house. Well, technically the second mortgage that Pop took out to finance his gambling habit before he up and died, leaving us with a boatload of debt. My job in construction pays well, but not that well.

Sure, money. That's a good reason.

"Um, yeah, I need the cash," I croak.

Sebastian shoots a glance over my head to Rhys, one that says he's not convinced.

"What about straight porn? Have you thought about doing that? Or even solo stuff? You can make cash that way too."

No. No freaking way. My body physically recoils at those suggestions, stuffing me into the corner of the chair where Rhys wraps his arm around my shoulders. The touch is so soothing, soft and strong at the same time. Safe and secure.

Sebastian looks both confused and amused. He lifts both hands, flicking them so his palms face out. "Or not. That's fine. I'm just throwing out suggestions. A little brainstorming sesh."

"Being comfortable is important," Hayden adds with a nod. "The last thing you want is not being able to get it up when everyone else is ready to roll."

The hands on my shoulders tighten a smidge, and I find myself leaning back with my head resting on Rhys's… chest? Shoulder? Stomach? I can't tell, but it feels… nice.

"You don't have to do anything you're not comfortable with," Rhys says. His voice comes from just above my head, edged with something steely and fierce. "You don't have to do any of this if you don't want to."

Sebastian and Hayden both nod in agreement, which just leaves me. Do I want to do this?

The rational, logical, sane answer is no. Of course I don't. I'm not gay. We're not about to go bankrupt. If anyone found out I was doing porn, I'd get into so much trouble with Mama. I have no good reason to do this.

And yet, there's been this seed growing inside me ever since that party. It's gotten bigger with every passing day, sinking its roots into me and latching on tight. I don't know what it is or what it wants with me. I don't know why this is happening to me now.

There's only one thing I do know—I can't ignore it.

I nod. "I'll do it."

CHAPTER
NINE

RHYS

Sebastian and his boyfriend, Christian, are in the kitchen, putting the finishing touches on the apartment we've rented for the shoot. They've hung up plastic sheeting and set out painting supplies. They've even covered the cupboards with removable contact paper that makes the doors look like they're half painted.

Meanwhile, I'm freaking the fuck out in the bedroom.

I'm never like this before a shoot. I've done so many of these with so many different people, I have my routine down to a science. Liquid diet for a couple days before-hand to make sure I'm completely cleaned out. Wax job so my skin is silky smooth. Extra-strength hairspray. Water-proof makeup. Cute lingerie. And I'm ready for the camera.

I didn't stray from my routine this time, and yet, I feel on edge, like I've forgotten something big, something important. My stomach is all twisted up in knots, and my heart is racing like I've just finished a pole routine. I'm crawling out of my skin and I can't sit still.

It's because of Angel, of course. I want today to go well for him.

He's put so much trust in me with this whole thing. So much naive and innocent trust that I now have a responsibility to protect. I introduced him to this world. It's my duty to make sure he's taken care of while he's here.

I want him to feel comfortable and relaxed. I want him to enjoy himself on set and get along with Sebastian and Christian. I want him to walk away with no regrets.

But if I'm honest with myself, it's not only that. Deep down inside, where I keep my darkest, most selfish desires, I want him to like it. I want him to like having sex with me.

Because I think I might have a teeny-tiny little crush on Angel.

Fuck.

What's the first rule of gay club? Don't fall in love with the straight boy. Trust me. Been there. Done that. Do not recommend.

"Uh… Rhys?"

I jump and yelp as I spin around. Angel is standing in the bedroom doorway, looking adorable as fuck. He must have gone to the barber's because his hair and beard are trim and neat. He's wearing a plaid lumberjack shirt on top of a thin, white dudebro tank top. The golden crucifix necklace lies on top of the tank. His jeans are paint-splattered and torn, and his boots are all scuffed up. With the hard hat Sebastian's got for him, he'll look every bit the home reno contractor he's supposed to play.

My cock roars to life, straining against the lace panties

I'm wearing. I shift on my feet and adjust the two sides of my robe, trying to hide my growing erection.

"Hey, Angel! You're here!" I wince at how surprised I sound. "I mean, of course you're here. You said you would be. I didn't think you were lying or anything." *Oh god, stop talking, Rhys.*

Angel scratches his jaw, lips curled into a sheepish smile. "Yeah, I'm here."

His gaze travels down my body in a slow perusal, his eyes bright with what looks like appreciation. If I didn't know better, I would think he's checking me out, that maybe he likes what he sees.

"You look good," he says, voice warm and soft, like the most comforting of blankets. It turns my bones into jelly and my cock into granite.

I tuck my hair behind my ear as the twisting in my stomach becomes more of a fluttering. "Thanks. You look good too."

He takes a few steps toward me, eyes locked on mine. Suddenly, the air in the room feels a little thin. My lips part as I try to suck in extra oxygen, and his gaze drops to my mouth. His eyes darken to a rich brown that makes it even more difficult to breathe.

He smells like fresh sawdust. I want to run my nose along his neck, rub myself against his body, and lick every single inch of his skin. I want to rake my fingers through all his fur. I want his beard to leave me red all over. I want his large, strong hands to hold me to him and never let go.

"Hey! You guys ready?"

We jump away from each other at the sound of Sebastian's cheerful voice. The tips of Angel's ears are tinted pink, and his gaze is cast down to the floor.

Sebastian looks from Angel to me, with a question in his expression.

"Yup!" I answer for both of us. "We'll be out in a sec."

Sebastian gives me an encouraging smile before disappearing again.

"How are you feeling?" I ask Angel, pulling him deeper into the bedroom.

"Um, okay? I think?" He rubs his palms on his thighs before curling his hands into fists.

"It's okay to be nervous."

He nods, Adam's apple bobbing. "Yeah, I am, a little."

"Do you have any questions?"

He blinks at me and I can see the millions of questions racing around inside his head. His mouth hangs open like he can't decide which one to ask first or how to ask them.

I know that Sebastian's already given him a truckload of information about safe sex, consent and limits, and blah, blah, blah. The boys and I joke that the only thing Sebastian loves more than Christian is paperwork.

Both Angel and I tested negative for STIs. I'm always on PrEP, but The Camboy Network covered Angel's prescription for him. Angel had to fill out a form about what sex acts he was okay with and what was off the table —not that we're doing anything especially kinky today.

We've even gone over today's shooting schedule, scene by scene, and rehearsed some of the lines Sebastian wrote for us.

The past couple weeks have been pretty intense, to be honest. More than any other video Sebastian's directed, and those have always been intense. But Angel is new to this, and Sebastian, being who he is, went the extra ten miles.

Which is why I'm pretty sure that Angel's questions have more to do with nervousness than how today will go down. I don't blame him—I'm nervous as hell too.

"You'll be with me, right?" he finally asks, and fuck if it doesn't make my heart swell in my chest.

"Yup. Every step of the way." I take one of his hands and unfurl his fingers to sandwich them between my palms. "I've got you."

He smiles, small and sweet, and I want to believe it's just for me.

Still holding his hand, I lead him out to the living room where Sebastian has the first scene set up. It'll be the pre-video interview where Sebastian asks us a bunch of questions so we can "connect" with our audience.

Angel takes a seat on the couch and I curl up next to him, turned toward him with my legs tucked under me. Sebastian sits opposite us and Christian hits the record button on the camera.

"Angelo, Rhys, thank you both for being here with us today." Sebastian uses the stage name we came up with for Angel. I had a bunch of out-there ideas, but Angel felt more comfortable using something closer to what he's used to.

Angel's ears flush as he smiles shyly and mumbles a hello.

I lean in, lifting my elbow onto the back of the couch and resting my hand lightly on his shoulder. Angel glances at it, then lifts his gaze to mine. We're inches apart and I'm caught in those soft, warm browns that make me feel all ooey gooey on the inside.

This keeps happening to me. Angel gets close, he stares into my eyes, and it's like I'm hypnotized, ensnared, trapped. I can't look away, I can barely breathe. I just want to bask in his attention, soak it all in until I burst.

Sebastian clears his throat. "So, uh, Angelo, this is the first time you're doing a video with The Camboy Network."

Angel turns toward Sebastian, but he keeps his eyes locked on mine until the last moment. "Yeah, it is."

"Fun fact, you're not actually gay, right?" Sebastian keeps his tone light and he smiles encouragingly. The question shouldn't take Angel by surprise. Sebastian sent them to both of us a few days ago.

Angel shakes his head. "No, I'm straight."

"Do you have a girlfriend?"

Angel scratches his jaw and shoots Sebastian a rueful look. It looks real, like almost too real. Like, if I didn't know Angel was the least disingenuous person on the planet, I would think he's acting.

"No, not at the moment."

"And this will be your first time with a guy?"

Angel sneaks another glance at me and my breath catches. "Yeah."

Sebastian lets the moment linger before continuing. "Rhys, how do you feel about being Angelo's first man?"

My heart thuds against the inside of my ribs. So hard and loud that I'm sure the microphone can pick it up. I feel… hungry for him, possessive, greedy. I want to be Angel's first. I want to be his only. I want to snatch him up and hoard him all to myself, so no one else can have him. I want him to be mine.

"I'm going to show him the time of his life," I say, still watching Angel as he watches me. I'm going for a fun and flirty tone, but my voice is a bit too husky for that. Angel's eyes go a little unfocused.

"Well, Angelo, you are in good hands!" Sebastian exclaims with too much enthusiasm, but neither of us react.

We're too wrapped up in each other, in this magnetism that keeps drawing us closer together. I lean in. My chest is pressed against Angel's arm. His lips part and his breath hitches silently. When he exhales, warm air blows across my chin.

I tilt my head and lean in a little more. My nose brushes against his. His beard tickles my skin. My lips slot into place against his.

No one moves. No one makes a sound. All around me is stillness and silence. But inside, fireworks are exploding, sirens are sounding, and my brain is screaming in excited and confused shock.

Angel lets out a whimper that shatters the quiet. I kiss him. Like my fucking life depends on it. I nip and lick. I'm gentle, but persistent, working my way into his mouth.

Angel kisses me back. Not quite as eagerly. But when I lick along the seams of his lips, he opens for me and his tongue reaches out tentatively. When it meets mine, he shudders from head to toe.

Fuck. I want to climb on top of him right now and explore every inch of his mouth with my tongue, video be damned. But I pull away instead. I'm supposed to be the professional here. I can't let myself get carried away.

"Whew! At least we won't need to worry about your chemistry," Sebastian teases.

We move to the kitchen where the first part of the scene

plays out. Sebastian walks us through the blocking and we recite our lines a few times before the camera starts rolling.

Angel pretends he's packing up his tools when I come in wearing my lacy panties and matching lace teddy. My short, silk robe is open and hanging off one shoulder.

"Where are you going? The kitchen's not finished yet," I say, acting confused.

"You haven't paid my last two invoices." Angel sounds a little stilted, but that's okay. We're not going for Oscar-worthy performances here. "I'm not doing any more work until you pay me."

"But… but…" I clutch the two sides of my robe together, lifting up my bare shoulder as I feign distress. "I don't have any money!"

Angel shrugs. "Then I'll have to leave your kitchen unfinished."

I let my jaw hang open for a moment before turning on the seduction. "I don't have any money. But there are other ways I could pay you."

I step toward Angel and reach out to draw a single finger down his front. The tip of my finger runs over the swell of his belly and down to his belt, then farther still to the impressive bulge in his jeans.

"I… I…" His voice is breathy and his hands are curled into fists by his sides. "I'm not gay."

Angel's protest is weak, and he looks so flustered that I'm having a hard time remembering that this is all an act. The real Angel isn't actually turned on by the prospect of sexual favors as payment. The real Angel isn't actually trembling because he wants my mouth on his cock. This is all fake. Make-believe. Pretend.

"You don't have to be gay," I say, hooking my finger

into a belt loop and tugging him closer. "Just close your eyes. You won't notice a difference at all."

Then I drop to my knees, and even though I told Angel to close his eyes, his gaze follows me down. I bite my lip, peer up at him through my lashes, and quickly undo the button on his jeans.

He shudders as I pull the zipper down and reveal the tighty-whities underneath. My cock throbs in my panties as I stare at the soft, white cotton straining over Angel's monster dick. So fucking innocent. So fucking pure.

I know Sebastian asked him to wear plain white briefs. Angel probably doesn't wear underwear like this in real life. But the line between the character in this scene and the actual man from my old neighborhood is getting dangerously blurred.

I hook my fingers under the elastic waistband of Angel's tighty-whities and pull them down. The sight that greets me makes my mouth water.

Angel's dick is hard, with thick, juicy veins. A drop of pre-cum runs down his length. He isn't very long, but he's oh-so girthy. He's going to stretch me beyond belief and my hole clenches in anticipation.

I grip him at the base and Angel lets out a soft whine. When I glance up, his eyes are squeezed shut, his teeth are clamped around his bottom lip, and his chest is rising and falling with each frantic breath. He looks like he's right on the edge, like he's about to blow if I so much as give him a lick.

I break character and squeeze his thigh. "Hey, Angel?"

His eyes fly open, darting around the room before landing on me.

"Do you want to wear a cock ring?" I ask. There's

always several in the boxes of supplies Sebastian brings on set.

Angel blinks at me like he doesn't know what I'm talking about.

"It'll help you last longer. You know, take the edge off."

Behind the camera, Christian hands something to Sebastian who holds it out to me. It's an adjustable cock ring made up of a length of elastic folded over on itself. A bead threaded through the ends controls how loose or tight it is around the cock.

Angel glances from me to the ring and back. He nods jerkily and I take the ring from Sebastian. Since Angel's already so hard, the adjustable ring makes it easier and safer for me to put it on him. I slip it over the tip of Angel's cock and slide it down to the base. Then I tuck it behind his balls and carefully adjust the bead so it's snug.

"How does that feel?" I ask, running my hand up and down his thigh to soothe him.

Angel nods. "Good," he croaks. "Better."

"Pull his underwear back up and do that part again." Sebastian instructs as he picks up one of the handheld cameras and gets himself into position.

I put Angel's dick away, and when Sebastian gives me the go-ahead, I draw his underwear down. The sight is just as good the second time around. Maybe better, now that there's a black ring around the base of his cock.

I can't help myself this time. I move in before thinking and lick him from base to tip.

CHAPTER
TEN

ANGEL

I'm flying. I'm falling. I'm floating somewhere in between. There's no way I'm still standing on my own two feet. Not when Rhys's hands are on my junk, moving me around with so much care and efficiency. The ring he put on me brought me down to earth a little, but that lick sent me right back up.

I've never felt anything like this before. Not when I'm giving myself a hand job. Not with my girlfriend in high school. Not even when I was first going through puberty and all I could think about all day was getting off.

This is a hundred times—a thousand times—more intense. It's not just my dick that's pulsing and throbbing. My entire body is on fire, burning with the need to come. There's already sweat rolling down my back, soaking through my shirt. An electric current runs along the surface of my skin. My head is spinning and I have a deep need to bury my dick into something hot and tight.

A ragged sound rips from my throat as Rhys takes me

into his mouth. Just the tip at first, which is good, because I can't take any more than that right now. His tongue swirls around the sensitive head, then wiggles into my slit. A zing of pleasure shoots through me before pooling in my groin.

Oh god, I'm going to come. I'm going to come.

But I don't.

Rhys takes in more of me, engulfing my dick in more wet heat. I still don't come. It's almost like I can't. Which is exactly what I need, because otherwise I would definitely blow my load the second I laid eyes on him.

There's barely an inch of my dick visible, with the black silicone tied around the base. Rhys's pretty, pink lips are stretched thin, and his cheeks are hollowed out. His eyes are heavily made up today, with long, dark lashes fluttering as he gazes up at me. His hair is a soft lavender color against the darker violet of the silk and lace he's wearing.

I've never seen a man in lingerie before, but I don't need to compare Rhys to anyone to know that he wears it well. The lace panties are a triangular patch over his groin. The top also has two triangular pieces that frame his pecs, then lots of flowy fabric around his middle. The robe hangs off his bare shoulders, revealing acres of creamy skin.

He's a vision. I can't take my eyes off him.

Rhys pushes forward until his nose is flush against my pelvis. My dick slides right to the back of his mouth and into his throat. He swallows around me and the tight squeeze around the sensitive head of my dick is almost painful.

I cry out as pleasure roils around inside me, searching

for a release valve. But there's nothing to ease the pressure. Instead, it just builds and builds and builds as Rhys works me over with his mouth.

My hands end up in his hair as I scramble for something to hold on to. Rhys moans when the lavender strands catch in my fingers. The vibrations travel deep into my groin, adding to the growing pressure until I think I'm going to pass out.

"Wait, wait, stop."

Rhys immediately pops off me. His chin is wet with drool and lines of spit hang between his lips and the tip of my cock. His eyes have been watering, making them gleam and glisten as he blinks up at me. He's still holding my dick with fingers tipped in the same lavender as his hair.

I squeeze my eyes shut, but it's no use. The image of him on his knees in front of me is already burned into my retinas. So lewd. So debauched.

"You okay, Angel?" Rhys's voice is hoarse and it sends shivers down my spine. I did that to him. He sounds like that because my dick was in his throat.

A whine escapes me as my body tries to chase down the orgasm that's out of my reach.

"I think that's good."

The unexpected voice makes me jump and only then do I remember we're not alone. Sebastian has been beside us with a camera in his hands this whole time. His boyfriend, Christian, is right behind him.

I didn't notice them while Rhys had his mouth on me. In fact, I completely forgot they were here. But now that I take in the cameras and lights set up around us, it dawns on me that they've captured everything. Every touch, every moan, every shudder. All of this, every reaction, will be on the internet at some point. Other people, strangers, will see what I did here today.

The realization should send me running for the exit. But my feet are planted firmly in place. I should be scared, terrified, sick with fear. But all I want is to haul Rhys up to me and kiss him like he kissed me earlier.

Tender and sweet. I had no idea kisses could be like that. In the past, it's always just been a pretty mechanical lips-on-lips situation. I never got why people made such a big deal about them. But Rhys's kiss was anything but mechanical. It was a full-body experience that I felt all the way down to my toes.

I want to do it again.

"Let's move things to the bedroom," Sebastian says, as he and Christian start carrying equipment from the kitchen.

Rhys gently tucks me back into my underwear, then gracefully rises to his feet. He's wearing a soft smile, but there's a hint of distance in his eyes. I hesitate, stopping myself from kissing him the way I want to.

He seems super into all this, eager and enthusiastic. But who am I kidding? Rhys is a professional, and this is all pretend. Of course he seems into it. It's his job to make it look convincing. That doesn't mean he wants to kiss me when the camera isn't trained on us. This is nothing more than an act.

I tamp down the unexpected disappointment rising inside me and let Rhys lead me into the bedroom.

It's pretty basic in there. A double bed sits against one wall with small nightstands on either side. The dresser that sat in the corner has been moved out to the living room to make space for one of the big lights sitting on a tall tripod. Generic art hangs on the walls.

I have to duck underneath a light and skirt around a camera to get to the bed. Once there, I gulp at the sight.

There's absolutely nothing special about the bed. The pillows and bedspread are covered in white linen. And that's it. Except it's where I'll be having sex for the very first time. Well, like, full-on sex. With a guy. With anyone. And it'll all be caught on camera.

My stomach feels all unsettled and weird. But that's becoming pretty normal whenever I'm around Rhys. He does things to me that I don't understand. Things that are way outside of my comfort zone, and yet don't scare me nearly as much as they should. Things that feel inevitable, that feel almost right.

"Angel, if you can stand right here." Sebastian points to a spot next to the bed. "Rhys will lead you through the scene, okay? Just let him do his thing."

Rhys gives me a wink. "You good?"

I nod and stand where Sebastian wants me, not sure where to look or what to do with my hands. I shift on my feet, wipe my palms on my jeans, and try to ignore how fast my heart is beating.

Sebastian calls action.

"Keep your eyes closed," Rhys says, voice airy and light. "I'll take good care of you. You're gonna have the best orgasm of your life."

My dick twitches at his promise and I slam my eyes shut so I won't accidentally peek.

His hands go to the waistband of my jeans, which are still undone from earlier. He pushes them down, along with my underwear, until they're pooled around my ankles.

He slips his hands under the hem of my tank, fingernails scraping lightly over my stomach and up to my chest. The shirt rides up and with a quick tug, he pulls it up and over my head. The fabric is caught around my shoulders. The plaid shirt I'm wearing over it has fallen halfway down my arms. I'm all tangled up in my clothes and yet fully exposed from chin to shins.

"Goddamn..." Rhys whispers, as his fingernails trail over my body. He's gentle, but the light scrape still leaves lines of fire in its wake.

Across my chest, around my nipples, quick flicks against the swollen nubs that make my dick jump. Down to my belly and around in circles, like he might be trying to comb my body hair into a special design.

Rhys guides me back a few inches to the bed, then down until I'm lying on my back with my feet still on the floor. His hands continue to move, fingers finding the tender skin at the crease of my hips, then the tops of my thighs that I never knew were so sensitive.

His hands brush up my thighs again. One wraps around my dick, stroking and twisting, while the other cups my balls, rolling them against each other. My erection had gone down a little when we moved from the kitchen into the bedroom, but now it's roaring back to life.

Pre-cum pumps out of me, giving Rhys more than enough to work with as he drives me crazy with his hands. Then he adds his tongue, licks and swipes and swirls.

With my eyes closed, I can't see what he's doing. Can't anticipate where he's going to touch and with what. Not knowing what's coming next makes everything way more extreme—hotter, tighter, wetter, better.

"Ahh!" My hips come off the bed as Rhys closes his lips around me again. He sinks all the way down in one smooth motion, taking every inch of me until I'm buried in his throat.

He still has my balls in his hand, massaging them like he's priming them to explode. But the ring around the base of my dick keeps me from ever getting there.

When he comes up for air, my dick feels cold for a second before he covers it with his hand again. It's wetter this time, more squelchy. He must've added lube.

The bed dips as he arranges himself above me, one knee on either side of my hips. Then there's a bit of fumbling before I lose my freaking mind.

It's just something blunt against the tip of my dick at first. I can't figure out what it is or what Rhys is trying to do. It only dawns on me when he lets out a moan and my dick is pushed into something incredibly tight and hot. He's taking me into his body.

Oh shit. Holy crap. This is happening. This is actually happening.

I grip the sheets under me as my entire body shakes and trembles. The pressure on my dick is more than anything I've ever experienced. The heat is scalding. It's so intense, so all-consuming that flashes of white light burst behind my eyelids.

"Fuck. Oh god, you're so thick. Fuck." Rhys's voice sounds strangled, almost like he's in pain.

Without thinking, my eyes fly open and the sight that greets me nearly kills me.

He's hovering above me, hands on my torso as he

holds himself up. The robe he was wearing is gone and so is the flowy top, leaving his stomach and chest and shoulders bare. But a scrap of lace still covers his dick.

Between his spread legs, I can see the fabric is bunched up and pulled to one side. My dick is harder than it's ever been, sticking up from my pelvis and disappearing between Rhys's butt cheeks.

Rhys's eyes are closed. His brow is furrowed. His jaw hangs open, lips glistening under the bright lights. He looks like he's in pain, the kind that borders on ecstasy.

A sound escapes me. Something between a growl and a groan. My hips shoot up before I can stop them, and suddenly, I'm buried in Rhys to the hilt.

Rhys gasps, loudly, his eyes opening then rolling toward the back of his head. He lets out a series of long, unsteady moans and hisses as he quivers above me.

"Oh no! I'm sorry! I'm so sorry!" I was supposed to keep my eyes closed. I was supposed to stay still and let Rhys take the lead. And now I think I've hurt him.

My hands come off the bed, to do I don't know what. Pull him off me? That might hurt him more than I already have. I freeze with my hips arched off the bed and my hands in midair, not knowing what I should do now.

Rhys takes a deep breath, then his expression becomes determined, and he thrusts himself down, shoving my hips back onto the bed.

CHAPTER
ELEVEN

RHYS

I'm so very, very full. Stretched so very, very wide. I fucking love this feeling, of being pushed to my limit and then a little bit more, of being stuffed to within an inch of my life.

The fact that it's Angel's cock doing the stuffing only makes it a thousand times better.

I roll my hips, savoring the sting, cataloging all the places inside me that he touches. He's so thick that he presses up against my prostate without even trying and if I angle myself just right, the pleasure is fucking exquisite.

This is why I love a thick cock. This is why I'm a greedy fucking bottom.

I shudder and shiver, letting myself get carried away by the sensation for a moment before tuning back into reality.

Angel's hands are in the air like he wants to reach for me, but doesn't know if he's allowed. His eyes are wide with alarm. His chest is rising and falling so fast, I think he might hyperventilate.

My own hands are braced against Angel's body. I have to shift and engage my abs in order to lift them and the movement increases the pressure of Angel's cock on my prostate. Another wave of pleasure crashes through me as I take Angel's hands and place them on my hips.

He immediately latches on, sliding his hands up and down, flexing his fingers, until he's found the perfect grip.

I hold onto his wrists, so thick I can barely wrap my fingers all the way around, and start moving. Just a little at first, as my hole loosens and my ass gets used to his girth. Then more when the sting fades and all that remains is fullness and pleasure.

Angel's eyes are glued to that spot between my legs. That spot where his cock meets my ass and disappears inside. He looks transfixed by it, like it's the most mesmerizing thing he's ever seen.

He's pretty mesmerizing himself. His necklace is nestled between his pecs. He's broken out into a sweat, his skin damp and sticky under my hands. His body hair is a couple shades darker now and when I rake my fingers through it, it feels so damn good. It's so tactile, smooth and wiry at the same time. My palms tingle at the touch, and the tingle spreads up my arms and down to my cock.

Which is begging for some attention. I pull my lace panties down to release my cock, leaving my balls trapped inside, and stroke myself as I bounce on Angel's cock. The dual sensations ricochet back and forth, ratcheting up the pleasure building inside me.

Fuck, I'm going to come if I keep this up. It's all so

good, so perfect. Like the whole scene was crafted just for me. Like Angel was made to be mine.

I pinch a nipple, hoping the pain will help ease me back from the brink. But it only adds to the pleasure.

I let go of my dick, bracing my hands on Angel's chest again. But the heavy thud of my cock against his belly sends vibrations straight to my prostate. The loud thwack each time it makes contact sends shivers down my spine.

It's hopeless. I'm too close. Everything is pushing me closer and closer to the edge.

I shoot a glance at Sebastian who is at the edge of the bed, camera in hand. I catch his eye and an unspoken message passes between us. I need to come. Now.

Sebastian nods, giving me the go-ahead, and my head falls back as I give into the desire.

"Fuck, yes! Oh god, Angelo! Fuck!" I slam myself down on Angel again and again. I slide my hands along his body, dig my fingers into his soft, rounded belly.

He grunts when I do that and his hands tighten on my hips. That's all I need to push me over the edge. I come hands-free, cum spraying everywhere as I keep fucking myself on Angel's cock. It lands all over his stomach and my hands. It flies up to hit me on the chin. I'm pretty sure a few drops even land on the camera lens since Sebastian moved in for a close-up.

I slow as the orgasm recedes, but I don't stop and I definitely don't let Angel's cock slip out of me. It's still hard as a rock and if I clench around him, I get another mini-orgasm.

Angel's holding himself stock-still under me, practically vibrating. His fingers are a vise around my hips and he's got his bottom lip caught between his teeth. His eyes are a little wild, like he's on his last strand of self-control.

But he doesn't move, doesn't fuck up into me like I'm sure he wants to. He doesn't flip us over and pound himself into me until I'm a pile of smithereens. Angel is too good for that, too gentle. I'll have to ask him for it, maybe even demand it, if I want him to wreck my hole. And I do, fucking hell, I want it so fucking bad.

I lean down, breath hitching as his cock shifts inside me, and lick up the cum I've painted him with. It's everywhere, which gives me a good excuse to lick everywhere. Every inch of his furry stomach. Every inch of his broad chest. I make a point of swirling my tongue around his nipples a couple times, and the way his body jerks in response sends another aftershock through me.

He tastes salty from the sweat, bitter from my cum. But beneath the scent of sex, he still smells like fresh sawdust, like a cedarwood sauna, like a walk in a pine forest. I want to lick him all over. I want to bury my nose in the crook of his neck. I want to burrow myself into Angel's softness and never leave.

"That's good," Sebastian says, interrupting my feast. "Switch positions?"

Reluctantly, I lift myself off Angel's dick. When it slips out of me, I'm left gaping and open. Empty. Bereft. My hole clenches around nothing and a sudden chill sweeps across my sweat-covered skin. I shiver, and not in a good way.

The bed dips as Angel pushes himself up to a seated position. I sense more than feel his big body behind me, and when I turn to look over my shoulder, he's *right there*.

Our gazes meet and the warmth of his eyes chases away all traces of cold.

Oh god, I'm in really dangerous fucking territory. It would be so easy to fall for Angel, to forget the first rule of gay club and throw my heart straight into a woodchipper. He's everything I want in a man, the perfect fantasy I dreamed up when I was a teenager and wanted to be swept off my feet. But despite the flirty conversations we've had over the past few weeks and what we're doing today, I can't assume that Angel is suddenly gay and wants to be in a relationship with someone like me.

Sebastian claps his hands once, jolting me out of my thoughts.

"Next up, we've got Rhys on his hands and knees on the bed. Angel, you'll be standing behind him. Make sense?" Sebastian gestures to where he wants us. "And you guys can take off the rest of your clothes too."

I only have the lace panties all twisted around my hips, so I quickly shimmy out of them. Angel takes a bit longer to untangle himself from his clothes. He folds each item and neatly sets them all on a chair in the corner. His boots are lined up perfectly under the chair, laces tucked inside. Watching him move so deliberately, taking so much care with something so simple, makes my heart do dangerous, ill-advised things in my chest.

I scramble into position so I don't end up making moon eyes at Angel. I've done enough of that already today, and I'm pretty sure Sebastian's noticed. He'll be on the phone to Hayden as soon as we're done here and I'll never hear the end of it when I get home.

Sebastian calls "Action!" and Angel steps between my legs, his thighs brushing against my ankles. He's supposed to grab me by the hips and fuck me from behind, but there's no grabbing.

Instead, one large, rough hand slides up the outside of my thigh, then covers my ass cheek. Another hand joins it on my other ass cheek. Together they pull me apart.

I moan and arch my back, tilting my ass up in his hands. His thumbs dip into my crease, running up and down the sensitive skin and tugging gently at my hole. I'm open and loose enough that he can probably see inside me. I bet I'm all pink down there, glistening from the lube.

"Wow." The single word comes out in a whisper. Astonished and amazed.

It sends a shudder running through me and my hole quivers with the need to be filled. "Fuck, Angelo, please!" I need his cock inside me. I need him stretching me wide.

But Angel seems too preoccupied with my hole to get to the fucking. He drags one finger down my crease, from my tailbone all the way to my hole. Then he pets me with the tip of his finger.

I whimper and wiggle my hips. I drop down to my elbows and push myself back. "Angeee—" A gasp cuts off my drawn-out whine as Angel dips his finger inside me.

Slowly, with just the tip, like he's testing the waters. I bear down like the experienced bottom I am and his finger slips deeper inside.

"Fuck, yesss! More! Give me more!" Did I mention I was a greedy little bottom? I might be a tad bossy too.

"Go ahead. Put another finger in," Sebastian instructs. "You can fuck him like that for a bit."

A second later, I feel the extra girth. Just like every other part of his body, Angel's fingers are thick, so two of his are more like three of anyone else's. And when he pumps them in and out of me, it's almost like I'm being worked over with a mini-dildo.

"More!" I demand.

When Angel inserts a third finger, I throw my head back at the delicious stretch. It's still nowhere close to having his cock inside me, but I'm pleasantly filled like this. If I could get a butt plug made in the shape of his three fingers, I'd wear it around every fucking day.

Behind me, Angel's breathing is getting louder and louder. The hand on my hip grips me tighter. But he keeps the pace of his fingers nice and slow, in and out, no rush, no hurry.

My dick is hard again, not that it went fully soft at any point. But it's now pulsing to the rhythm of Angel's finger-fucking, one gentle swell of pleasure after another. He's driving me fucking mad.

"Angelo! Fuck me! Just fuck me! Please!"

His fingers pull out and are immediately replaced with the blunt tip of his cock. But he doesn't shove it in me like I want him to. No, Angel is much too gentle for that. He feeds it into me, inch by fucking inch.

I moan, again and again, unable to stay silent as Angel fills me. It's so good. So full. So sweet. I just had him inside me a handful of minutes ago, but I'm still a little shocked at how wonderful he feels, how perfectly he fits. He hits all my pleasure buttons without trying, turning me into a trembling, quivering mess.

Angel stops when he bottoms out. His hips are flush against my ass. I can feel the movement of his rapid breaths and hear his open-mouthed pants. He sounds like he's barely holding on, like he's at the very limit of his self-control.

I want him to *absolutely* fucking lose it.

CHAPTER
TWELVE

ANGEL

I'm gonna come. I'm gonna come. If I move a single inch, I'm going to explode and it'll all be over.

I don't want this to be over. I want this to last forever.

Rhys clenches around me, his already-tight hole squeezing my rock-hard dick.

I let out a strangled sound, throwing my head back and slamming my eyes shut.

He feels so dang good. So much better than anything I could've imagined. No wonder people are always going on and on about sex. If this is what the guys are getting from their girls, I'm surprised they don't quit their jobs just to have sex all the time.

Except Rhys isn't a girl. I have to remind myself of that. I've never been with a girl like this, so technically, I have nothing to compare him to. But the vision of him bent over in front of me, rounded butt, gracefully arched back, long hair spilling over his shoulders… it wouldn't be difficult to mistake him for a girl.

Maybe his shoulders are a little too broad. Maybe his hips are a little too narrow. But I'm only noticing these things because I'm looking for them.

In fact, the view is almost as overwhelming as the physical sensations. Watching my dick disappear into Rhys's hole. Seeing how he reacts when I move inside him. Hearing the sounds he makes, the filthy moans, the high-pitched whines, the demands he throws at me. It's a full-frontal assault on my senses.

"Okay, Angel, we need to see a bit of fucking," Sebastian says. He's been moving around us with the camera held up close to his face.

I didn't notice him or Christian or the big lights earlier when I was on my back and Rhys was doing most of the work. After we switched positions, it was impossible not to see Sebastian hovering so close. But the reminder that this is all being recorded hasn't been as jarring as I thought it would be. Weirdly enough, it's almost reassuring to have him here, giving me encouraging nods and quiet directions when I'm not sure what to do.

Like now.

I can't just stand here all day with my dick in Rhys's butt. I need to move.

I start slow, the motion strange and unfamiliar. How much do I pull out? How forceful should I be going back in?

"Yes! Faster! Harder! I can take it! Give it to me!"

Apparently, I'm being too cautious.

Rhys thrusts himself back onto me, so much harder and faster than I thought was allowed. It's staggering, driving me to new, dizzying heights of pleasure. All I can do is hang on to his hips and try to match his speed.

The sound of skin slapping against skin fills the room. It mixes with my heavy breathing and Rhys's cries. The scent of sex, of sweat, is tangy and sharp in my nose.

Rhys shifts, reaching one arm under himself, and Sebastian leans down to get a shot from below.

Is he jerking himself off? I wish I could see that. He came hands-free earlier, spraying both of us with his cum. I didn't know that was possible, that guys could come without any direct stimulation.

It was fascinating to watch. His dick bouncing up and down as Rhys moved on top of me. The slap of it against my stomach each time he hit bottom. The look on Rhys's face when the climax overtook him. The heat of his cum, scorching my skin.

Then he licked it off me, every single drop, that tongue winding its way over my body.

Oh god, oh no, I'm going to come. I'm so close. "Ah, I'm gonna… I need…"

"Pull out!"

Sebastian's instructions filter through the roaring in my ears, and I pull out of Rhys's body without a second to spare. My hand flies over my dick as cum shoots out of me in thick, creamy white ropes, landing all over Rhys's butt.

My vision goes blurry and I'm literally unsteady on my feet. I've never come so hard before, like my entire body is getting siphoned out through my dick. My head is stuffed with cotton. My limbs are weighted down with lead. And yet, I feel completely weightless. I collapse onto my back next to Rhys.

He shifts to lie on his side, facing me, braced up on one elbow, while still stroking himself with his other hand. He leans over and attacks my mouth with his lips, teeth, and tongue. He's forceful and aggressive and all I can do is lie there and take it.

He cries out into my mouth, and I swallow it down. A second later, he hooks his leg over mine and hot spurts of cum land on my thigh.

"Oh my fucking god," Rhys mutters, as he drops his head to my shoulder. His exhale is a cool wash over my heated skin. The weight of his body against mine is solid and anchoring. I let my eyes drift shut, basking in all the warm, tingly feelings.

"That was awesome, guys," Sebastian says. "You can get cleaned up when you're ready. Then we'll shoot the exit interview."

Rhys lets out one last sigh, then rolls away from me. I immediately miss the press of his body, but I stop myself from reaching for him. The cameras are off already. There's no reason for me to want him close.

Rhys sits up and stretches, his lithe body arching and bending like a work of art. Then he hops off the bed and grabs the silky robe he was wearing earlier. Sebastian and Christian have turned away too.

No one is watching me. No one will notice.

I swipe my fingers through Rhys's cum on my thigh, then quickly stuff my fingers in my mouth. Bitter. Salty. Musky. Delicious.

I suck my fingers clean, but when I'm about to go back for more, Rhys turns to face me again. I freeze with my fingers in my mouth.

His eyes narrow a fraction, flitting between my face and my cum-splattered thigh. Then the corners of his lips lift in a suspicious smile.

My ears burn hot as I yank my fingers free and clear

my throat. Shit. Crap. I scramble to sit up and act normal, but it's too late. He totally caught me sneaking a taste of his cum.

"Here." Rhys's voice is soft and gentle as he hands me a towel. "Just wipe down. No need to dress for the last interview. Fans like to see us disheveled." Then he plants a quick kiss on my cheek before disappearing out to the living room.

Sebastian and Christian are out there already, moving equipment around for the last part of the shoot. I do as Rhys said, wiping myself down as best I can with the small hand towel. But I still slip on my underwear before going to join them.

Rhys's gaze rakes down my body when I step out, lingering for a moment at my crotch.

"Is it okay?" I ask when I sit down next to him on the couch. "It feels weird being completely naked."

"It's great," he says, settling in beside me so we're pressed nice and close.

I lean into the contact, trying not to be too obvious. I let out a silent sigh of relief when he practically drapes himself over me.

"You look super cute in tighty-whities. Like a cuddly teddy bear," he murmurs quietly into my ear.

I squirm a little at the description. No one's called me a teddy bear before. What does that even mean? And why does it make me feel all weird and fluttery inside?

Sebastian sits down across from us before I can really dwell on it. "Angelo! That's a wrap on your first gay-for-pay scene. What do you think?"

What do I think? I think it was... a lot. Overwhelming. Surreal. A dream. How do I explain that it's the craziest thing I've ever done in my life, and yet, it felt so normal, so natural? So good?

"Yeah, it was… cool."

My hand settles on Rhys's knee before I even realize I've moved it from my own. I stare at it for a moment, marveling at how nice it feels. It's such a casual touch, and yet so intimate at the same time. I can be a pretty touchy-feely person with Mama, with Sabrina, with friends like Mario. But it's different with Rhys—everything's different with Rhys.

"How about you, Rhys? How was Angelo?"

Rhys props his chin on my shoulder so he can peer up at me through his thick lashes. "He was fantastic."

I doubt I was fantastic. I barely knew what I was doing. He's just saying that because the camera's rolling. But my ears still get warm at the scripted compliment, and the fluttering in my tummy grows stronger.

"Would you do it again, Angelo?" Sebastian asks.

My stomach clenches. I forgot he was going to ask that question. I'm supposed to say maybe so we're not committing to anything, but we're not ruling anything out either. Keep things open and ambiguous. It's supposed to heighten anticipation or something.

But the word gets caught in my throat and my hand tightens on Rhys's knee. I can feel his gaze on me, weighty and constant and oddly soothing.

I should say maybe. Just say it. What's so hard about that? It's two syllables. I say the word all the time. It doesn't even mean anything. It's just a word that's been scripted out for me.

But I can't. My body won't let me.

Because I want to say yes instead.

Because… I need the money. Yes, that's right. That's what I told Sebastian when he asked me that day at Rhys's apartment. A bit of extra cash to help make ends meet before Sabrina gets herself a job.

Sebastian's paying me pretty well for today, but one video won't make much of a dent in the house's two mortgages. I'll need to make a bunch more in order to pay off the house. And give Sabrina more time with Jonah before she has to go back to work. Then build a cushion so things aren't always so tight.

It's the smart thing to do, right? It's not like this was a horrible experience or anything. It's actually kind of fun? How else would I be able to make so much money so easily? Yeah. Yeah, it is the smart thing to do.

"I, uh, I think so?" My heart is hammering against my ribs as I speak, sending blood rushing past my ears.

Sebastian blinks in surprise, gaze flitting to Rhys.

Next to me, Rhys is stock-still, unmoving. I glance toward him and our gazes collide, stealing the air from my lungs.

There's surprise in his eyes too, but also something else. Something that reaches into me and wraps itself around my heart. It tugs so hard I can feel the physical sensation in the middle of my chest as it reels me in.

We're already so close, pressed up against each other. And yet we're not close enough. I want to be closer. I want to draw Rhys into my arms and get so tangled up with him that I can't tell where I end and he begins.

I'm here for the money. I'm here for the money. I'm here for the money.

And *only* for the money. I gulp.

"And Rhys?" Sebastian sounds like he's a world away. "Would you do another video with Angelo?" he asks.

Rhys doesn't hesitate. "In a heartbeat."

———

After wrapping up the shoot, Sebastian and Christian start packing away the equipment while Rhys and I get dressed again. He emerges from the bathroom in a light blue floor-length skirt with black boots peeking out from under the hem. His white shirt is loose enough to hang off one shoulder and cropped to reveal a band of smooth stomach. He's touched up his makeup and added a fresh coat of gloss to his lips.

I stare at him, speechless, as he twists left and right, making the skirt swish around him.

"So, um, what are you up to for the rest of the day?" He winces like he hadn't expected to ask me that question.

I blink, drawing a blank. Suddenly, the only thing I want to do is grab Rhys and tumble onto the bed in a pile of limbs. But I did have something planned for tonight... what was it?

Oh, yeah. "I, um, have Sunday dinner with Mama."

Rhys's brows draw up and together, and his eyes soften with tenderness. "That's so sweet!"

I shrug. It's really not a big deal. I have dinner with Mama all the time. It's easier than having to cook for myself. But Sunday dinners have always been special— and mandatory. "I go every week."

Rhys nods. "I get it."

"Do you want to come?" Ah, shoot. I had not meant to ask that. I mean, yeah, a part of me wants to keep spending time with Rhys, but bringing him to Sunday dinner feels… inappropriate?

I don't usually bring friends over for the weekly family dinner, but then, most of my friends have their own to go to. I'm pretty sure Rhys doesn't, but still. You don't just bring anyone home for Sunday dinner. And I don't even know if Rhys and I are actually friends.

Rhys smiles and tilts his head. His hair brushes over his bare shoulder, and all of a sudden, I need to know what it would feel like on my skin. I tamp it down and drag my gaze from his shoulder back to his face.

"Thanks. You're such a teddy bear. But I've already promised Hayden we'd order in."

I nod as disappointment and relief fill me at the same time.

"But, um, are you free on Wednesday night?" Rhys takes a step closer. "I dance at The Bronzed Rail on Wednesday nights. If you want to come, I can get them to waive the cover charge for you."

Images of Rhys dangling from a pole flash through my mind. I've watched a bunch of videos of him online, but I never thought I'd get to see him dance in person.

"It's a gay nightclub, though, just so you know. In case that makes you uncomfortable or anything. No worries if it does. It's totally cool either way. Oh, and I go on kind of late. At elevenish. And I know you have to work early the next day. I also dance on Fridays if that works better for you. Just let me know and I'll put your name on the list. Or not. Either way. It's cool." His hand waves as he speaks and he shuffles backward, turning slightly as if he's about to escape out the door.

"I'd love to."

Rhys freezes, already halfway to the door. "Really?" he breathes.

Nightclubs aren't really my scene. I haven't been club-bing in years. Most days I'm in bed by the time eleven rolls around. And I definitely haven't been to a gay nightclub before.

But none of that matters. Rhys invited me and every cell in my body is screaming yes.

CHAPTER
THIRTEEN

RHYS

> TEDDY BEAR
>
> I'm so sorry I couldn't make it tonight.

I was a tad upset when Angel messaged me this afternoon, saying that he wouldn't be able to come to The Bronzed Rail tonight for my show. Something to do with his sister and baby nephew.

He's already apologized three times, and I'm starting to feel guilty about how guilty he feels.

> RHYS
>
> No worries! Stop apologizing!

I type out "family comes first" before shaking my head and deleting it. I'm the last person who should be saying something so inane. "Found family comes first" is more like it.

Although, it is kinda sweet how devoted he is to them. Sunday dinners and mowing the lawn and last-minute babysitting. It's so… domestic. I've never found that attractive before, never been drawn to that kind of life, but something about Angel makes it look way more appealing than it has any right to be.

TEDDY BEAR

Is it still okay if I come on Friday?

RHYS

You can come any day. *winky face emoji*

"What are you smiling about?"

I drop my phone face down on the dressing table. "Hmm?" I blink up at Hayden through the lit mirror in front of me. He's leaning against the back of my chair, trying to peer over my shoulder.

We're backstage at The Bronzed Rail and I'm in the middle of getting ready for my set. Hayden isn't a dancer, but he's here often enough that the bouncers all know him, so he comes backstage whenever he wants.

"Who were you texting?" Hayden asks.

"No one," I say, laying a hand over my phone so Hayden doesn't try to snatch it and check. He already did that earlier this week when I was texting with Angel on the couch at home.

"Could it be one cuddly teddy bear?" Hayden teases.

I huff. "Maybe."

"Is he still coming tonight?"

I pout, feeling more disappointed than I expected. "No… he has to babysit or something."

In the mirror, Hayden's expression goes tight. This isn't the first time it's happened, but I haven't asked him about it because I'm pretty sure I won't like what he has to say. But there's only so much concern and pity I can take.

"Ugh," I exclaim, throwing up my hands. "Whatever you have to say, just say it already!"

He pulls out the chair next to me and sits down, like this is some kind of intervention or something. I roll my eyes and cross my legs and arms for good measure.

"I'm just worried, that's all."

"There's nothing to worry about."

He arches an eyebrow, clearly not believing my claim.

"There isn't!" I insist. "What is there to worry about? We're just friends."

"Uh huh. Friends who filmed a video together. And you've been texting each other all day every day for the past couple weeks. And you invited him to watch you dance." Skepticism drips from Hayden's voice.

"Yeah, so? We've done several videos together," I say, gesturing between us. "And we text all the time. And you come watch me dance almost every week."

Hayden scrunches up his face. "That's different."

I stick out my chin, defiant. "How is that different?"

"Because I'm not doing gay porn while claiming I'm straight."

My jaw hangs open as my brain scrambles to figure out how to respond. Because Hayden has a point. For someone who is supposed to be straight, Angel seemed to really enjoy gay sex. I mean, I give a damn good blowjob, so there is that. But then the whole licking-up-my-cum thing? Yeah... even gay guys don't always like doing that.

Still. Angel says he's straight. It's important to believe him until he tells me otherwise.

"Gay for pay is a thing, you know. There are straight guys who do gay porn for the money."

"What straight guys are doing gay porn for money?" Anna Conda, the drag queen who hosts the show every night, bursts into the dressing room, bringing four other dancers with her.

They must have just finished their group number because they're all bouncing off the walls with energy.

"Straight guys doing gay porn? Where? Sign me up!"

"Eww, no thank you. Keep those straight-boy cooties away from me."

"What? You've never wanted straight-boy dick?"

"Everyone wants straight-boy dick."

The little side conversation doesn't distract Anna like I hoped. She looms over me and Hayden, hands on her hips.

"Hmm? So? Are we talking about straight guys doing gay porn in general? Or is there a specific straight guy you're doing gay porn with?"

"The latter," Hayden confirms, while I groan and bury my face in my hands.

"Is that so? And does this straight guy have a name? A face?"

Hayden grabs my phone off the table before I can stop him.

"Hey!" I lunge for him, but he's already jumped out of the chair and out of my reach. "Give that back!"

He completely ignores me and unlocks my phone instead. Note to self: change the passcode on my phone.

Hayden holds out my phone to Anna. Her carefully drawn eyebrows shoot clear to her hairline.

"You get to fuck this guy?" She points to the phone while shooting an astonished look at me.

"I already did." I march over to them and pluck my phone out of Hayden's hand. On the screen is the selfie Angel took while he was mowing the lawn, and I can't help gazing at it for a second before swiping away.

"Oh lord!" Anna exclaims.

"See what I'm dealing with?" Hayden gestures vaguely in my direction.

"Uh huh. I do, I do."

I glare at both of them. "What?"

"You, hunny, are smitten." Anna declares.

I scoff. "I am not smitten."

"That's a good word for it, actually," Hayden says to Anna with a nod.

"No, it's not a good word for it, because I'm not smitten. I'm not anything." But even as I say it, I know it's not true. I'm totally smitten by Angel. Utterly. Helplessly smitten.

But that's fine. It's *fine*. Because it's just a little crush, an infatuation. This happens sometimes between performers who find themselves with really good chemistry. If they vibe off-screen as much as they do on-screen, it's easy to mistake that chemistry for actual feelings.

That's all this is. My heart's getting ahead of my head. It doesn't help that I know Angel from the old neighborhood. But it's fine. It'll blow over. A couple weeks, maybe a few months. Once the video is out and the hype is over, we'll lose touch and my life will go back to normal.

My hand flies to my chest at the sudden and unexpected ache. I spin away from Hayden and Anna, grabbing the bottle of water on my dressing table and chugging a few mouthfuls.

Fuck. What is going on with me? I need to keep my shit together.

My phone buzzes and despite myself, I grab it, heart lurching at the prospect of another text from Angel.

TEDDY BEAR

Good luck with your show tonight!

Or am I supposed to say break a leg? *leg emoji*

Fuuuck. The guy is too damn sweet for his own good.

RHYS

Thanks, teddy bear. *kissing emoji*

TEDDY BEAR

blushing emoji

When I set my phone down again, Hayden and Anna are behind me, watching me in the mirror. Anna looks amused, but Hayden looks worried.

"I just don't want you to get hurt," Hayden says.

"I won't," I answer.

He doesn't believe me. To be honest, neither do I.

"Come on." Anna points her thumb over her shoulder toward the stage. "It's time for you to go on."

I stand and slip my dressing gown off my shoulders. Hayden gives me a hug and kiss for good luck, then follows me and Anna out to the stage. He slips through the stage door so he can watch from the front of the house, and I wait behind the curtain for Anna to announce me.

Then the curtain rises and the crowd cheers. Music flows from the speakers and I step out onto the stage. I'm Rhys Rawlings. Pole dancer. Camboy. Performer. Entertainer.

I move to the music, bending and stretching, rolling my body and spreading my legs. I've done this routine dozens of times, so many times I could run through it in my sleep. The trick to keeping it fresh is to perform it for one person, a single audience member who is seeing it for the first time. Make it about him. Make him feel like he's the only person in the room. Make him feel like he's the only person who matters.

I could pick any random guy in the audience. Someone from the table of dress shirts and ties. Or the younger group who all look like they're still in college. But the guy in my mind is big and burly, with a luxurious beard and rich body hair. He's got a sweet, shy smile and eyes like pools of chocolate. He scratches his jaw when he's nervous, which is often. And his ears turn red when he's embarrassed, which is all the time.

I perform for him, for Angel, my teddy bear. And the routine flies by.

I blink as the last of the music dies, and the audience is on its feet. There should be one last rush of adrenaline at this point, the thrill of a live performance in front of an appreciative crowd. I take my bow and strut off the stage, waiting for the high to kick in. But it still hasn't by the time I get back to the dressing room.

I drop into my chair, heart racing and fingers tingling. But there's something missing. I feel hollow, empty. The euphoria I usually feel after performing isn't kicking in.

I scramble for my phone, desperate for it like I need

another hit. There's a notification waiting for me, a message from Teddy Bear. I swipe the screen and it brings up a new selfie he's sent me.

He's sitting on a couch or in an armchair, and he's holding his nephew in one arm. The baby is in a onesie covered in cartoon bears, thumb in his mouth, giant eyes staring straight into the camera. Angel's got his head tilted to the side and he's grinning into the camera too.

TEDDY BEAR

> We're matching! Get it? Bears! *bear emoji*

My heart swells so big in my chest that I can barely breathe. God. Fuck. I can't. I squeeze my eyes shut and drop my face into my hands. It should be illegal for anyone to be so goddamn adorable.

Then the adrenaline hits and I'm soaring. Everything is light and bright. I'm on top of the world and I can't stop grinning.

It was just a delayed reaction, that's all. It had nothing to do with the selfie, nothing to do with Angel's message.

It's fine. Everything is totally fine.

Right.

CHAPTER
FOURTEEN

ANGEL

Wednesday night is Mama's weekly cards night with the neighborhood ladies. So when Sabrina made plans to go out with her girlfriends, she just assumed that I would be around to babysit. It was midmorning by the time she texted me at work, "reminding" me that I had to look after Jonah.

For a split second, I considered telling her no. I'd already agreed to go to The Bronzed Rail to watch Rhys dance. Why should I have to cancel my plans when Sabrina's the one who didn't ask me ahead of time?

But then I'd have to explain why I wouldn't be home on a weeknight and I don't think I'm ready to do that. Not that there's really anything to explain. I'm certainly not telling Sabrina or Mama that I did gay porn. And there's nothing wrong with going to a nightclub—they don't have to know it's a gay one.

Still, I'm a terrible liar. Even the thought of lying by omission gives me the sweats. So babysitting it is.

I don't really mind hanging out with Jonah. As long as he's not crying, he's a really cool baby. I even got to put him in that cute bear onesie after I gave him a bath.

Mama gets home around eleven, kicking off her shoes and easing into the recliner. I'm sprawled out on the couch where I've spent the evening texting with Rhys.

"How was cards?" I ask.

"Eh, Maria cheated."

I stifle a laugh. "Maria always cheats," I say, typing a quick message back to Rhys. He's been giving me a play-by-play of the shenanigans going down in the dressing room backstage. Who knew drag queens were so funny?

Mama waves away my comment while pulling on the lever at the side of her chair. The footrest pops up and the chair reclines back. She peers at me from her stretched-out position. "Why are you smiling like that?"

I pause, realizing only then that I've got a giant grin on my face. I drop my phone onto my chest, face down. "Smiling like what?"

"Angel."

I don't need to glance at Mama to know what expression she's wearing. A very not impressed one. "No reason. Just chatting with a friend."

"A friend?"

I do glance at her this time. Why does she sound so suspicious? Like chatting with a friend is a weird thing for me to do. I have plenty of friends. Look at all the guys I grew up with.

"Mario?"

Oh no, she wants to know which friend? What should I say? I can't lie to save my life. "Uh, no."

Her eyes narrow even more, and I swear she's trying to see inside my brain. "Nico?"

My ears go hot. Shoot. Crap. Don't blush, dang it! "Uh, no?" My voice goes up at the end, like I'm asking a question. Ugh.

"No? You're not sure if it's Nico?"

"No, it's not Nico."

She studies me for another long, tense moment before her eyes widen. Reaching for the lever on her chair, her voice is tinged with excitement as she asks, "Is it a girl?"

"What?" Why would she think it's a girl?

Mama shifts forward in the arm chair. "A girl, Angel. Are you seeing someone finally? Are you dating?"

I push myself upright and scoot a few extra inches away from Mama. "No, I'm not dating anyone, Mama. When would I have the time to do that?"

She grows suspicious again. "You've been acting strange lately. Glued to your phone all the time with that dopey grin on your face."

My pulse skyrockets as my hand flies to my cheek, as if the grin is a speck of food that accidentally got caught in my beard. "I don't know what you're talking about."

Mama shakes her finger at me. "Don't give me that, Angel-boy. I know you better than you know yourself."

I sputter, ears heating and palms growing clammy. "What— I don't— I'm not—"

"Angel," Mama says, voice admonishing. "You're such a good boy. Handsome and strong. Kind and gentle. I want to see you settled down with a sweet girl. I want some grandchildren before I die."

"You already have a grandchild," I mutter, pointing toward the bedrooms where Jonah's already asleep.

Mama tsks at me. "More grandchildren. *Your* grand-children. You'd make such a good papa. Nothing like your father."

My stomach churns with a sickly, sour feeling. Mama doesn't bring up this topic often, but when she does, it always leaves me feeling a little panicked. Like there's a clock ticking somewhere, counting down the days and hours before I run out of time.

Like there's a universal deadline for getting married and having kids. Except I haven't been told when that deadline is, or how long it takes to do all the things I need to do before it arrives. I keep waiting for someone to let me in on the secret, but then Mama says things like "I want to hold your grandchildren", and I wonder if I've missed the announcement somehow.

Everyone else makes it look so easy. They meet girls all over the place. They know how to act and what to say, and the next thing I know, they've got girlfriends who turn into wives.

I don't know how they do it. Is there some kind of manual I don't know about?

I hardly ever meet girls I don't already know. Either they're related to me or they're already dating one of my friends. There are a few I grew up with, but they feel more like sisters to me than potential girlfriends.

The few times I've met someone who I think I could like, they never like me back. They think I'm nice, and maybe they'll hang out with me a few times, but no one ever wants to take things further.

The only girlfriend I've ever had was Claudia in high school. But that was mostly because every other football player and cheerleader had already paired up, and we were the only two left. She was kind and we got along okay. We went to parties together, hung out after school together, went to prom together.

But after we graduated, she moved away for college, and we ended things as friends. I haven't spoken to Claudia in years. I think she's married now.

"You should bring her to Sunday dinner." Mama pushes herself slowly to her feet.

"Sun-Sunday dinner?" I stammer.

Mama waves a hand toward my phone. "The girl you're dating. Bring her to Sunday dinner so I can meet her."

She says that like it's not the most terrifying thing ever.

"Uh, I'm not dating anyone." I scramble off the couch and follow her into the kitchen.

"It's okay if you're not dating yet. You can still bring her. It's probably better this way. I can tell you if she's any good. If she's not, you won't need to waste your time."

There's so much wrong with what she said that I don't know where to start. But I don't get a chance to say anything because Mama cracks open the door to the room Sabrina shares with Jonah. Slipping inside, she quietly shuffles up to the crib and peers over the side to gaze lovingly down at her grandson.

She smiles so sweetly, with so much tenderness. Guilt seeps in through the cracks of my panic. She's such a great nonna to Jonah. She's got so much love to give. And I want to give her more grandchildren, I do. I just… I don't know how.

Suddenly, an image flashes in my mind.

Long, rainbow-colored hair and a slim figure. A gurgling baby held adoringly close.

"Teddy bear, come here."

I step in closer and the baby smiles up at me with big, brown eyes that bring me to my knees.

"He looks just like you, teddy bear."

My breath hitches as I recognize the voice. Then the bowed head lifts, and Rhys's glowing face turns toward me.

I grip the doorframe as my knees actually go weak at the vision my imagination feeds to me. What the heck? Why? How? That's not... I can't...

"Angel? You okay?" Mama's in front of me, holding the door with one hand, waiting for me to back up so she can close it.

I nod and stumble backward. "Yeah, I'm just tired. I'm gonna go upstairs."

I'm already halfway to the door when Mama calls, "Don't forget Sunday dinner!"

Yeah, that's not happening. Because there's no girl to bring. There's only Rhys. Who's a guy. Who I imagined holding a baby—our baby. What the actual heck?

I'm numb by the time I've climbed the stairs up to my apartment, and I head immediately to my bedroom where I collapse onto my bed. It groans under my weight, the squeaking sound reminding me of another bed that squeaked loudly while I was on it. While Rhys was on it with me.

Oh good heavens, what is wrong with me? I give myself a few knocks on the head, as if I can somehow reset my brain and stop thinking about Rhys.

But I'm not just thinking about him, am I? I'm imagining him as—what, the father to my child? Like we're married?

I'm not so sheltered that I don't know that gay couples

can have babies these days. But that's a far cry from putting Rhys in the role of my husband and turning us into dads. It's like my brain has gotten its wires crossed, conflating my conversations with Rhys with Mama's pestering about finding a nice girl.

That's it. My brain is just confused. I just need to untangle these two things and put them into separate boxes in my mind. Rhys in one. Wife and kids in another. They have nothing to do with each other. They have no reason to interact. If I'm thinking about one, I'll make sure the other is sealed up tight.

Tonight was just a momentary mix-up. I'm tired and Mama caught me at a bad time. It won't happen again. I'll explain to her that there is no girl and I'm just catching up with Nico's brother after we reconnected at that party a few weeks ago. No big deal. No need to mention porn or nightclubs or pole dancing.

I drag myself from the bed and listlessly change into a t-shirt and boxers. Once my teeth are brushed, I crawl under the covers and turn onto my side, pulling a pillow to my chest. I hug it and my thoughts drift automatically to Rhys.

He's probably still at the nightclub. I wonder how many times he's performing tonight. He says he always goes on stage at least twice, usually three times, and sometimes four. He likes to try out new routines on Wednesday nights because there are fewer people.

Friday is when things get kinda rowdy. I'm not a huge fan of crowds, mostly because I tend to be the one knocking into other people. But if I find an out-of-the-way spot, I don't mind hanging out for a few hours.

Rhys says Sebastian and Hayden will be there, and

maybe a couple others too. They've all been so nice to me and at least I won't be completely alone in an unfamiliar environment.

Two more days and I'll finally get to see Rhys dance in real life. I wonder if it'll be as good as the videos I've watched. Who am I kidding? It'll probably be better.

My eyes drift shut as I snuggle into the bed, and my dreams are filled with rainbow-colored hair.

CHAPTER
FIFTEEN

RHYS

"What are you doing?"

I jump clear out of my skin, yelping loudly as I spin around. Hayden is behind me, wearing a smirk that is partially amused and partially concerned.

"Nothing," I answer, stepping away from the stage curtains I was peeking around, trying to get a view of the club's front of house.

Hayden knows me too well for me to fool him. "You're looking for Angel, aren't you?"

I cross my arms over my chest and lift my chin. "No."

Hayden lifts an eyebrow at me.

"Okay, fine, I was," I huff, stomping past him and back toward the dressing room.

He doesn't say anything, but I can feel the disappointment rolling off him as he follows close behind.

The dressing room isn't empty, thank god. The second the other performers spot Hayden, they drag him into the middle of their circle for a little flirting. It gives me a minute to sort myself the fuck out.

I smooth out a few flyaways in my hair, then hit them with a blast of hairspray. Then I add a coat of sparkly lip gloss over the color I applied earlier. All the while, my attention is glued to my phone, as if I can *will* the screen to light up with a notification from Angel.

When Hayden finally extricates himself from his admirers and drops into the chair next to mine, I ignore him. He doesn't speak, just watches and waits, knowing I'll crack sooner rather than later.

And I do. "I don't know what you have against Angel. He's a literal angel."

"I don't have anything against him. He seems like a really nice guy."

I shoot Hayden a sidelong glance. "So what's the problem?"

"The problem is you." He nudges my foot with his.

"What's wrong with being his friend? I'm allowed to have other friends, Denny."

Hurt flashes across Hayden's face, quick enough that anyone who didn't know him as well as I do would've missed it. Hayden's the golden retriever of our group of friends. He's always sunshine and smiles, and hardly anything ever gets to him. Sometimes, when I'm being terrible, I forget that he's got soft, vulnerable spots too.

"I'm sorry, I didn't mean that." I reach across the space between us and take his hand. "You're my bestie and I love you."

Hayden quirks a smile. "I know. I love you too."

I wait for the unspoken "but" that hangs in the air

between us. I can see it in his eyes, in the tightness at the edges of his smile.

"What is it?" I say with a resigned sigh. There's no point in turning away or denying it. I can't keep fending him off with unfriendly jabs.

"I'm worried about you."

I pull my hands back and study my nails. The pink ombre is a couple days old now and still looking good. But my nails are a lot safer than letting Hayden see how much I'm worried about myself too.

I double and triple-checked with Angel that he was still coming tonight. And even now, I'm low-key anxious that he'll cancel last minute again. Honestly, what is up with that? Why do I care whether this random guy from the old neighborhood shows up at the club?

So we've been chatting and it's been fun. So we did a video together and that was fun too. We're just friends. We can't be anything more. Why am I acting like a teenager getting all flustered over a first crush?

"I don't like him," I say, voice small. "He's straight."

"That's never stopped a gay boy from falling for a straight boy."

He's right, obviously. It wouldn't even be the first time it's happened to me. Except none of my previous crushes or infatuations have ever felt like this. Those were fleeting, fun, a dizzying high that fizzled quickly. This is… something else entirely.

It's not only that I can't stop thinking about Angel. It's more like I crave him. There's been an ache lodged in the middle of my chest since we filmed our video and the ache's only grown bigger and stronger with each passing day.

I want to see him. I want to touch him. I want to sit in his lap and bury myself in him. But I'd settle for just being in the same damn room as him. Anything to ease this thing sitting on my chest and making it difficult to breathe.

It doesn't help that Sebastian sent me a rough cut of the video. I might have spent most of yesterday watching it on repeat.

The look on Angel's face during the blowjob scene is utterly priceless. So much obvious pleasure tempered by confusion. The conflicting emotions etched into every twitch of muscle, every deep groan, every heated glance.

If I close my eyes, I can still taste him on my tongue. I can still feel the stretch of my jaw and the way he hit the back of my throat.

Then at the end, when he was fucking me from behind… I hadn't been able to see his face when we were doing it, and that was probably a good thing. I would've come prematurely a second time if I'd seen that look of reverence while he had his massive cock inside me. Like it wasn't just fucking, not just dick in hole. Angel looked like he was going through a religious experience, one that shook him to the core.

I've been telling myself that none of it was real. It was a video and our job is to pretend we're enjoying ourselves, even if we aren't. But if I know anything about Angel, it's that he's not much of an actor. I seriously doubt he could fake that kind of reaction. No, I'm pretty sure what the camera captured was exactly what was going through his mind at that moment.

How can I not be "smitten" with him, as Anna so delightfully pointed out the other day? Angel is the epitome of smitt-able. It's a wonder he isn't already taken. The girls in the old neighborhood obviously don't know a good man when they see one.

Hayden nudges me with his foot again when I've been silent for too long. "The thing is, I'm not convinced he's as straight as he claims."

My heart clenches so tightly it hurts. I haven't let myself consider that possibility. But Hayden is right, damn the man, because the more I chat with Angel, the more my gaydar needle inches upward.

Hayden continues, "If he keeps saying he's not gay, he might just be really deep in the closet. And honestly? That's almost worse than falling for a straight boy."

My head drops back as Hayden goes and drops one truth bomb after another. "I know," I groan. "It is." Because yeah, been there and done that too. Fuck.

"And yeah, you're not super close to your parents, so maybe meeting his family isn't that big a deal. But like, you deserve better than that, babe. You deserve someone who wants to parade you around on his arm. Someone who wants to show everyone he knows how much he loves you."

Tears prickle my eyes and I frantically wave my hands in front of my face. I've just gotten my makeup on and I don't have time to redo it all. "Denny! You're gonna make me cry!"

Hayden chuckles and shifts to the front of his chair. "I'm sorry. I didn't mean to make you cry. Come here."

"Bitch," I say, with more affection than heat, and let him pull me into a hug.

"I just don't want you to get hurt."

I sniffle and blink back the moisture in my eyes. "I know. Thanks for always looking out for me."

He gives me a squeeze. "Always."

Anna appears in the doorway of the dressing room. "Rhys, baby girl, you're up."

I give Hayden a light kiss on the cheek before pulling away. I double-check my hair, my face, and my outfit, then take one last glance at my phone. Nothing. Sigh. Maybe something came up after all. I won't be disappointed. I won't. We're just friends. If we're even that. It's fine. I'm fine.

I'm already turning away when the screen suddenly lights up again. And there it is in all its blue bubble glory.

TEDDY BEAR

I'm here! Near the bar. I overheard someone say you're performing next. Break a leg!

My heart thunders as I read the message. He's here. He actually made it. He's in the audience. Waiting for me.

I gulp as I'm attacked by an unexpected burst of nerves. It's not the typical excitement of going on stage—I get that all the time. This is different. This makes me want to hide in the dressing room.

What if I fall? What if I make a fool of myself in front of Angel? What if he thinks I'm a bad dancer? That I've been exaggerating how good I am? That I'm pathetic?

"Rhys," Hayden steps in between me and the dressing room table, blocking my view of my phone. He takes me by the shoulders and gently turns me toward the door. "It's time to go."

He directs me out to the stage and it's a good thing I'm

an expert in walking in these platform boots, because I can't really feel my feet at the moment. I'm basically floating, staying upright by sheer muscle memory.

"You've got this." Hayden plants a quick kiss on my temple before disappearing through the door that leads to the front of house.

Anna gives me a concerned once-over. "You okay, baby girl? You're not gonna hurl, are ya?"

I grab for one of the water bottles we keep stocked back here, twist the top off and take a quick sip. The water isn't cold, but it's enough to shock me back into some semblance of normalcy.

I can do this. I've done it hundreds of times before. It's just a more pronounced case of stage fright. Once I get out there, my body will remember what to do, and it'll all go off without a hitch.

There's a buzzing in my ears as Anna heads out to announce me. It's so loud I barely hear the music when it starts playing. The curtains rise, the spotlight zeroes in on me, and the audience goes wild.

With the lights shining in my face, it's difficult to look past the edge of the stage, but that doesn't matter. It's like I've got a homing beacon on Angel and my eyes immediately seek him out in the crowd. He's by the bar, tucked into a corner, holding a pint of beer, with his free hand stuffed into his jeans pocket. He pulls it out when he realizes I'm looking at him and gives me a little wave. It takes everything inside me not to wave back.

How terrible would it be if I jumped off the stage right now and ran into Angel's arms? Pretty terrible, I think. I'd never hear the end of it from Anna. Angel will have to wait. But that doesn't mean I can't dance for him. I can dance the fuck out of it for him.

Deep breath. Here we go.

The strains of Sia's "Chandelier" courses through me, jump-starting each cell as I start to move. Every sweep of my arms feels larger, every kick of my legs feels higher, every twist and turn is more pronounced as I dance to the very tip of every finger. I pour myself into the performance, into every twerk of my ass, every flick of my hair.

The buzzing in my ears turns into a roar, though I can't tell if it's from the thumping of my heart or the excitement of the crowd. It fuels me, though, the adrenaline pumping through my veins as I lift myself up onto the pole and spin.

I lean my shoulder against the pole, feet planted a few feet away, and slide down, letting my body arch with my groin pushed out. The skimpy fabric of my thong leaves very little to the imagination and the audience shows its appreciation with wolf whistles.

When the song finally ends, I'm in my final pose, hanging off the pole. I unfold myself and rise to my feet to take my bow. My gaze immediately flits to where Angel was standing. Except he's not there anymore.

During my performance, he moved closer to the stage, skirting around a couple tables like he wanted to get a better view. From the look of awe on his face, I'm pretty sure he saw plenty.

I take my bow, then holding Angel's gaze, I blow him a kiss.

Anna's already on stage, shooing me off so she can introduce the next performer. I scurry off and rush back to the dressing room for my robe. I've been out front in my practically nonexistent dance outfits before, but I often get waylaid by handsy guys who want to cop a feel. After several years of performing, I've accepted that it's a part of the job.

But I don't want to get sidetracked today. I'm making a beeline for Angel because his hands are the only ones I want on me.

CHAPTER
SIXTEEN

ANGEL

I think I was more nervous turning up at The Bronzed Rail than I was when shooting gay porn. There was a part of me that wondered whether I should manufacture another babysitting emergency so I could beg off tonight too.

But in the end, my need to see Rhys in person, to see him dance, overruled the nerves that threatened to make me upchuck my dinner.

I held my breath while the bouncer at the door checked my ID. He kept glancing from my driver's license to my face, to the list he had on the iPad, like he didn't quite believe that I wanted to go into a gay nightclub. I swear it took him several minutes of double-checking before he let me in.

It's only marginally better inside. It's crowded, obviously, but more than that, it feels like everyone knows everyone. Guys greet each other by name and with kisses on the lips. They're so casual and comfortable with each other, which makes me feel like I've got a flashing neon sign on my chest. It says, "Straight Dude. Does Not Belong Here."

Actually, I probably don't need a sign. I bet they can tell just from what I'm wearing. And people are definitely watching me, their gazes heavy as they scan me from head to toe.

I'm in my nice jeans and a freshly ironed button-down shirt, but I might as well be going to a business meeting compared to the other outfits in here. See-through shirts, leather pants, scraps of fabric that look almost like bras, tiny little shorts that leave half the butt hanging out.

There's also an alarming amount of glitter everywhere and everything sparkles in the light reflecting off the disco ball hanging from the ceiling.

I gulp and wipe my clammy palms on my thighs, then head toward the bar. I need a drink, or at the very least, something to hold on to so I know what to do with my hands.

Trying to move through the space only adds to how awkward I feel. I'm so big and bulky that I keep bumping into people as I squeeze through the crowd. I get sly looks over shoulders and a few people mutter something about daddies. My stomach churns, but I can't tell if it's plain old nerves or the fluttering feeling I get whenever I'm around Rhys.

By the time I get to the bar, my heart is racing and my tummy is all tied up in knots.

The bartender looks bored and annoyed when he gruffly demands my drink order. I ask for a beer and he brings one over, setting it in front of me with a *thud*, not even sparing me a glance. He's a little rude, to be honest, but I don't mind—this is the most normal and familiar interaction I've had since walking up to the club's front door.

There's a little pocket of space a few steps away from the bar, behind a group of guys sitting at a table. I tuck myself into it and plaster my back to the wall. I take a long swig of beer and almost chug down the entire bottle of cold, hoppy brew, stopping with the back of my hand pressed to my lips.

If I finish the beer too quickly, I'll have to get another. And I can't quite brave the crowds around the bar again so soon.

I'm wondering how long I'll have to wait for the show to get started when the house lights dim and the stage lights up. The music switches to something upbeat and electronic, almost like a game show of some kind. The people around me start shouting and cheering, adding to the noise.

Then the rainbow velvet curtains rise, and a drag queen struts out onto the stage. She's tall and shapely, with her curves on full display in a bright blue bodysuit. The shiny material hugs her thighs, her waist, her arms, and plunges down her front to reveal ample cleavage. Her orange boots give her a few extra inches of height and extend all the way up past her knees. Giant lightning bolt earrings dangle from her ears, and her elaborate hairstyle looks like a halo around her head.

I've seen drag queens before—of course I have. But I've never seen one in person. She's stunning and I have to remind myself to pick my jaw up off the floor.

"My darlings!" she drawls in an weird accent, like she's from Brooklyn, but trying to pretend she's English. "Welcome, welcome to The Bronzed Rail, where we all like to get railed." She turns sideways and sticks out her bum.

The audience bursts into another round of shouts and catcalls.

"My name is Anna Conda and I will be your host tonight. Strap in, boys, because you are in for a show!"

I watch the people around me go wild. They're having so much fun. They're so immersed in the moment. There's an energy coursing through the place that builds with every passing minute. Slowly, it tugs at the nerves that have me wound so tight. As they loosen, I find myself breathing a little easier, relaxing against the wall rather than trying to disappear into it. My lips curve into a smile and the fluttering in my tummy settles into a comfortable warmth.

The first few acts are cool. A lip-syncing drag queen duo, a burlesque dancer, and a group number.

As the group takes their bows, someone next to me shouts to his friend, "Rhys Rawlings should be up next!"

I immediately straighten, anticipation spiking as my heart thunders in my chest. Rhys. He's next. He's almost here.

I pull out my phone, only now realizing that I didn't text Rhys to tell him I'm here. I do it now, shooting him a quick message. I have no idea whether he'll see it. He's probably already behind the curtain, ready to come on stage.

Anna Conda introduces Rhys and I swear the audience goes berserk. Louder than ever, everyone's on their feet, clapping and shouting and stomping. It's almost like Rhys is the headliner, like he's the one they've all come to see.

The whole place goes dark, except for one circle of light

directed onto the rainbow curtains. They rise, revealing Rhys, perfectly framed in the spotlight. He's magnificent. Beyond magnificent.

He's wearing a shimmering gold outfit that's barely more than a few strips of fabric strategically wrapped around his body. What is there blends so well with his skin tone that it almost looks like he's naked. Naked and glowing.

The leg openings are cut high enough to reveal his hip bones, and the fabric is pulled so tight around his crotch that the outline of his dick is visible. There's a cutout on the left side, a large triangle that crosses from his left hip all the way to his right, leaving most of his stomach bare. Then a narrow piece of fabric stretches from his right hip up toward his left shoulder. At his sternum, the fabric splits into two, one for each shoulder, leaving both his nipples on display.

His gold boots look like weapons. There's a good four inches under his toes and an extra three in the dangerously pointy heels. The boots extend all the way up his calves, to his knees. He's dyed his hair blond and it falls in waves around his shoulders. Even his makeup is golden, heavy enough across his eyes that it looks like a mask.

He looks like a superhero. A shimmering, scantily clad, pole-dancing superhero. Beware of his heels.

Rhys takes a step forward, kicking his heel up behind him in an exaggerated motion. His hips and shoulders twist with the movement. The expression on his face is pure sex, pure sin, everything I shouldn't want and yet I've never wanted anything more.

He looks to his right, making eye contact with people

in the audience. His lips curl up in a seductive invitation as his gaze sweeps across the room.

He looks straight past me and my heart plummets to my feet. It doesn't mean anything, obviously. It's probably hard for him to see anything with the bright lights shining in his face like that. Besides, I'm all the way at the back of the room, tucked into a corner. It would be difficult to find me, even without the lights.

But then his gaze snaps back. It zeroes in on me. My breath catches in my chest and my feet itch to carry me forward. I pull my hand from my pocket instead, and give him a little wave.

Rhys's smile widens, gaze still locked on me, and it feels like this whole place just got ten degrees hotter.

When he reaches the pole, he grasps it with one hand and pauses. Then my brain shuts down. There's no thinking, no understanding, no trying to figure out why I'm responding the way I am or what it could mean. I just soak in Rhys's performance. The way he tilts his head to show off his long neck. The way his long legs sweep through the air. The positions he contorts himself into while hanging from the pole. The way his body undulates when he's sprawled on the floor.

He's captivating. Mesmerizing. It's impossible to take my eyes off him—I wouldn't want to, even if I could.

The back of his golden outfit is practically nonexistent. The fabric disappears between his butt cheeks, and when he bends over, I'm reminded of our video, when I was taking him from behind. My dick has been stirring since the moment Rhys stepped on stage, but now it's growing steadily plumper at the memory of how those glutes felt in my hands.

When he's climbing the pole, all the little muscles in his back flex and stand out in sharp relief. His thighs look carved from stone and his forearms sculpted by a master artist.

He's so freaking strong. So amazingly talented. Every move is breathtaking. Every pose staggering.

When the music fades and Rhys stands to take his bow, his gaze drifts to me. I'm not back in that little corner anymore, I realize. I've made my way between the tables so I'm nearly at the stage. If I reach out my arm, I could probably touch him.

He blows me a kiss and something bright and beautiful, happy and bubbly bursts open inside me. It's cracking me open, struggling to be set free, and I'm powerless to resist.

What has Rhys done to me? What kind of spell has he cast over me? I don't feel like myself anymore. Something's changing inside me and I can't stop it. I don't recognize the person I'm becoming.

Rhys bows and disappears backstage. Anna Conda comes back out to introduce the next act.

With my heart in my throat and my lungs struggling to function, I stumble back to my dark little corner. But it's no longer empty. Hayden's taken my spot, arms crossed and frowning.

I haven't seen him since that first afternoon at Rhys's apartment—*their* apartment. Maybe he doesn't remember me? Maybe that's why he's staring at me like I spilled my drink on his pants.

"Oh, uh, hey, I'm Angel, uh, Rhys's friend?"

He studies me for a moment before sighing. "Yeah, I know all about you, teddy bear."

He uses the nickname Rhys has for me and it makes my hackles rise. Strange—it never bothers me when Rhys uses it. Why does it sound so wrong coming from Hayden?

"We weren't sure if you would show up today," Hayden says.

I flinch at the subtle accusation in his words. "Yeah, I'm sorry about Wednesday. My sister…" Um, how do I say she wanted to go out with her friends and didn't bother to ask if I was free?

"Needed you to babysit, yeah, I know." Hayden dismisses the rest of my comment.

Silence falls between us as the next performer takes the stage. Hayden keeps studying me and my ears start growing hot. Why is he looking at me like that? Why won't he say anything? Should *I* say something? What should I say?

"I hope you know what you're doing." Hayden finally breaks the silence.

Except I have no idea what he means. "What I'm doing?"

"With Rhys," Hayden clarifies. "He's fun and flirty and he can let a lot of things roll off his back. But that doesn't mean he can't get hurt. I don't want to see him get hurt."

Oh. Shoot.

I nod jerkily, at a loss for words. Because I *don't* know what I'm doing. I have absolutely no freaking idea. I've never done anything like this before. I've never met anyone like Rhys in my life. I've never felt the way he makes me feel.

I'm in uncharted territory without a map. Rhys has

become my North Star. All I know is I want to follow him to the ends of the earth.

CHAPTER
SEVENTEEN

RHYS

Pulling the short, silky dressing gown tightly around me, I rush out front in search of Angel. He's on the other side of the club from the stage door, so it takes a bit of weaving through the crowd to get to him.

I'm stopped a few times by men who compliment me on my routine, and a couple more by guys who flash me flirty smiles. I manage to politely put them off before I continue toward Angel.

Then there he is. He looks amazing. The jewel-toned green shirt hugs his wide shoulders and shows off the little swell of his belly. It's unbuttoned at the collar, dipping low enough for some dark chest hair to poke out. A thick gold-link chain lies flat against his chest. The shirt-sleeves have been rolled up to reveal his forearms, and dear fucking god, those forearms! They should be illegal, with how strong and furry they are.

Angel looks up as I approach and his eyes brighten

when he sees me. He breaks out into a grin so wide it throws me off balance.

I didn't bother to stop and change my boots, so I'm still tiptoeing in my sky-high performance heels. Normally, I can saunter around in them without a second thought. But the things Angel does to me are entirely abnormal.

I stumble toward him and he catches me, drawing me flush against his deliciously cushioned chest. With the extra six-or-so inches on my feet, I'm eye level with him. And even though it's dark in the club, I can still see the deep, rich browns of his irises.

So close to him, I'm completely enveloped in that distinctly Angel scent. Fresh sawdust cuts through the sour, alcohol-soaked air of the club. I breathe deep, greedy for more.

"Hey," I breathe, just loud enough for the sound to travel the few inches from my lips to his ears.

"Hey," Angel replies, and I feel the rumble in his chest more than I actually hear the words.

"You made it."

"I wouldn't have missed it for anything."

I blush. At least, I think I do. Blushing isn't really my thing, I'm too shameless for that. But the heat in my cheeks is undeniable. See? Angel does abnormal things to me. He turns everything on its head, changes all the rules, makes me want things I've never wanted before.

Next to us, someone clears their throat loudly. I drag my gaze away from Angel to find Hayden standing right there, arms crossed, eyebrow lifted.

"Oh, hi, I didn't see you there," I say, guilt creeping in.

"Yeah, I know." Annoyance mixes with amusement in his voice and our earlier conversation comes back to me.

Reluctantly, I pull away from Angel so we're not blocking Hayden out. But I can't stop myself from keeping a hand on his shoulder, and Angel keeps one of his on my lower back.

Fuck, that's so hot. There's something so possessive about a man touching me like that. Like he can't bear to lose the contact. Like he's making a public declaration that I'm his.

I lean into it. The heat from his palm seeps through the thin fabric of my robe and directly into my skin. The weight of it is perfect, just solid enough for me to know he's there. It sends a sumptuous shiver through me, and I think I might have discovered a new erogenous zone.

Hayden looks back and forth between us, gaze lingering on the hand I still have on Angel's shoulder. I can see the concern in his eyes, but he doesn't say anything. More guilt creeps in, ruining the high I've been riding since spotting Angel from the stage.

I know he's worried about me. He doesn't want me to get hurt. I appreciate how much he cares, I really do. It's just that…

Angel's not like any of the other guys I might have foolishly pursued in the past. He's gentle and tender. He's innocent and sweet. There isn't a single malicious bone in his body. I'd bet my entire wardrobe that he's never had a single negative thought about anyone.

How am I supposed to stay away from him? How am I supposed to resist? Even if he is straight or so deep in the closet he'll never see daylight. There's just something about Angel that calls to me and I can't ignore it.

"You were amazing up there," Angel says, interrupting the silent conversation Hayden and I are having.

Gratefully, I turn my attention back to him. "Aw, thanks, teddy bear."

"It's really cool to see it in person instead of in a video." The earnestness in Angel's eyes is breathtaking.

Just how many videos of me has he watched? How many times has he watched them?

"You've seen videos of Rhys dancing?" Hayden asks.

Angel nods. "Yeah, that first time at your dad's birthday. And then... I looked up more on my own." He scratches his jaw a little sheepishly.

The look Hayden shoots me is conflicted. As if he wants to like Angel—because, come on, who can resist him?—but then remembers why he has his reservations.

"Just the dancing videos?" Hayden continues.

Angel flushes red, visible even in the dim and flashing lights of the club. "Uh, no, I've also seen... the other ones." He sneaks a glance at me before dropping his gaze. "You were in some of them," he says to Hayden.

"Oh." A slight furrow appears between Hayden's brows as he turns to me. "I didn't know that."

Shit. Hayden knows I've been talking with Angel a lot, obviously. But I didn't tell him that Angel's apparently been watching videos of me—dancing and fucking—almost nonstop since that party. It's the type of thing I would normally share with Hayden. In fact, it's something I'd usually brag about to all the boys. But I haven't mentioned it because, well, I wasn't sure how Hayden would react.

More evidence of Angel's abnormal effect on me.

The hurt that flashes across Hayden's face upends the bucket of guilt that's been steadily dripping on me the past several minutes. But he quickly replaces it with one of his broad smiles, the same one his fans have dubbed his golden-retriever smile.

"I'm glad you got to come and see Rhys in person tonight," Hayden says to Angel.

I have no doubt he's sincere. Hayden is nothing if not always sincere and gracious. But I can still hear the tightness in his voice, the hint of discomfort.

His gaze suddenly shifts over my shoulder and a spark of relief colors his expression. "The guys are here. Let me flag them down."

Hayden moves to slip past me. Angel's arm around my waist draws me closer to give Hayden a couple extra inches of space. It leaves me pressed against Angel again, and I let myself melt into his body.

"Is he okay?" Angel asks, and I blink in surprise.

"Uh, what do you mean?" I'm usually the only one who can read Hayden's microexpressions. And that's because we've been best friends for years. Most people—even Sebastian and Noel—can't read him nearly as well as I can.

"I dunno." Angel scrunches up his face. So damn adorable. "He just seemed… off."

My heart is already in danger of falling head over heels for Angel, and this only inches me closer. He pays attention. He notices the little things. He cares about someone who is basically a total stranger. I never realized how fucking sexy kindness could be.

I glance over my shoulder to where Hayden is saying hello to Sebastian and Noel and their respective boyfriends. He looks fine now, his typical grinning and cheerful self.

When I turn back to Angel, he's watching me like he can't tear his gaze away.

I don't know what to do. Hayden is the most loyal friend I could ever ask for. He only wants what's best for me. I understand where he's coming from, and under any other circumstances I would wholeheartedly agree.

But I can't help it. Maybe Hayden's right and I'll end up getting hurt. But that's a risk I have to take.

The guys come over and I introduce Angel to Noel and Bellamy. Then we grab the VIP booth that's usually reserved for The Camboy Network as part of the sponsorship deal Sebastian negotiated for us.

Angel and I sit next to each other, squished into the booth so tight I'm practically in his lap. He's got his arm looped around my waist, hand resting on my opposite hip, and I'm leaning back against his chest.

Every now and then, I catch Hayden regarding us, wary and guarded, and I feel myself getting tugged in opposite directions. I keep fending off his concerns with claims that Angel is straight and there's nothing but friendship between us. But the truth is, it's frighteningly easy for me to forget that Angel's not mine.

He's so free with his touches, so casually intimate. He's always looking at me like I'm some rare and precious jewel. How am I supposed to keep my defenses up? How am I supposed to stay away?

I leave the table for my second act of the night. It goes off without a hitch and my attention stays on the VIP booth the entire time. After I take my bow, I hurry back to the dressing room to change into my street clothes. I'm just behind the privacy screen, tugging on my shirt, when I hear Hayden's voice.

He says hello to Anna and the other dancers hanging out back here.

"Oh my, and who is this you have with you?" Anna asks

I freeze. Did Hayden bring Angel to the dressing room? Why would he do that? I poke my head around the edge of the screen to find Angel with his ears glowing pink.

"Hi." He waves shyly. "I'm Angel."

"The newest addition to The Camboy Network," Hayden adds.

That sends them all atwitter, shooting a barrage of questions at Angel.

"That's supposed to be a secret," I jump in, pinning Anna with a look. "Our video's not out yet and Sebastian wants to do this whole launch thing, so you can't tell anyone."

Anna's eyes grow even wider than they already were. "Our? You mean…" She points between me and Angel.

Ah, fuck. I didn't mean to let that slip. And there's no point in denying it now that Angel's ears have gone fire-engine red. I move to stand in front of him, as if I can physically block him from view.

"It's a secret!" I hiss at Anna, who just breaks out in laughter.

"Down girl, I wasn't about to out your man."

Longing surges through me at the description of Angel as my man. God, I want that so much, it's staggering.

I glance cautiously back at Angel, not sure how he'll take being called my man. But his only reaction seems to be the flush that has spread across his cheeks. His gaze is cast to the side and he scratches his jaw. Does it not bother him? How come he's not denying it?

"Anyways, it's lovely to meet you, Angel." Anna holds out her hand, palm down.

After a moment of hesitation, Angel takes it and brings it to his lips for a quick brush.

"What a gentleman!" Anna exclaims. "I wish I could stick around longer, but the show must go on!"

She can't leave fast enough, in my opinion.

I take Angel's hand, the same one he used to hold Anna's, and drag him over to my makeup station. It makes zero sense, it's completely irrational, but I want Angel to kiss my hand, not Anna's. I want him to hold my hand, not hers.

"I, uh, should probably get going," Angel says quietly, looking sheepish.

I step closer to him, a mild panic seizing me at the thought of Angel leaving so early. "Do you have an early morning? You don't work on Saturdays, do you?"

"I told Mama I'd clean up the garden first thing."

"Oh." My disappointment is so thick, it feels suffocating.

"I was going to offer to drive you guys home, but it's probably a little early for that, huh?"

"No!" In my excitement, the word comes out a tad too loud and the rest of the dressing room falls silent. Hayden and the other dancers are staring at us now. "I mean, I can leave now. I'm done for the night." *And not at all desperate to spend every last second with you.*

"I'm going to stick around a bit longer."

My head snaps around when Hayden speaks, and only then do I realize that Angel's offer had been for the both of us. Oops. I totally forgot about Hayden, totally forgot he was still in the freaking room. Ugh. I'm a terrible friend.

"Are you sure?" I ask, torn between loyalty to my best friend and this wild, untamed thing I feel for Angel.

Hayden's smile is strained around the edges. He knows what's been running through my mind. "Yeah, I'm sure. I can split a ride with Sebastian and Christian."

I try to telegraph my apology and Hayden gives me a slight nod to say he's received the message.

"In that case," I say, turning back to Angel. "Let's get out of here."

CHAPTER
EIGHTEEN

ANGEL

Rhys keeps up the chatter all the way from The Bronzed Rail back to his place. He tells me about the club and the other performers, about Anna Conda and how she auditioned for *Drag Race*. He asked me if I watch *Drag Race*—I don't, but I might need to start.

He tells me about how Sebastian and Christian got together, and how Noel and Bellamy did too shortly after. There's a wistfulness in his voice as he recounts their stories, and it makes me wonder whether Rhys is looking for his own love story.

My stomach twists uncomfortably and something hot and uneasy takes up residence in the middle of my chest. I rub at it. Maybe I drank those beers too fast tonight, and they're not sitting well for some reason.

"It's very romantic," I say when Rhys finishes.

Rhys sighs. "It really is."

"So, uh, are you and Hayden...?" The burning in my

chest increases and I cough, trying to clear the constricted feeling.

"You okay?" Rhys reaches across the center console and rubs my shoulder. He's sitting sideways in the passenger-side seat of my truck, one knee bent so he can face me. The touch sends a completely different kind of heat spreading down my arm and through my chest.

"Yeah, uh, yeah, I was just saying…" I cough again.

"Something about me and Hayden?"

I nod as my throat kind of feels like maybe some beer went down the wrong tube.

Rhys tilts his head and his hair falls in a silky cascade over his shoulder. "Me and Hayden…" Then his eyes widen and his jaw drops. "Are we together? Oh god, no! Not even a little bit!"

The tightness in my chest starts to ease and my coughing subsides. "I just thought maybe… you know, because of your videos… and what you said about Sebastian and Christian."

Rhys laughs, bright and bubbly, and I smile at the sound. "Hayden and I are only friends. Period. I mean, yes, we've got decent chemistry on-screen, and I love the guy to death, but it's not like that."

I take a deep breath and my lungs expand like I didn't just have a weird coughing fit a second ago. "Great! I mean, not great, but like, not *not* great. Just that, it's cool that you're friends, you know, and that, like, you can… do… stuff."

Oh dear heavens above, god, please strike me down now. My ears are on fire.

Rhys laughs out loud again, leaning over the center

console to rest his head on my shoulder. "Teddy bear, you're amazing. And yes, I do know."

His words wind around me, wrapping me up, all warm and snug. He thinks I'm amazing. Rhys thinks I'm amazing.

And right then, we pull up in front of his apartment building. I don't know if this is perfect timing or the absolute worst.

Rhys unclips his seat belt, which gives him more room to sit up straight, facing me. His lips are curled in a gentle smile and his eyes are so dark and mysterious, lined with the heavy stage makeup. I stare into them, letting myself get lost in their depths.

"Thanks for the ride," he says softly after a moment of silence.

"No problem. It's on my way home." Well, sort of. With a forty-minute detour. Close enough.

"I'll talk to you soon?" he asks, as if he doesn't want to get out of the truck.

If I'm honest with myself, I don't want him to get out either. I want to drag out this moment for as long as I can. I want it to stretch into eternity.

I nod. "Yup."

Then, as if the heavens are actually listening, time slows.

I see Rhys coming toward me and I know he's about to kiss me on the cheek. It's how he said goodbye that first time in his childhood bedroom, and how he's said goodbye the other times we've met in person.

I watch as he draws near, closer and closer, and at the very last second, I turn my head.

I don't know why, or even how, but suddenly, it isn't

my cheek that's in the path of Rhys's oncoming kiss—it's my lips.

He gasps quietly when he makes contact, and the same surprise ripples through me. But the gasp is quickly followed by a tender moan that sends desire straight to my dick.

I'm not sure who moves next, whether Rhys climbs into my lap on his own, or if I haul him to me. It doesn't really matter, because the end result is the same. I have an armful of Rhys and my dick is as hard as a rock.

I fumble for the lever on the side of my seat and when I yank it, the seat goes sliding backward. We hit the end of the rails with a jerk and I let out an *oomph*, but Rhys doesn't miss a beat.

His hands bracket my face, holding me still as he plunges his tongue into my mouth. It's so commanding and so powerful, I'm completely helpless against the onslaught.

I try to chase his tongue, but he nips at my lips in response. I try to lick into his mouth and he sucks on my tongue, holding me captive. With every touch, every movement, pleasure zings through me, pooling in my groin.

It doesn't help that Rhys is grinding his own hard-on against my erection. My hands *might* be on his butt, encouraging him along.

Somewhere in the back of my mind, I know we're in the cab of my truck and I'm double-parked in the middle of the street. It's late, so there aren't many people around. But this is a busy part of Brooklyn, so someone will wander past eventually.

But I don't care about any of that. Because Rhys is in

my lap and his tongue is in my mouth and—oh dear lord. His hands slide down my front, undoing the buttons of my shirt along the way. He rakes his fingernails—glittering gold tonight—down my chest, my stomach. My nipples harden into tight nubs, my dick presses painfully against the metal zipper of my jeans.

Or at least, it did. Because now Rhys is undoing my jeans and reaching into my underwear to pull me out.

I shudder as he licks his palm, then wraps his hand around me. That's so… dirty, so… debauched, and… it's so freaking hot.

"Rhys." His name comes out wispy and strangled. It's a question and a plea at the same time.

"Shh, teddy bear, relax. I've got you."

Rhys has his own tight red leather pants undone and his dick out before I even realize he's moved.

Then his dick is on my dick and oh lord, oh heavens, oh. Oh. Oh. It's mind-shattering, the sensation of our dicks rubbing together. We slip and slide against each other, spit and pre-cum easing the way. The tip of his dick bumps against the ridges of my glans and I think I might actually die from how good it feels.

Rhys's fingers aren't long enough for him to wrap around both of us with one hand. He has to use both, one stacked on top of the other, to stroke us from base to tip. His hips move at the same time, like he's dancing to a silent soundtrack that only the two of us can hear.

Rhys's lips cover mine, his tongue diving between my lips again. The kiss sends my head spiraling just as his hands on my dick make my body tremble with need.

He leads this dance, guiding me with his tongue and his hands, making me spin until I'm dizzy, flipping me upside down and inside out. I'm lost to the sensations he wrings from me, but I don't actually feel lost. Rhys knows where we are and where we're going, and I trust him to lead the way.

It should scare me, and it does, but not the way I would've thought. I'm not scared of what I'm turning into. I'm scared of never finding out what I could become.

That truth sparks deep inside, a flickering light in the darkest parts of my soul. It's small and fragile, but it's brighter and clearer than anything I've ever felt.

"Jesus, Angel," Rhys murmurs against my lips. There's a slight hitch in his voice that makes my entire body shudder.

"Rhys," I whine.

His rhythm accelerates. The music swells. Pleasure courses through me. Pressure builds in my balls.

"Rhys! Rhys!" Every muscle in my body draws tight. There's a hum in my ears as the air vibrates around us. I hang on, fingers digging into Rhys's thighs.

He focuses his strokes on the tip, squeezing the head of my dick against his. The tightness sends tingles right down into my balls, toward the base of my spine. It's too much, I can't take any more. I'm going to come. I can't hold it back.

"Yes, yes, that's it, baby. Come for me, teddy bear, come for me. Now."

It's as if he hits the detonate button and I explode on command. My insides liquify as cum erupts from my dick, shooting up between us, hitting me on the chin.

Rhys comes at the same time. His hands clamp down on our dicks, creating an impossibly tight vise. Both of us twitch, and the feeling of his dick moving against mine spurs on my orgasm in wave after wave.

I've come undone, ripped open and left in tatters. I thought filming the video with Rhys was hot, but it was tepid compared to this. Getting sucked off by Rhys, getting to be inside him—those were the most amazing things I'd ever felt until now. And now, they're merely okay compared to this.

This—this intimacy. Holding Rhys so close to me in this small space. Kissing him, tasting him, drowning myself in that flowery scent of his. With no one watching, no cameras pointed in our direction.

This is… amazing. Simply amazing. I feel like I'm flying. Like I've stepped off the roof of a skyscraper and I'm soaring.

We stay like this for long moments, panting into each other's mouths. Rhys's hands are still on our dicks as we grow soft together. Even as I get sensitive, Rhys's dick touching mine feels good. Like they're cuddling together, basking in the afterglow.

The smell of our combined cum is strong. It fills my nose and reminds me of the taste of Rhys's cum. And just like the day of our shoot, I don't think before I act.

I take Rhys's hand. It's wet and sticky. I bring it up to my lips and lick it. Rhys gasps as I clean his hand with my tongue. The combined flavor of our cum is bitter and earthy, and knowing that it's both of us mixed together only makes me want more.

Rhys's jaw hangs open as he watches me lick every inch of his hand, then scoop up the drops of cum that are starting to dry on our stomachs and chests. Then he attacks me, shoving his tongue between my lips like he wants to eat our cum straight from my mouth.

We kiss like we're starving men fighting for the last scraps of food. But eventually—still too soon for me—Rhys pulls back. His eyes are lowered as his deft hands make quick work of putting us both back together.

I'm still dazed when he finishes, resting his hands on my clothed chest. He studies me, searching my eyes for something. What is he looking for? I'm suddenly anxious to help him find it. Whatever he wants, whatever he needs, I want to be the one to give it to him.

I don't know what that means, or how I could possibly have what it takes. But I want it. From the core of my being.

"I'm sorry," he says.

The words are a splash of cold water to the face. I blink as my stomach twists in one hard wrench. "You are?"

He quirks his lips. "Not really."

It takes a second for his response to sink in and for my tummy to settle. "Good," I whisper, sliding my hands over his hips and to the small of his back. "Me neither."

His smile widens and my heart skips a beat. He bends forward for another quick kiss on my lips, so fast it's over before I can savor it. Then he climbs back into the passenger seat and is out of the truck.

Rhys practically skips to his door and once he pulls it open, he casts one last look over his shoulder. He waves and disappears inside.

I take a deep breath and let it out slowly. I think something important just happened.

CHAPTER
NINETEEN

RHYS

Angel is sitting with his back against the headboard. I'm straddling his lap, riding him. He's inside me, filling me up, stretching me wide. Every time his cock hits my prostate, I leak a drop of pre-cum onto his stomach.

This is my favorite position with Angel, I've decided. He's so solid and strong between my legs. I have full access to his broad shoulders, his furry chest, his rounded tummy. His hands brace me and support me. He's so gentle and so tender.

And the best part: watching him as he watches me, like I'm the most beautiful thing he's ever set his eyes on.

I know this is a dream. The bed floats in a nonexistent room. There are no lights or cameras around us. Sebastian isn't hovering at the corner of my eye.

This is my imagination indulging itself, fantasizing about what-ifs. What if Angel were actually mine? What if we could have a repeat of what happened in his truck, but in the luxury of a bed? I don't want to let it go. I don't want to wake up and face reality. I want to stay in this make-believe world forever.

My body drags me back to consciousness against my will and when I open my eyes, it's worse than I expected.

Guilt hits me like a train, stealing my breath. Fuck. What did I do? Jesus motherfucking Christ, what did I do?

I didn't plan on jumping Angel last night. The thought hadn't even occurred to me. I was so happy just getting to sit in the truck next to him, getting that little slice of alone time together.

But then he turned his head at the last moment. I still can't tell if it was an accident or on purpose. And when our lips met, I couldn't help myself. Something came over me, possessed me, and suddenly I was in his lap. And holy fucking heaven did it feel so right being in Angel's lap.

He didn't hesitate for a single second. He didn't need to be coaxed or convinced. He was as eager to kiss me as I was to kiss him. He held me so close, so tight. The sexy little gasps of pleasure he makes when I touch him... oh god, I don't think *he* even knows he makes them.

I've never wanted someone the way I want Angel. I've never hungered for someone like this, craved someone like he's fundamental to my survival. It's like a beast has sprouted inside me, clawing and scraping at me, demanding that I go find Angel, that I plaster myself against him, that I crawl into him and lose myself there.

Hayden was right. I'm going to get hurt. There's no way I'm coming out of this unscathed. I wouldn't go so far as saying that I love Angel. But at this point, it's practically inevitable. All it'd take is another sweet smile from him, another cute, oblivious text message, another flash of red across the tips of his ears. And I'm a goner.

Reluctantly, I force myself out of bed and to the bathroom. When I stumble out to the kitchen, Hayden is already there with a steaming mug of coffee in hand. He slides a second mug toward me and I gratefully chug it down.

He watches me with a wary eye. I know he wants to ask about Angel. I also know he won't. He'll wait for me to bring it up on my own.

"He didn't come up," I say, annoyed at how defensive I sound.

"Okay."

"He didn't," I insist. I'm not sure why my hackles are rising.

"I believe you," he says calmly, which only makes my hackles rise even more.

"Well? Don't you have anything to say about that?"

Shit. What's wrong with me? Hayden is being understanding and I'm trying to pick a fight with him.

Hayden's expression tightens around the edges. "What do you want me to say?"

I deflate. I don't know what I want him to say. Maybe that I'm not making the biggest fucking mistake of my life? Maybe that it's okay to be selfish and greedy and there won't be any consequences later?

I set down my half-finished mug of coffee and shuffle toward Hayden. He opens his arms in time for me to help myself to a hug.

"I'm sorry," I say, resting my chin on his shoulder. "I just…"

Hayden doesn't make me say the words out loud. "I know."

"You're the best. I don't deserve you."

He chuckles softly. "You're not so bad yourself."

I sigh and pull away so I can give Hayden my best puppy-dog eyes. "Seriously. What am I going to do, Denny?"

He gives me a lopsided smile. "I don't know, babe. I wish I did."

He plants a quick kiss on my forehead before extracting himself to make breakfast. He's been doing these overnight oats things with chia seeds and other healthy stuff that sound gross. I'm just thankful I have a fast metabolism that combined with my dancing lets me eat pretty much whatever. Hayden, on the other hand, is a bit of a health nut.

I leave him to his breakfast while I get ready for my dance class. I try to make it to two or three classes a week —pole or modern or ballet. I need the training to stay on top form for The Bronzed Rail. More importantly, it's how I de-stress. I can't obsess about Angel when I'm focused on moving my body.

At least, that's how dance classes usually work. Today, though, Angel keeps hovering at the edge of my mind, distracting me so much I nearly collide with another student while we're practicing our pirouettes. Oops.

I rush out of class the second we've finished our bows and head to Sebastian's apartment. A message comes in from Angel just as I'm climbing the stairs, and I pause on the landing to read it.

Angel: I had a lot of fun last night. *grinning emoji*

My heart somersaults so wildly in my chest that it takes a second for me to catch my breath. Fuck. How do I respond? What do I say?

We had sex in the cab of his truck. While double-parked outside my apartment building. It's a miracle no one saw us.

He's supposed to be straight. He's not supposed to want to kiss a man or have sex with a man. Let alone do all that out in public where anyone could have stumbled on us. And yeah, maybe I have long hair and like to wear makeup and skirts, but it's kinda hard to miss the dick I was rubbing against his.

Straight boys don't do the things we did last night. So maybe Angel isn't so straight after all. And if he's a late bloomer, only now exploring his sexuality, maybe he'll be willing to come out of the closet too. He probably just needs time to process. These things aren't easy to figure out, especially when he grew up in the old neighborhood.

Yeah, that's it. I'll just keep telling myself that.

The door to Sebastian's apartment opens. "Rhys? What are you doing standing out here? Are you okay?"

My head snaps up and I blink, pushing my spiraling thoughts aside. "Yeah, I'm fine. Just club-scheduling stuff. Someone wants me to fill in for them next week." I slide my phone into my bag and go to give Sebastian a quick hug.

He gives me a quizzical look, but doesn't press—thank god. It's bad enough having to talk about this with Hayden. I wouldn't even know where to start if Sebastian started asking questions.

"Where's Christian?" I ask when he ushers me inside.

"At Mars Fitness. He's got clients back-to-back until close today."

"Busy guy," I say, helping myself to a seat on the couch.

Sebastian puffs up a little, looking all proud. "Best personal trainer in the city!" he calls out as he disappears into their second bedroom, which they turned into a filming studio slash office for Sebastian.

He comes out holding his laptop. "Okay, so, I got an idea this morning."

"Uh oh," I tease. Sebastian is known for his ideas—most of them are crazy, but they almost always work out. The guy has a knack for business-y things that the rest of us don't. We learned early on not to question him and just go along with whatever he says.

"Hear me out!" He sets his laptop down on the coffee table, then holds his hands up, palms out, eyes flashing with excitement. "I'm calling it *12 Toys of Christmas: The Camboy Network's Official Holiday Gift Guide.*"

I blink at him. "Sebby, girl, you know what we do isn't exactly kid-friendly, right?"

He drops his hands and gives me a flat look. "Yes, of course, I know. I don't mean kids' toys. Jesus, who do you think I am? I mean sex toys! For adults!"

"Oh." I roll the idea around in my mind again, but nope, still doesn't make sense. "So... how exactly would it work?"

"I'm putting together a list of twelve toys. We'll divvy them up, then film ourselves as we use them. It'll be like video reviews as we're using the toys. The videos will go out every other day in December, like an advent calendar!"

My jaw kind of drops as I'm stunned into silence. "That's... genius."

"I know, right?!" Sebastian looks smug as he pulls his computer onto his lap. "So, you in?"

I shrug. "Why not? Sure."

"Awesome. I've got you down for a giant dragon dildo and then a metal cock sleeve, also shaped like a dragon."

He turns the laptop toward me so I can see the two toys he's talking about.

The dildo is huge, like the size of a giant's forearm. It'll definitely be one of the bigger ones I've stuffed into my ass. The cock sleeve, however, is… weird. In the picture Sebastian shows me, it covers the entire length of the dude's cock. It looks more decorative than anything else. I can't see how it'd feel very good to wear it, and there's no way I'd be able to fuck anyone with it.

"Uh, what am I supposed to do with that?" I point to the metal sleeve.

"Right, so, I was thinking. You could wear it while doing a pole routine!"

I glance at Sebastian, whose smile is so wide, it looks a little manic. "You want me to wear that thing while I'm on the pole?"

"Yep!"

"It'll be in the way! Or I'll crush my dick!" My hand goes to my crotch where my cock shrivels up a little bit at the thought.

"It'll be fine! You don't have to do anything too fancy. Just think. It'll look so cool if you're spinning around the pole wearing nothing but that."

I cross my arms and pout. The problem is, Sebastian's probably right. If I could figure out the right moves to use, it would look really cool.

"And… I was thinking, if Angel wants to do a second video, you could be giving him a private show."

My dick goes from not-at-all-interested to raring-to-go. A private show for Angel? Wearing nothing but a metal cock sleeve shaped like a dragon? Maybe a pair of my platform heels? Yes. Yes. And yes. My dick is one-hundred-percent on board with that.

"Speaking of which! I just finished editing your video this morning. Wanna watch?"

Do I want to watch the video of me and Angel fucking? Yeah, of course I do. But I already feel so raw and off-kilter, and watching the video will make it worse.

But Sebastian isn't waiting for my answer. He's already got the video pulled up and the cursor hovering over the play button. He clicks it before I can object.

As with all The Camboy Network videos, it starts with our interviews. And from just a few seconds of Angel on the screen, I'm done for. He's so fucking cute, it should be illegal. The way he blushes and stammers. The way he peeks at the camera shyly. This is Angel at his most adorable.

The scene switches to the kitchen, and after we deliver our super-cheesy lines, I drop to my knees. Jesus. Angel looks so innocent standing there, hands gripping the counter behind him so hard his knuckles are white. And I look so slutty, with my robe hanging off my shoulders, tears running down my cheeks, spit dripping off my chin.

The sucking sounds are loud and obscene. I moan as I worship Angel's cock. He whimpers and gasps like he doesn't know what to do with the pleasure he's feeling.

I was there when this was filmed, obviously. I remember the taste of his pre-cum, the weight of him on my tongue, the stretch of my jaw as I swallowed around him. And yet, sitting on Sebastian's couch, my gaze is glued to the screen. I can't look away.

My lips part. My tongue swipes across them. My mouth waters in anticipation.

Heat slithers through me and my cock swells, a bulge forming in my leopard-print leggings. I shift on the couch as I struggle to take in a full breath.

The scene switches and we're in the bedroom now. Angel's on his back and I'm climbing on top of him. The camera zooms in for that first breach of his cock in my hole. I can see every bulging vein and watch as they disappear into the glistening pink skin of my hole.

When the camera zooms back out again, it captures the look on my face. Eyes shut and head thrown back. Hovering right on the brink of ecstasy. Then Angel's face, eyes wide open, staring straight at me. I come, spraying him with my cum. There's no mistaking me for anything other than a man in that moment. No pretending I'm a woman.

The scene switches again. I'm on my hands and knees now, and Angel is touching me with such reverence, like he's handling something priceless, something precious. My throat grows tight with emotions I don't want to examine too closely. Emotions that will only get me in trouble and confuse me even more.

Then Angel's pounding into me from behind. His rough, construction-worker hands are so big around my narrow hips. On the couch, my hole twitches at the memory, at how well he filled me, at that incredible feeling of being whole.

Want slams into me so hard, so suddenly. Want for Angel, for him to fill me like that again, for him to fill me with his cum.

My hands curl into fists from how overwhelming the desire is. So strong, it steals my breath away.

The video switches to the last scene. Angel's on his

back again, spent this time. I'm curled around his side, chasing my second orgasm.

A part of me wants to look away from the laptop, or at least squeeze my eyes shut so I don't have to watch. But I can't. My eyes are riveted to the screen as it shows me spraying my cum onto Angel's thigh.

Then I look up at Angel and he gazes down at me. I don't remember this part. I don't remember the feelings that are so clearly displayed on both our faces. Neither of us are trying to disguise them, and neither of us are that good at acting.

The video ends and silence settles in the apartment. Sebastian doesn't speak, doesn't move. I should probably say something, compliment him on his editing or the lighting, but I'm at a loss for words.

The video isn't merely hot. It's… intimate and vulnerable. It's unlike anything I've ever put on the internet. It's unlike anything I've ever experienced.

"Rhys?" Sebastian finally says in a quiet voice. "You okay?"

I swallow around the lump in my throat and nod.

"Do you want to talk about it?"

I shake my head jerkily.

"Do you want me to shelve the video? Angel's already been paid and I don't mind eating the cost."

The offer brings tears to my eyes and I blink rapidly to chase them away. "No," I croak. "I mean, don't shelve it just for my sake."

Sebastian's smile is understanding and sympathetic. "I'll send the video to Angel and make sure he's okay with it too."

Then he reaches for my hand and gives it a squeeze.

"Hey, if it makes you feel any better, my first video with Christian was like this too. Same thing with Noel and Bellamy."

I furrow my brow in confusion.

"You know, before any of us were ready to admit our feelings about the other person? It's hard to hide love."

My eyes sting with unshed tears and no matter how fast I blink, I can't keep them at bay. They spill over my lashes as Sebastian pulls me into a hug.

"Oh, Sebby, I'm in so much trouble."

CHAPTER
TWENTY

ANGEL

One of the most important rules when working on a construction site is being aware of your surroundings. There are hazards all over the place—vehicles backing up, cranes swinging things through the air, heavy materials being moved around—if you're distracted, you'll get hurt.

"Angel!" Mario grabs my arm, pulling me to an abrupt halt right before I walk straight into the path of an oncoming forklift. "Jesus, man, that's the third time today. Where the hell's your head?"

In Brooklyn, with Rhys. But I can't tell Mario that. "Sorry, just… have a lot on my mind."

"Yeah?" He nudges me forward once the forklift passes. "Like what?"

Shoot. I shouldn't have said that. "Nothing, just stuff at home."

"Sabrina and the baby?"

"Uh, yeah." It would've been a good excuse if my ears

weren't my own personal lie detector. They heat up, the tips turning red.

I hope Mario doesn't notice as we run across the street to grab coffees from the local deli.

"How are they doing?" Mario asks as we wait our turn to be served at the counter.

"Uh, they're fine?"

He casts a sideways glance at me, clearly confused. "But you just said…"

Crap. My ears burn hot and I scratch my jaw through my beard. "Yeah, uh…"

Mario turns to face me fully, arms crossed over his chest. "Dude, you okay? You look like you're about to pass out."

"I'm fine, I just—"

The guy behind the counter waves us forward, thank the lord, and we place our orders for coffees. But if I think the short break will distract Mario enough to forget his question, I'm wrong.

It's the middle of September and the hot summer weather has cooled into a breezy fall. It's the perfect temperature to stand outside, sipping our coffees and watching pedestrians walk past. Mario and I take up spots at the end of a row of other guys taking their breaks.

"So," Mario starts up again the second we're settled. "I got a feeling this ain't about Sabrina and the baby."

I scrunch up my face. I mean, I could technically make it about my sister and my nephew. Needing extra money to support them was the reason why I agreed to do gay porn in the first place.

But I didn't get paid to go watch Rhys at The Bronzed Rail. I didn't get paid to drive him home. I wasn't even thinking about money when Rhys and I… in my truck… yeah.

The extra money is nice, but who am I kidding? It isn't about the money anymore.

The video went live this morning. Rhys and Sebastian both sent me texts to let me know that the initial reception has been good. Exceeding expectations even. I don't know how I feel about that.

On the one hand, that's good, right? We want the video to do well. But on the other hand… the video is out there now, and hundreds and thousands of people are going to watch it. I don't think I really understood what that meant until this morning.

Sebastian had sent me the video and asked if I was still okay with it being released. I said yes without giving it too much thought. It's not that I regret saying yes, it's just…

"Dude." Mario bumps me with his elbow. "What's going on?"

I glance up at Mario, my friend since high school. I wouldn't call us best friends, since I don't know if I've ever really had a best friend. But we both played defense on the football team and we both started working in construction at the same time. Of all the guys in the neighborhood, he's the one I'm closest to.

And I suddenly want to tell him everything. Every. Single. Thing. From following Rhys upstairs at his dad's birthday party, to doing the whole gay-for-pay thing, to the texts we've been sending each other and what happened in my truck.

The words scramble up my throat, demanding to be let out. But I can't. Mario wouldn't understand. No one from the neighborhood would understand. It's why Rhys moved away the second he turned eighteen. It's why I never knew that half this stuff existed until he came back.

A strangled sound escapes me as I try to swallow the words back down.

Mario's expression grows alarmed and he grips my shoulder, giving it a shake. "Jesus, Angel, is someone dying? Are you dying?"

"What? No! No. Nobody's dying," I choke out.

"Then why do you look like your nephew's got cancer or something?"

"What?! No! Jonah doesn't have cancer. It's nothing like that." I shake my head while my tummy ties itself into knots. I take a sip of my coffee, but it just burns when it hits my stomach.

"You're gonna give a man a heart attack. Christ. Just tell me what it is."

I open my mouth and nothing comes out at first. Then something that sounds like a dying duck escapes me. I clap my hand over my mouth as Mario bursts into laughter.

"Oh my god, Angel. You're killing me. Whatever it is, it can't be that bad." He punches me on the shoulder. "You know we always got your back."

And that's the thing, isn't it? I don't know if they will, not about this. With anything else, sure, the people I grew up with wouldn't think twice. But this might be their one exception.

I grip my coffee cup with both hands, hoping Mario won't see how much they're trembling. It's hard to believe that I'd rather tell Mario that my nephew has cancer than tell him that I did gay porn and now I'm sleeping with a dude. I'm really, truly messed up.

"Alright. If you're not gonna tell me, I'm just gonna start guessing." His brow furrows like this has turned into a trivia game and he's determined to win.

"No—" I feel slightly nauseous as he starts guessing.

"Nobody's sick or dying. How about debts? I know your pop wasn't great about that."

"No, no new debts." I drain the rest of the coffee, wincing as the hot brew burns down my throat and into my churning stomach. I toss the empty cup into the trash bin next to us, then stuff both my hands into my pockets.

His face lights up with another idea. "What about Sabrina's baby daddy? I heard he was trouble. He sniffing around again? We wouldn't mind showing him out of the neighborhood."

"No, he hasn't shown his face since they moved in," I mutter, turning to walk back to the worksite. We still have a few more minutes on our break, but maybe if I get back early, Mario will stop asking questions I don't know how to answer.

He falls into step next to me. "Good. Oh, wait a minute!" Mario hits my arm with the back of his hand. "You seeing somebody? You got a girl?"

That's not exactly it, but it's close enough to the truth that panic makes me trip over my own feet and I stumble a few steps before catching myself.

"That's it, ain't it!" Mario laughs, giving me a friendly shove. "Angel, you sly dog, you! You got a girl and you haven't said a word. Who is she? You got pictures? Where'd you meet?"

"No!" I grab Mario and pull him away from the other dudes on site. "No, there's no girl!"

Mario gives me a "come on" look. "Dude, you're the worst liar I've ever met."

Except I'm not lying this time. There's no girl. There's… a boy.

The thought rings through my mind and my heart hammers against my ribs. There's a boy—Rhys. These things I feel for him, these confusing feelings that I don't understand, they're feelings I should have for a girl. But I've never felt them before. Not for my high school girlfriend, Claudia. Not for anyone. Only Rhys.

What does that mean? Does that mean I'm gay? Can I do gay for pay if I'm not straight? Or maybe I'm just bisexual—that's a thing, right? People who are attracted to both men and women? Am I that? How do I know? How can I tell?

"Aw, Angel, you don't gotta be embarrassed or nothing." Mario slings his arm around my shoulders. "It's about time you hooked up with a chick. Shit. How long has it been? Not since Claudia? I don't know how you went so long without getting your dick wet."

My nausea worsens at Mario's crude description and I forcefully shrug him off of me.

"No!" The word bursts out of me from nowhere as blood rushes in my ears. Rhys isn't just a hookup. At least, not to me. What we have is so much more than that—I think. I'm just not entirely sure what.

Mario holds up both of his hands in surrender. "Whoa, easy, so it's a serious thing? You just had to say so. What's her name? You gonna bring her around to meet everyone in the neighborhood? Where she from, anyway?"

"There's no she!" My heart is beating so hard, my

whole body shakes with the force of it. My fingers are curled into tight fists, but that doesn't stop the trembling.

Mario pauses, then tilts his head in confusion. "There isn't?"

"No." My heart ricochets around, lodging itself in my throat. "There's a he."

The words come out so garbled I'm not sure Mario hears them at first.

But then his expression goes slack, his jaw drops, and he takes a step away from me. "You mean… you mean… you fucked a guy?"

I flinch at the f-bomb and clench my jaw to keep myself from hurling.

"But you…" He waves his hand in my direction, as if that's supposed to mean something.

"I'm what?" I bite out.

He drops his hand, letting it slap against his thigh. "Nothing. You just… don't… have that… vibe."

My hackles rise and an unfamiliar anger trickles through me. This is what Rhys goes through whenever he's in our neighborhood, isn't it? The look Mario's giving me, a little confused and a little suspicious. The way he's stepped away from me, leaning away from me.

"What kind of vibe am I supposed to have?" I practically growl.

"Nothing. No vibe," he backtracks quickly, then sighs. "I'm just surprised."

Yeah, well, him and me both. I never expected to feel like this, especially not for someone like Rhys. I never thought I'd tell anyone from the neighborhood, and definitely not like this.

"Does anyone else know?" Mario asks.

I shake my head jerkily right before I'm seized by a new fear. "You gonna tell people?"

He actually looks a little offended. "Nah, man, why would I do that?"

"Because. It's gossip." And anyone from the neighborhood knows that the place runs on gossip.

Mario gives me a grim look. "Nah, I won't tell anybody."

"Hey! Mario! Angel!" Our foreman calls us over for a quick meeting.

Mario shoots me one last glance before spinning around and walking away. I follow after him, hoping I haven't just lost a friend, hoping I haven't just lit the fuse on a bomb.

CHAPTER
TWENTY-ONE

RHYS

At four o'clock sharp, my phone rings.

Teddy Bear.

I scramble for it, swiping at the screen a few times before it connects.

"Hello? Angel?" I call out before the phone is even at my ear.

"Hey."

The single word is filled with so much emotion that my heart immediately seizes. I jump to my feet.

"What's wrong? What happened?" If he's hurt... if someone hurt him... I won't be held responsible for what I do in retaliation.

"Nothing happened," Angel says with a tired chuckle. "I just, um, finished work, and um, wondered if you were..."

"Yes! Yes, I'm at home. You want to come over?" I bounce on my toes, excitement skittering over my skin.

"Yeah, if that's okay?" The shyness in his voice makes me simply *ache* for him.

"Of course it's okay! You can come whenever you want!" I slap my hand over my eyes as my mind helpfully provides an image of Angel's O-face. *Not* what I meant, but also, applicable.

"Yeah?" He sounds so hopeful and oh god, I want to make him come right now. Hard. Multiple times.

"Yeah."

"I can pick up dinner along the way, if you haven't eaten yet?"

I drop my head back and smile up at the ceiling. This is starting to sound an awful lot like a date, and god, I want it to be. So bad. If Hayden were here, he would be so disappointed. But I can't help it. I just can't say no.

"That sounds amazing. Pick up whatever you want. Surprise me."

"Okay, see you soon."

That simple phrase shouldn't fill me with so much joy, but it does.

It takes about an hour for Angel to get here and I pace around the apartment the entire time, too amped up to stay still. I buzz him into the building, then wait at my door for him to climb up the stairs.

I've never had a construction-worker fetish before, but fuck me, I definitely have one now. Angel's come straight from work, with his scuffed-up steel-toed boots and tattered jeans. He's wearing a reflective vest on top of his fall jacket and his hair is flattened against his head from wearing a safety helmet all day. He's covered in dust, dirt, and splatters of concrete. I've never seen anything sexier in my whole life.

His steps are sluggish and slow, like he's been carrying something heavy for a really long time. Fatigue rolls off him in waves. And yet, when he sees me, he smiles, like I'm the finish line and he's on the home stretch.

I step back to let him inside and the door swings shut behind him. Then I push him up against it and plaster myself to his front. I don't care that my clothes will get dirty. I don't care that he's sweaty and gross from a whole day at work. All that matters is that he's here.

Whatever this is between me and Angel, whether he's just experimenting or he's bi or gay or whatever. There's no way I can walk away from him. However he wants me, for however long he wants me, I'll take whatever I can get. Consequences be damned.

Standing on my tiptoes, I pull him down to meet me halfway. It's a gentle kiss, a hello kiss, a melt-into-each-other-and-rest kiss.

The takeout bag he was carrying hits the floor and his hands come to my waist, around to the small of my back. He holds me to him, carefully at first, then more tightly. His arms wind around me and he bunches up the back of my shirt in his hands until he's clinging to me. His knees give out and he slides down the door a couple inches.

"Angel? Babe? Teddy bear?" I brush my fingers across his cheeks, his brow, his lips. I comb them through his hair. "What's wrong?"

His eyes are closed, thick dark lashes fanning across his rosy cheeks. "I told Mario," he says softly.

It takes me a second to connect the dots, then the world narrows to this small space between us. There's only one thing Angel could have told Mario that would have him acting like this now. But if he did… what does that mean? Why would he do that?

"Mario?" I ask, voice tight, heart pounding. "From the old neighborhood?"

Angel nods.

"What did you tell him?" I hold my breath, not sure I want to know the answer to my question.

"That… I've been seeing someone," he speaks so quietly I can barely hear him even though I'm an inch away. "Seeing a guy."

My fingers tighten on either side of his face.

He told Mario. That he was fucking a guy.

My heart swells with joy even as fear strikes deep. It can't be that simple. There has to be a catch. It can't be as easy as me wanting Angel to be gay and suddenly he is.

"Uh huh," I croak.

"I didn't tell him it was you, though. I…" He blinks, lashes fluttering, then hesitantly meets my gaze. "I didn't know if you'd be okay with that."

I swallow again, forcing the jumble of emotions down, and nod. "Yeah, I get it. Thanks for thinking of me."

Angel stares at me, rich brown eyes so full of something I'm afraid to identify. "I'm always thinking of you."

My heart stops. Oh god. Fuck. How am I supposed to resist that? How am I supposed to not fall for that? I send a silent apology to Hayden, wherever he happens to be right now.

I don't know what this means or how Angel's confession to Mario will change things. Maybe Angel will decide I'm not worth the risk of getting ostracized from the neighborhood. Maybe I'll still get my heart broken. But it doesn't matter.

Angel's here now. And as long as he's here, he's mine.

I lean in for one more hard kiss, using the moment to get my heart beating again. We're both panting when I break the kiss, and there's a noticeable bulge in Angel's jeans. But he's been working all day, so my teddy bear needs food. Eat first. Sex later.

"Come on." I slide my hand into his, intertwining our fingers. Grabbing the takeout bag, I lead him to the living room.

Angel unpacks the food on the coffee table while I grab plates and napkins and utensils.

"I got barbecue, I hope that's okay," he says when I drop down on the floor next to him.

"Yup. Love barbecue." I mean, it's fine. It's not usually my go-to, but I enjoy it when I have it. But if Angel likes it, then I'll have barbecue every freaking day.

He got us ribs and brisket, plus corn, mashed potatoes and Swiss chard. It's way more than the two of us can finish and when I say so, he smiles shyly.

"I wasn't sure if Hayden was here. And I figured you could have leftovers."

I pause in the middle of scooping mashed potatoes onto my plate. He thought of Hayden. Hayden, who disapproves, who has been polite, but nowhere near as friendly as he usually is. Angel knows how important Hayden is to me and remembered to include him.

I lean over and plant a kiss on his cheek. "Thank you," I murmur, and warm satisfaction spreads through me when his ears go pink.

"It's nothing." He gives me a little shrug.

I put a hand on his shoulder and wait for him to glance at me. "It's *everything*."

He holds my gaze for a moment before his Adam's apple bobs and he drops his gaze.

I set my plate aside and pull Angel into my arms. It's a little awkward, with him sitting on the floor, back against the couch, and me kneeling next to him. His arms come around my waist and he buries his face into the crook of my neck, but my knees are in the way. He makes a small, frustrated sound while trying to tug me closer.

So I swing a leg over his thighs and settle myself snugly in his lap.

"Better?"

He nods, beard rubbing on my collarbone as he gives me a squeeze.

I hold him. Or we hold each other. In silence, for long moments. My eyes drift shut and I savor the feel of Angel against me, the thickness of his arms, the soft yet scratchy texture of his beard, the scent of sawdust that clings to him, fresh even after a full day of work.

I hold him until the tension in his body dissolves, until he breathes deep, full breaths.

"Do you want to talk about it?" I ask, as I continue carding my fingers through his hair. "About Mario?"

He shrugs, his big body moving under me.

"How did he react? When you told him?"

Angel pulls back, but keeps his eyes downcast. His hands play with the hem of my shirt at my back. "He was surprised. Said I didn't give off a vibe."

I still as my anger surges. At the same time, a little voice at the back of my mind calls me a hypocrite. Isn't that what I thought at first? Angel's a rough, burly construction worker from the old neighborhood, so he has to be just like everyone else from there. Judgy and a tad homophobic, not so blatant that it's obvious, just enough to make things uncomfortable.

But Angel's nothing like them. He's sweet, kind, caring, selfless. He's special.

"Do you think he'll tell anyone?"

Angel slowly shakes his head. "He said he wouldn't."

"Do you believe him?" Because I sure as fuck wouldn't.

He takes a moment to think before answering. "I don't know. I think so."

Angel knows Mario a hell of a lot better than I do, but he's also way more trusting than I am.

"Well, if he does, you tell me, and I will shred him." I give Angel's chest a poke to make my point. "I will tear him limb from limb. Don't underestimate me because I'm small. These nails are reinforced and I know how to use them." I hold my hand up and wiggle my fingers. The nails are a bright orange today to go with the peachy-pink color of my hair.

My threat—uttered in complete seriousness—draws a smile from Angel. "I know. I would never underestimate you."

His vote of confidence makes my chest feel all warm and fuzzy. It makes me feel like I can do anything, overcome anything. Anything except...

Another question hovers on the tip of my tongue, one that I don't have the guts to ask. Why did he tell Mario in the first place? Why now? Why today?

If this is just a phase, if this is just Angel exploring his sexuality before he meets a nice girl, gets married and has kids... then I don't want to know. I don't need to know. I'd rather live in my little make-believe world and pretend that Angel is mine forever.

CHAPTER
TWENTY-TWO

ANGEL

My chest has been tight all afternoon. Ever since that conversation with Mario, all through the drive to Rhys's apartment, even after he kissed me by the front door. I've been wound up so tight, bracing myself for something bad to happen.

But then Rhys crawled into my lap and pressed himself to me. I breathed him in, held him, was held by him. Gradually, the tension eased.

The worry is still there. How will Mario treat me now? Will anyone else in the neighborhood find out? But the longer I have Rhys in my lap, the less panicked I feel about it. I might not know what to do if people find out about me, but Rhys does. He'll be there. He'll help me.

My stomach grumbles, loudly, and we both glance down at my belly.

I didn't have much of an appetite on my way over, but my body disagrees.

"I guess we should eat?" Rhys asks.

"Yeah, I guess," I say, with a sheepish smile.

He moves to climb off my lap, but I pull him back down. I like having him here. I don't want him to move.

"Is it okay if we…?"

"Eat like this?" Rhys finishes my question. "Of course, babe."

He turns to grab a plate—mine or his, it doesn't matter. Then he picks up a bit of brisket on a fork and holds it up for me. I open my mouth and let him feed it to me.

Smoky barbecue flavor bursts on my tongue and I moan in appreciation. Rhys's eyes darken in response.

"Good?" he asks breathily.

I nod.

This is silly. I'm not a baby. But there's something soothing about sitting still and letting him feed me. I don't have to think, I don't have to do anything. Just chew and swallow while holding this beautiful man in my lap.

His hair has a variety of peachy colors today, half of it pulled up and half of it hanging around his shoulders. It reminds me of a creamsicle. I want to lick him up. His pants are also orange and peach and white, loose and flowy, riding so low that his hip bones poke out the top. And his white t-shirt is cropped above his stomach.

"Does Mario know about the video?" Rhys asks as he feeds me another bite.

The video. That's what I was distracted by all day. It's what led to me telling Mario about sleeping with a guy.

"I didn't tell him." I can't even imagine how Mario would react to something like that. His head might explode.

Rhys's lips twitch into a wry grin. "And it's not like he'll find it on his own, right?"

A snort bursts out of me unexpectedly. "No, I don't think so. None of those guys are looking for gay porn."

"Do you want an update on how it's doing?" Rhys asks as he feeds me another bite.

I take a deep breath to calm the fluttery feeling in my tummy. To be honest, I don't know how I feel about it being out in the world. I can't really wrap my head around it. It doesn't seem real. Like, what do you mean other people can watch it now? How? Why? Who?

But Rhys seems excited about it, so that's good, right?

"Um, yeah, sure."

Rhys scoops up a forkful of mashed potatoes for me. "It's doing amazing. Like, really, really good. Sebastian says he wants to give you extra royalties on top of the set fee he's already paid you."

"He doesn't have to do that," I say without thinking.

Rhys pauses for a moment before peeking at me through his lashes. "Wouldn't the money be helpful?"

Oh. Right. I'm doing gay porn for the money. Supposedly. "Uh, yeah, it would." I scratch my jaw. Oops.

Rhys's lips quirk to the side. "He also mentioned a second video? If you're open to the idea?"

A second video.

Rhys sets the plate down and picks up a rib with his fingers. Holding the two ends, one in each hand, he brings the whole thing to my lips. I lean forward and take a bite, gaze locked with his as I do.

Am I open to another video with Rhys? There's no reason for it. I mean, yeah, the money is nice, but who am I kidding? This isn't about money anymore. This is about so much more.

It's about me, who I am, who I want to be. And all the

strange feelings Rhys stirs up inside of me. It's about this —sitting here with Rhys, comfortable, peaceful, full of joy despite the worries that are still plaguing me.

I don't need to do another video to get more of this. And yet… something inside me perked up at the mention of it. It was fun when I wasn't freaking out. Sebastian and Christian are nice. It was unbelievably hot. I kinda liked watching it back afterward.

If Sebastian thinks it's a good idea, if it'll benefit Rhys's career… I don't feel too weird about it being on the internet, at least not yet. So… am I open to doing another video? "Yeah? I think so?"

Rhys beams. The smile breaking across his face so bright and shiny it sears my eyeballs.

"Yeah? You sure?"

With a reaction like that, how could I possibly say no? I squeeze him, savoring the shape of him in my arms. "I'm sure."

I finish off the rib and Rhys drops the bone back onto the plate. He starts licking his fingers clean, lips pursed as he sucks the finger into his mouth. Then the subtle pop when he pulls the finger free. When he moves onto his other hand, I grab his wrist.

His glance is confused and surprised at first, but then he gasps silently when I bring his sauce-covered finger to my mouth instead. I lick up the sticky sauce, wrap my lips around his finger, swirl my tongue around it.

Rhys's eyes lose their focus and his lips part, tongue peeking out.

I clean one finger, then move on to the next. Rhys lets out a little whimper and his hips shift forward, dragging his pert bum across my growing erection.

I spend extra time on his last finger, sucking on it the way I imagine I would suck on Rhys's dick. I've never wanted to suck on a man's dick before. The thought has never even occurred to me. But with Rhys's finger in my mouth, I think I can understand the appeal.

It's almost soothing. Meditative. I think I could lose myself in it.

Rhys pulls his finger from my mouth and replaces it with his tongue. He shoves it between my lips so fast that I don't have time to react. He moans as I continue the sucking, as I draw his tongue deeper and twirl mine around his.

His hips rock forward and the length of his dick presses against my belly. I grip his butt, helping him grind himself against me. He groans into my mouth and I swallow down the sound.

We kiss. It's messy with lots of tongues swiping everywhere and shivers keep running down my spine. My dick is so hard, aching in the confines of my jeans, and the thought of maybe giving Rhys a blowjob makes it throb.

"Fuck, teddy bear, you drive me crazy." Rhys pants, forehead resting against mine, both of us trying to catch our breath.

I drive *him* crazy? That can't be true. There's nothing all that interesting about me, nothing very special. But Rhys... jeez, I don't even have the words to describe him. He's so vibrant, so full of life. So sincere and genuine and accepting. From that first day in his childhood bedroom, I've felt more seen than I ever have before.

He's introduced me to a whole new world. He's shown me a side of myself I didn't even know existed. He's literally turning me into a different person, and I think I might like this version better than the old one.

"Rhys." I can't help all the emotions I pour into his name.

"What is it, baby? Tell me what you want. Tell me what you need."

"I… I…"

"It's okay, whatever it is, you can tell me." He places his hand in the center of my chest. "In here. What do you want in here?"

No one has ever asked me that before. No one's really cared. They've always assumed that I want the same things that everyone else wants, and I've never stopped to question it. But do I? Do I actually want the nice girl, the house next to Mama's, and a bunch of kids? I don't know.

I search myself, pushing aside everyone else's expecta- tions. Deep in my gut. What do I want?

"I… I want to suck you."

Rhys stills. Then he pulls back enough to stare into my eyes. His irises are a rich brown that sparkles and dances.

"Really?" he says in a hushed tone, like he's not sure I meant it.

Suddenly, a bout of nerves attacks. Maybe he doesn't like being on the receiving end? He knows I'm new to this, so maybe he doesn't want a total newb anywhere near his dick? "Is… is that okay?"

Rhys laughs out loud, eyes wide, smile even wider. "Yeah! Yeah, it's definitely okay. Come on." He scrambles to his feet and drags me along with him.

We stumble into his bedroom and he starts tearing at my clothes. I help him, kicking my boots off and peeling off my shirt, my jeans. The second I'm naked, Rhys shimmies out of his pants and whips his t-shirt over his head.

"Come here."

He takes my hand and guides me toward the bed. But instead of climbing on, Rhys sits on the edge and pushes me down to my knees.

His dick is hard, sticking out from his pelvis. The tip is already glistening with pre-cum, and the shaft is straight and smooth. His balls sit at the base, two little round orbs. It's... cute?

Rhys is a small guy and so his junk is proportionally on the small side. But it looks so perfect, like it was made in a mold. There are no weird bumps, no wonky angles. The skin all around it is flawless.

I've had brief glimpses of his dick before, but this is the first time I've really seen it up close. This is my first chance to really examine it, learn the feel of it, the taste of it.

Rhys leans back, hands braced behind him. His knees fall out to the sides, giving me plenty of room to work with.

I set my hands on his thighs and pause, heart hammering as I stare at the gorgeous man in front of me. "I don't know what I'm doing," I confess. I don't want to mess this up, or god forbid, hurt him. I want this to be good for him.

"It's okay. Just do what feels good."

"What if I hurt you?"

"I'll tell you if you do." Rhys combs his fingers through my hair, cups my cheek, presses his thumb into my lower lip. "But I don't think you will."

His hand drops away and he leans back again.

Slowly, I draw my hands up his thighs, toward my prize.

Rhys shudders when I wrap my hand around his dick. His stomach and thighs contract, but otherwise, he doesn't move.

My hand is big enough that it almost entirely engulfs his dick. Only the head sticks out of my fist, the glans engorged and shiny, enticing me to taste. I bend forward and lick it experimentally.

Salty and bitter, the flavor takes me right back to the day of our shoot. At the end, when Rhys was getting dressed and I tasted the cum he splattered on my thigh. To the day in my truck, when our cum mixed together, landing all over both of us.

I lick his dick again, running my tongue all over the head. He grunts, his breaths coming in fast and shallow. His eyes are heavy-lidded as he watches me. His fingers dig into the messy bedding underneath him. He's either incredibly turned on, or I'm completely mangling my first blowjob.

"Is this…?"

Rhys groans. "I swear to fucking god, Angel, if you don't keep going, I'm going to die."

Warmth spreads through my chest at his words and a thrill runs through me. He likes what I'm doing. He wants more. Unfamiliar feelings of power and pride give me a fresh boost of confidence.

I take the head between my lips, the same way I did with his finger, with his tongue. And I suck.

"Oh, fuck!" Rhys's body goes taut, every muscle flexed. But he doesn't stop me, doesn't try to take control.

I'm doing this. I'm actually doing this. Me, Angel, a

nobody from a sleepy suburb. I'm making Rhys feel good, making him shudder and jerk in pleasure.

I slide my lips down toward the base, marveling at the girth of Rhys's dick. It's not super thick, but my jaw still stretches more than I'm used to. He's heavy on my tongue, heavier than I expected for his size, and that contrast makes my balls tingle.

I only get a couple inches before my gag reflex kicks in and I hurriedly pull myself off. "Sorry," I pant, wiping up spit with the back of my hand.

"Don't be. You don't have to deepthroat for it to feel good." Rhys's fingers are in my hair again, comforting, soothing.

"But I want to," I object.

He chuckles. "You'll get there. It just takes practice."

I think about that for a moment. Yes, he's right. I *will* get there. And I will practice on his dick every chance I get.

CHAPTER
TWENTY-THREE

RHYS

I know Angel's never given a blowjob before. But honestly? He could do nothing but drool on me and I would come my brains out.

When he asked if it was okay for him to suck my cock, my head had nearly exploded anyway. It's easy to pretend I'm a girl when I'm the one giving him a blowjob or when he's pounding me in the ass from behind. But the fact that he wants to put his mouth on my dick… straight guys don't do that, right?

He wouldn't want to suck cock if he's just experimenting or indulging his wild side. Right? I mean, sucking cock is pretty gay. Even with frotting, he could close his eyes, ignore the other dick, and focus on how good it feels. But you can't really ignore the dick when it's in your mouth. You can't pretend you're not sucking cock when you're actively sucking it.

Jesus, Mary, and Joseph, I'm going to strangle myself with all the thoughts racing frantically through my mind.

Although, it might not matter in the end, not if Angel sucks my brains out through my cock. Which he is doing a very decent job of.

It's taking every ounce of self-control I possess to sit still and let him do his thing. Let him lick where he wants and suck however he wants. The roughness of his hands on my sensitive flesh is deliciously painful. The scrape of his beard sends pleasure radiating through me. And when he palms my balls, both of them fitting neatly into one hand. Holy hell, he could crush them with one squeeze, and why the fuck do I find that arousing?

He's slow at first, exploring and getting used to my size and shape. He makes these curious "aha" sounds when he figures out something new—like digging his tongue into my slit or wriggling it on that delicate spot under the head.

But once he gets going, there's no stopping him. He sucks like he's trying to drink the cum from my balls. He laps at me, from base to tip, like I'm a fucking ice cream cone. He mouths at my balls, almost like he's chewing on them.

I feel like I'm being devoured, and fuck, I am here for it.

Angel's got his lips sealed around the head and he's working the base of my cock with one hand. The other one is between his legs, and I don't have to guess to know what it's doing down there.

He sucks and sucks, tongue swirling and dipping. My balls are drawn up so tight, they might end up inside my body.

I'm going to come. There's no helping it. Even if he

stopped now, dropping me and stepping away, I'd still come. I'm too close to the edge. I can't pull back.

"Angel!" I push at his head, but he lets out a stubborn grunt and sucks even harder. "Angel, I'm going to come! Fuck, I can't hold it back anymore. Fuck! Fuck! Angel!"

My orgasm starts deep in my groin, rocketing through me and destroying everything in its path. My body folds in on itself and I curl around Angel's head, holding him in my lap.

I erupt directly into Angel's mouth, but he doesn't pull off, doesn't even flinch. There's no hesitation before he starts swallowing it down. Every spurt, every gush, every single drop. He takes it all and greedily eats it up.

Goddamn. Jesus Christ. Lord Almighty.

I collapse back onto the bed, still quivering from the orgasm. My skin is electrified, with sparks dancing along the surface. My hole twitches, wanting to be filled despite how wrung out I already am. I want his cum inside me, the way my cum is inside him.

The bed dips as Angel joins me on it. He props himself up on an elbow and gazes down at me. The gold chain dangles from his neck and the crucifix is warm where it touches my shoulder. He looks worried. "Was it okay?"

I chuckle, or at least try to. I can't manage any more than a couple huffs. "It was more than okay."

My hand floats up and he catches it, bringing my palm to his mouth. He plants a kiss on it, then I reach around to the back of his neck. I pull him down to me for a kiss. Lazy and slow. I lick between his lips, tasting myself on him, and even though I'm spent, my dick stirs.

I can't believe he swallowed. But I suppose I shouldn't be surprised. He's scooped up my cum and eaten it more than once—completely unprompted. Makes sense that he'd want to drink it from the source. Goddamn. It's so hot, I can't even. My Angel, my shy, cuddly teddy bear, seems to have developed a taste for my cum.

"Give me a second and we can go again," I say.

He's still hard, hot to the touch and leaking. When I grab his cock with my free hand, he thrusts into my fist with a whimpering gasp. I stroke him, light and easy, keeping him primed as I catch my breath.

As the daze of my orgasm clears, I push Angel onto his back, bracketing his body with my hands and knees. He gazes up at me, so open and trusting. I can read every emotion as they flash across his face. Excitement, a touch of nerves, desire. But more than any of that is wonder, awe, reverence. It's not the first time he's looked at me like that. And god, what I wouldn't give to have him look at me like that every single fucking day for the rest of my life.

Mentally, I pull back. Nothing good lies in that direction. Just focus on now, on this moment. Enjoy what we have today and don't think too much about tomorrow.

I lean to the side to grab my bottle of lube and a strip of The Camboy Network branded condoms. I hold the condoms up.

"I haven't been with anyone since our shoot," I say to Angel with a question in my eyes.

He shakes his head. "Neither have I."

"So?" I dangle the condoms over the edge of the bed.

Angel nods and I drop them to the floor.

Impatient, I squeeze out a dollop of lube onto my fingers and hiss at the cold when I reach back to prep myself. But before I can get even the tip of one finger inside, Angel stops me.

"Can I watch?" he asks, shyly, as if he thinks I'll say no.

Pfft. As if. Of course I want Angel to watch. I climb off him and flop down onto my back, then lift my legs into a V that perfectly frames my body. Angel scrambles into position in front of me, kneeling, eyes glued to my hole.

Slowly, I probe myself with one finger, then bear down so it slips inside.

Angel gasps, mouth hanging open.

I sink my finger in as far as it'll go before pulling it all the way out. In. Then out. Slowly at first, then faster. The lube squelches and a visible shudder runs through Angel.

I add another finger, stretching myself easily. My muscles relax into the familiar invasion.

Lying on my stomach, my dick is well on its way to fully hard again. But it isn't the fingerfucking that's making it grow. It's the expression on Angel's face. The rapt attention and unabashed eagerness.

He reaches out, almost like he's in a trance, and touches me, right where my fingers disappear into my body. It's just a single finger, a tiny spot of contact, but it sends heat coursing through me.

"Fuck. Angel."

He pushes on the muscle, as if testing how firm it is. It shouldn't make me squirm with want, but it does. I buck, trying to chase that feeling, wanting more of him.

"How does it feel?" he asks, with so much innocent honesty that I laugh out loud.

I kind of sound pained. I kinda am. Angel's gaze flicks to mine. The expression on his face fucking takes my breath away.

"It... it feels... fucking amazing." It's a poor description that completely fails to capture everything I feel. But it's all my lust-addled mind can come up with at the moment.

Angel glances back down to where I've still got two fingers stuffed in my ass. "Can I?"

Jesus Christ. Angel and his totally innocuous questions. They're going to kill me. They will literally murder me.

I nod, then move to pull my fingers out.

"No, wait, stay there."

What the fuck?

Angel grabs the lube and slicks up his fingers, then brings them back to my hole.

Oh. Motherfucking goddamn. I squeeze my eyes shut as he gently places a finger next to mine again. It's all I can do to lie still. I'm vibrating. My entire body is twitching.

My eyes fly open when Angel starts pressing his finger into my ass alongside my own. I bear down, letting him in and a moan escapes me as he slots into place.

"Fuck," I breathe.

He wiggles his finger so it slips between the two I've got in there, then curls it so we're hooked together and intertwined.

The feeling is like nothing I've ever experienced before. It feels like we're holding hands. Inside my body. The shifting and twisting of our fingers against each other is incredible. It's unbelievable.

Then it gets better.

Angel pulls his finger out. But since it's all tangled up with my fingers, we both end up pulling out. With just the tips inside, he pushes back in. And now he's fucking me with our fingers. Yeah, because that's a totally normal, completely not-gay thing for a straight guy to do.

How am I still alive? How have I not expired and gone to heaven? Or maybe Angel has brought heaven down to earth.

He fucks me—makes me fuck myself. Then he adds another finger to our woven digits. The stretch is divine. The fullness is so satisfying. The strange bumps and dips of our knuckles as they slide past my rim is unlike anything I've ever experienced.

But it's the way our hands are locked together, the way Angel's directing the movement with so much deliberate care. If I hadn't already come once, I'd probably be coming right now.

"Fuck, Angel." The words come out in barely-there gasps

"Is this okay?" His voice is lower and a little more rumbly than usual.

I nod, unable to speak. I don't think I could handle it if this was any more okay.

He picks up speed and I practically sob. We bottom out hard and the impact against my ass sends reverberations up through the rest of my body.

I've never been fucked like this. In all my years as a camboy, never have I ever thought to get fucked like this. How is this possible? How did Angel, with less than a month of gay sex under his belt, come up with something so bizarre and so incredibly hot?

Jesus. Fuck.

"Angel!" I whine. I can't take much more of this. Either Angel sticks his cock in me or I'm going to have to tap out. "I need you. Please. Fuck me. I need your cock."

Gingerly, Angel eases our fingers out of my ass. My

hole gapes open, quivering with nothing to bear down on. It needs to be filled. It needs Angel filling it.

I reach for Angel's cock, coating it with the lube on my hand. He tops up with a squirt from the bottle, and I direct him to my hole.

There's no waiting, no easing him in. I lower my legs and wrap them around his waist. As soon as his cock touches my hole, I push my heels into his ass and drive him forward. I'm impaled in a nanosecond.

"Yesss." I sink into the sensation of being stuffed. Angel's cock fits so perfectly, it hits all the right buttons inside me.

I run my hands up and down Angel's sides, down toward his hips, then up his back. His body hair tickles my palms and the tingles travel along my arms.

He props himself up with his hands on either side of my head. His necklace hangs between us, bumping into my chin. My cock is trapped against his stomach.

I don't usually love missionary, and not because it's boring like some people think. I like being on top, taking charge, being in control. I like teasing my partner, giving them pleasure, watching them fall apart and knowing it's because of me.

But with Angel, everything is different. I mean, yes, I still want all those things, but I also want things the other way around.

I want his weight on me, pressing me firmly into the mattress. I want to be smothered by him and engulfed in him. I want to lose myself in him and let him have control over me. I want him to feel powerful, to feel strong, to feel like he's in charge.

I yank him down to me, and we both grunt when he

drops to his elbows. I catch his lips with mine, tangling our tongues together the way our fingers were earlier. I fill my lungs with the scent of our sex, of my cum, and underneath it all, that fresh sawdust that is Angel himself.

I wrap myself around Angel like a fucking octopus, arms and legs snaking around his back. "Fuck me, teddy bear," I whisper against his lips.

And he does. He takes me apart, inch by careful inch. Not with hard, bone-shattering thrusts. But with slow and equally soul-destroying ones. It's definitely Angel-style fucking and I am here for it.

He rocks against me, barely pulling out before pushing back in. The movement has the underside of my cock rubbing against the soft hairs on his belly. He peppers my face with kisses before licking his way to my neck. I crane my head to give him better access. He nips my earlobe, laps at my pulse point, then buries his nose into the crook of my neck.

I cling to him, reveling in the exquisite torture, letting myself drift in the pool of pleasure he's creating for us. I could die like this and be happy. All wrapped up in Angel, inside and out, feeling loved, cherished, precious.

My eyes sting suddenly as emotions surge, unbidden, to the surface. No. No. Not now. Not like this. When I can't run away, when I can't hide from him.

I squeeze my eyes shut, willing the tears to go away. This is just fucking. This is just sex. It's only physical. I'm just guiding Angel through his exploration of gay sex.

There's nothing personal about this. Nothing emotional. I'm definitely, absolutely, one-thousand-percent not in love with my teddy bear.

A tear escapes.

CHAPTER
TWENTY-FOUR

ANGEL

I bury my face into the crook of Rhys's neck and snuggle down into him as much as I dare. I don't want to crush him. Although he seems intent on crushing himself with how tightly he's clinging to me.

If that's any indication of how he feels, then I feel the same way too. I want to cling to Rhys and never let him go. I want to burrow into him and pretend the rest of the world doesn't exist. All I need is Rhys and his light. All I want is to bask in him—forever.

Or at least, for as long as he'll let me. I'm under no illusion that this will last. Rhys has his pick of guys. Dudes who will stumble over each other for just one chance with him.

I'm everything he left behind the second he was old enough to move away from home. I'm everything he's run away from and cut out of his life. Why would he invite any of it back in?

I tilt my hips forward, sheathing myself all the way inside his body. Then I wiggle my hips back and forth a bit. He clenches down around me, and twin shudders run through us.

I like this kind of sex. Soft and gentle is much more my speed. Slow enough to savor, to imprint every moment, every sensation into my memory. So that in the future, when Rhys has moved on, when I'm back to my boring old life, I have something to remember, something to cherish.

Rhys sniffles. He turns his head to the side, away from me. He doesn't stiffen underneath me, but his movements become jerky, rather than the smooth, flowing dance we've been doing.

I lift my head and what I find triggers alarm bells and flashing lights.

"Rhys? What's wrong?"

Tears trickle from his closed eyes, over the bridge of his nose, and down into the pillow. There's a growing wet spot on the fabric.

"Am I hurting you?" I move to climb off him, but he only clutches me tighter.

"No," he says, voice thick with tears. "You're not hurting me."

"Then why… why are you…" I try to lift off him again, but he digs his fingernails into my back.

"I just… got something in my eye." He blinks a few times and takes a deep breath. "I'm fine. I'm okay."

He's clearly not. Crying during sex isn't normal, is it? It's supposed to be fun and pleasurable. Not sad.

"Are you sure? Can I… do something?" Although I

have no idea what I can do when he doesn't want me to move.

Rhys keeps his gaze lowered, his lashes still clumped with moisture. "Let's flip."

I don't know how he does it since he's so much smaller than me and I'm basically smooshing him into the mattress, but being small doesn't mean he's weak. All those dancer muscles are stronger than I've been giving them credit for.

He leverages himself somehow, then shoves. And in one swift motion, we've rolled so I'm flat on my back and he's straddling me. My dick is still firmly buried in his butt.

It takes a moment for me to orient myself, and in those few seconds, Rhys has taken control. He braces his hands on my stomach, and starts bouncing on my lap. It's like what we did in the video, and at the same time, it's not.

The position is the same. Rhys's quads are flexed and fully on display. His dick smacks against my stomach in loud *thwacks*. His head is thrown back. His body is beautifully arched.

But there's something else too. Something raw and unfiltered, primal and potent. Rhys's nails scrape over my front, almost painfully, leaving red, burning trails in their wake. The sounds he makes are deep and guttural. His face is screwed up tight. The pace he sets is punishing, driving, like he's chasing something that's just out of reach.

It's so good that my mind spins. Too many sensations coming at me from too many directions. Too fast for me to catalog, too fast for me to capture any memories. All I can do is hold on to Rhys's thighs and let him ride me toward the edge of the cliff.

He slaps his hands on top of mine, then moves them up so I'm palming his pecs. I squeeze them, his nipples hard against my palms.

"Yes, yes, that's it. Almost there, teddy bear. You with me?"

"Yes! Yes!" I'm not sure what I'm agreeing to, but if Rhys is asking, my answer will always be yes.

He reaches down for his dick, and his hand flies over it, stroking so quickly it's nothing but a blur. His hips never falter, only going harder, faster.

"Come for me, Angel. Come now. Now!"

My orgasm rips through me, sending me right off the cliff and into the air. With a roar, my hips come off the bed. Rhys's hole clenches tight around me, a hot vise that milks my cum from my balls. At the same time, scalding liquid shoots from Rhys's dick and lands on my skin, branding me.

We both freeze, locked into those positions by utterly paralyzing pleasure. Wave after wave until I'm battered, bruised, and broken.

Sluggishly, Rhys lays himself down on me, face hidden between my pecs. I run my fingers through his long, damp hair, down his toned, sweaty back.

The high of the orgasm clears slowly, but even then, it's much too soon. And in its place is a niggling worry. Rhys cried. While I was inside of him, on top of him. I must have done something wrong, something he didn't like.

Maybe I'm too heavy. Maybe he doesn't like being coddled. Or it makes him feel trapped. Guilt eats away at me as the words burst from my lips.

"I'm sorry!"

Rhys stills before pushing himself up to gaze down at me. The tears are gone, but there's a hint of pink rimming his eyes. "You don't have to be sorry," he says, voice strained.

He sounds like he's only saying that so I don't feel bad, but that only makes me feel guiltier.

"Was it something I did?"

Rhys lets out a strangled laugh, then rolls off to the side. My fingers itch to drag him back to me. I want to hold him. I want him to hold me. The scant inches of space between us feels like miles.

"No, it's not you."

I don't believe him. What else could it have been? I shift onto my side, hoisting myself up on an elbow, leaving enough room so I'm not hovering over him.

Rhys regards me for a moment, then raises a hand to cup my cheek. I turn into his palm, eyes drifting shut as I lean into the contact.

Maybe he's had enough of me. I remind him too much of all the people he left behind in the neighborhood. I knew this wouldn't last forever, but I was hoping it would last a little longer than this. I feel like I just found him, I'm not ready to lose him yet.

"Do... do you want me to leave?" I ask in barely a whisper.

When Rhys doesn't answer, I blink my eyes open, bracing myself for the rejection. But that's not what I find in Rhys's expression.

I don't know how to describe it, really. It's tender and affectionate, so much care and fondness. Rhys's eyes are glassy again, but there's no hint of rejection in them. He pulls me down to him, and after a second of hesitation, I let him arrange me how he wants me.

My arm is slung over his waist. My face is tucked into the crook of his neck. I'm half on top of him.

"I don't want to crush you," I say, still keeping my weight off him.

"I want you to crush me." He tugs me more snugly against him.

I give in. To him and to the overwhelming desire I have to be as close to him as possible.

It feels *so good*. Better than anything I've ever felt before. Maybe better than kissing. Maybe even better than sex. It's hard to believe how something so simple can make me feel so light and joyful, calm and peaceful.

I soak it in. Every single drop. I'm hungry for it. Starving for it. For that connection I've found with Rhys that I never knew was possible.

He doesn't want me to leave now. But that doesn't mean he won't change his mind later. I don't know what I'll do when that time comes.

———

I drift back toward consciousness, and the first thing that registers is that I need to pee.

The second thing is that I'm not hugging my pillow. No, the thing in my arms is much bigger, much warmer, and fits against my front much better than my pillow ever could.

I'm hugging Rhys. My heart rate skyrockets at the realization. We're both on our sides, him facing away from me, his body tucked snugly into the curve of mine. I think this is called spooning? Which would make me the big spoon and Rhys the little spoon.

Delight races through me and a smile tugs at my lips. I'm spooning with Rhys. I memorize the feel of him, of his bum against my morning wood, the tickle of his hair in my nose, the way his chest expands with each breath. Another memory to add to my collection. Another moment I'll be able to recall once this is all over.

We fit really well together—is that coincidence? I want to think that it's not, that we were made for each other, custom-built to slot right into place.

My bladder protests and I reluctantly uncurl myself from around Rhys. He turns over as I ease off the bed, grabbing the pillow where my head was and nuzzling into it like he's trying to find my scent again. If my bladder wasn't bursting, I would slide right back into bed with him.

Instead, I grab my boxers from the floor and slip out of the room. I'll just relieve myself and go right back to bed. I want to squeeze in every last second with Rhys before this ends and he kicks me out.

But on my way back to his room, I hear the front door opening.

I freeze, seized by sudden panic. Oh no. Is someone breaking into the apartment? What do I do? I'll need to fight off the intruder. I've never fought anyone before.

Footsteps come down the long hallway. I plaster myself against the wall so I can jump the bad guy when he comes around the corner. But before anyone materializes, the living room lights flick on.

I hiss as the bright lights blind me. I press my fingers into my eyes to ease the sting.

"Uh… hey."

I force my eyes open to find Hayden standing with his hand still on the light switch.

Oh. It's not an intruder. It's just Hayden.

"Uh, hey," I parrot back at him.

We stand there, me in my boxers, Hayden with his coat still on, staring at each other.

"Um, I was just going to the bathroom," I say, pathetically.

Hayden nods. "I'm just coming home."

I nod back. "I, uh… I'll just…" I point toward Rhys's bedroom, not waiting for Hayden's response before pushing myself off the wall.

"Wait."

I stop in my tracks and slowly turn around.

He looks conflicted, with a furrow in his brow. He opens his mouth, then shuts it again. Open. Shut. Then he plants his hands on his hips, dropping his chin with a short, frustrated chuckle.

"Are you okay?"

Hayden shakes his head. "It's not me I'm worried about. It's Rhys."

My stomach drops to my knees. "Rhys?"

Hayden glances up at me, his green eyes wary. He studies me, and I wrap my arms around myself defensively.

"I'm worried about Rhys," Hayden repeats. "He's had to put up with a lot of shit in his life—you probably know. His parents aren't the greatest, and he stands out everywhere he goes. The straights think he's too gay. The gays think he's too femme. Despite all that, he's still himself. No matter how hard it gets. He's tough, strong, resilient, but…"

My stomach isn't at my knees anymore. It's all the way on the floor. I agree with everything Hayden has said. A lot of it is why I like Rhys so much. But I don't think I'm going to like what comes next.

"Look, if you hurt him, it won't be the end of the world."

My hackles rise at the thought of hurting Rhys. I would never. Not on purpose. But Hayden doesn't let me talk.

"He'll get over you. He'll bounce back. But the thing is, he shouldn't have to. He shouldn't have to be strong all the time. He deserves to be the soft one for once and have someone else be strong for him."

I'm stunned. Speechless. Every single one of Hayden's words is a nail shot directly into my heart. They're painful to hear, especially because I know they're true.

This whole time, I've been so preoccupied with myself, with all these new feelings sprouting up inside me. I've been confused about what it means about who I am. I've been afraid of Rhys getting bored with me and kicking me to the curb.

I never stopped to think about Rhys. What does he want? What does he need? He's done so much for me, and what have I done for him in return? Nothing, dang it. I've given him nothing.

"I…" I'm not great with words on a good day, never mind in the middle of the night while wearing nothing but my boxers.

I force myself to meet Hayden's gaze, to look him right in the eyes so he can see how sincere I am. I swallow around the ball of emotion that's lodged in my throat. "You're right. About everything."

Hayden's eyebrows lift a fraction, as if to ask what I'm going to do about it. I haven't a clue. But I want to. I want to be there for Rhys the way he's been there for me. I want to support him, care for him, protect him.

He's shown me what it feels like to be the soft one. Now it's my turn to show him I can be strong too.

CHAPTER
TWENTY-FIVE

RHYS

I wake up to the scent of coffee. Dark. Rich. It makes my mouth water before I'm fully conscious.

I roll over. Wait. Something's wrong. I'm alone in my bed, but I wasn't earlier. The mattress is still a little warm under my hand.

Angel. My teddy bear. He spent the whole night with me, hugging me to him like I'm *his* teddy bear.

Where is he now?

I scramble out of bed and take a second to pull on the clothes I was wearing yesterday before bursting out of my room. The fragrant aroma of coffee hits me in the face and I breathe in deep. Following my nose, I end up in the kitchen with my jaw on the floor.

It's Angel. Wearing his boxers and undershirt, necklace nestled in his chest hair. He's got two mugs of coffee in front of him, and he's in the middle of doctoring them. Well, one of them. Two heaping spoons of sugar and enough milk to make the whole thing go white.

That's the way I take my coffee.

Angel finishes stirring, taps the spoon lightly on the edge of the mug before setting it aside, then holds out the mug to me. I take it with both hands, bringing it to my nose for another deep inhale.

"How did you know how I like my coffee?"

Angel hides his shy smile behind his own mug of black. "I asked Hayden."

"Hayden?" My head snaps around and only then do I notice that his door is closed. He must still be asleep.

"He came home when I got up to go pee," Angel explains.

My heart skips a beat. It's stupid. It's just coffee. But the fact that Angel thought to ask, in the dead of night, when he was probably still half asleep…

I busy myself with taking a long gulp of the sweet, milky brew. If I dwell on how sweet Angel is, I'm going to start crying again. Ugh. I still can't believe I did that. In the middle of fucking sex. I mean, probably the best fucking sex I've ever had in my life… but still. God.

Angel sets down his mug, then turns to open the fridge. He ducks to peer inside, then starts pulling things out onto the counter. Butter. Onions. Mushrooms. Green peppers. Eggs. Cheese. The leftover brisket from yesterday.

"What are you doing?" I ask suspiciously. The kitchen is Hayden's domain. I'm pretty useless in here, but Hayden gets all fancy with his food. Our fridge is always fully stocked, even if I don't know what to do with the stuff in there.

"I'm making you breakfast."

I bite back the "why?!" that's hovering at the tip of my

tongue. Then I fight back the tears prickling my eyes again. How is he so goddamn sweet? That's not normal, that's inhuman, that's… I sniffle. Fuck. Fuck!

What in the holy hell is wrong with me? Did I take something that threw my hormones out of whack? That has to be it. There's *no reason* for me to cry!

"Rhys?"

Ah, shit.

Angel comes toward me, concern etched on his face.

I take a step backward, holding up one hand to keep him away. "No, I'm fine! I'm totally okay! There's nothing wrong!"

He freezes mid-step, his concerned expression growing more hurt.

Ah, god-fucking-damn it!

"No! I don't mean… I mean… fuck, I don't know!"

Now Angel looks worried again, like he might have a freakout on his hands. And to be honest, he might. I don't know why I'm reacting this way and that scares me just as much as the love I feel for Angel.

"Rhys?" He takes a cautious step forward, slow and measured, like I'm a skittish animal he's trying to soothe.

I'm torn. A part of me wants to run away and hide from him and from my feelings. Just bury my head under a pillow until this whole thing resolves itself and I can lick my wounds in peace.

Another part of me wants to run into Angel's arms and bury my head in that little space between his shoulder and his neck. I want to pretend just a little bit longer, put off reality for another day. Let myself live in this fantasy world until real life comes knocking.

Make-believe wins out.

I rush into Angel's arms, careful not to spill any of the coffee he so tenderly made for me. He cradles me to him, one big hand wrapped around the curve of my waist, the other tangling in my hair. I nuzzle the bare skin of his neck, breathing in the scent of fresh sawdust. Mixed with the coffee, it makes me feel like we're enjoying the early morning in a cabin hidden in the woods.

Angel doesn't ask me what's wrong. He doesn't ask why I'm all teary and acting weird. He just holds me, rocking me back and forth until my emotions finally settle. Thank god, because I wouldn't know what to tell him. I certainly can't say that I've fallen in love with him. Dear lord, that would be worse than bad.

Eventually, Angel kisses me on the head. "Breakfast?"

I nod.

He pulls away, keeping his hands on my arms until he's sure I'm steady on my feet, then he goes back to sorting all the ingredients he pulled out of the fridge.

"What are you making?" I ask, inching a little closer.

"Omelets?" He glances at me with a question in his eyes. "Is that okay?"

I smile and beat back my emotions. "Yeah, they're my favorite."

"I know."

His ears go pink and *ngh*, I want to kiss them so bad. I want to nibble on them to see if they're as sweet as they look. Christ, I'm fucked. So very fucked.

Angel chops up the veggies and beats the eggs. He looks like he knows what he's doing in a kitchen, and I watch with my chin resting in my hand. My stomach is filled with butterflies trying to escape, and my heart is beating erratically. Yearning stirs deep in my soul, yearning for this: simple mornings with someone who knows how I like my coffee, who makes omelets because he knows they're my favorite, whose mere presence makes me feel all gooey inside.

I want to wake up every day with Angel's scent lingering on the pillow next to mine. I want to watch his ears go pink when I tease him. I want to melt into the strong comfort of his embrace.

Angel plates up two perfectly folded omelets and piles on a mountain of hash browns. The finished product looks like something I'd order from one of the brunch places the boys and I go to. It looks amazing and smells divine.

He sets a plate down in front of me at the small table tucked into the corner of the kitchen, then takes the seat across from me.

"This is…" I shake my head, overwhelmed by him, by my feelings, by everything.

"It's nothing." Angel shrugs.

I reach across the table to grasp his hand. "It's not nothing."

He flips his hand over so we're touching palm to palm, then gazes into my eyes like he's trying to memorize how they look. I pour everything I feel, every ounce of affection and adoration into my expression, hoping he'll see them and recognize them for what they are. Love. Unexplainable. Unexpected. But so real it hurts.

"We should eat before it gets cold," Angel says, and I reluctantly let go of his hand.

The omelet tastes even better than it smells, an orgasm of flavors exploding on my tongue. I don't usually eat right after waking up, but I gobble this up like I haven't eaten in days.

"Is it okay?" Angel asks.

"Teddy bear, this might be the best thing I've ever tasted."

His ears flush pink, and his cheeks scrunch into a smile. God, why does he make it so hard to not love him?

"Do you cook a lot?" I ask, before scooping up another mouthful of omelet.

Angel nods. "I've been cooking with Mama since before I can remember. We do big family dinners every Sunday. It was just the two of us for a long time, but then my sister and nephew moved back in with Mama last year."

The mention of Sunday dinners makes my heart twinge. "My family does Sunday dinners too. I don't go, though."

Angel shoots me a concerned look, but he doesn't ask why. It's so obvious, he doesn't have to. Why torture myself with hours of awkward eating every week? They stopped bugging me to go not long after I moved out, and I've never bothered inviting myself.

"How is it? Having your sister and nephew around, I mean?" I remember Angel's sister. She's older, I think. Pretty, popular, and smart, too.

"It's okay," he says with a shrug. "She disappeared with her boyfriend for a while. But he left her after she had Jonah."

"Jerk."

Angel's lips twist into a sad half-smile. "Yeah, he is."

"Do you like having them around now?"

Angel blinks like he doesn't understand the question. "Um, I guess I do?"

Under the table, I nudge his leg with my foot. "You don't sound so sure."

He squirms a little. "I dunno. I've never thought about it. They're family, so..." He shrugs, like that's all the answer that's needed.

I get it, even if I don't agree. Family is everything in the old neighborhood. You do anything for family. Bend over backward, deny yourself, sacrifice. It doesn't matter if they're assholes or abusive or don't deserve it. Loyalty is paramount.

Which is bullshit, in my humble opinion. But then, no one from the old neighborhood has ever asked for it. Whatever.

"How did you..." Angel trails off, gaze lowered as he pokes at a few of the last hash browns on his plate. "When you moved out, how did you... you know?"

"How did I survive?" I clarify, keeping my tone light and teasing. I know what he's asking. How did I do it? How did I break away from everything that was familiar and set up my own life without the support of family and the neighborhood?

It's not something that happens back there. People don't up and leave. You grow up there, get married there, have kids there, and the cycle never ends.

The pink on Angel's ears darkens. "No, I mean, well, actually, yeah, kinda?"

"Simple. I didn't fit. They didn't really want me around. So it was a win-win situation." I flick my wrist, like I'm waving off an annoying fly. That's what it felt like sometimes. Getting out of the neighborhood was like finally killing the incessant buzzing in my ears.

Angel's brow furrows. "It was that easy?"

I chuckle. "Well, no, I said it was simple, but it wasn't easy. I started camming to support myself. You know, just my dick, my hand, and my phone. I'd throw a few dildos in there sometimes." I smile at the memory of the early days, trying to figure out how to get the right angles, how to upload the damn videos...

"It was only supposed to be a temporary thing to help pay rent and cover the bills until I could support myself with dancing. But then, the porn took off and there was no way I could make as much as a dancer, so..." I shrug, then continue, "Plus, it's a really welcoming environment. I know that sounds weird, but I've never had anyone in the industry look at me strangely or say anything hurtful. It's surprisingly inclusive and respectful."

Angel's ears have faded to a mostly normal shade of pink. His expression is thoughtful, with a hint of curiosity and a dash of wistfulness. "Your family doesn't know, do they?"

Laughter bursts from me at the thought of my parents finding out how I've been supporting myself for the better part of the past decade. "Oh god, no, can you imagine? They'd have aneurysms. I think Nico knows, though. He's never asked me about it, and I never mention it. But he's always had this... 'I'm cool with whatever, I just don't want the details' thing with me."

Angel nods in understanding. "Nico's a good guy."

"Yeah, he is."

We fall silent with me watching Angel while he's lost in his thoughts. There's so much longing in his eyes, but for once I can't read any more than that. What is he longing for? What does he want? I want to give it to him. I want to shower him with every good thing he could possibly desire.

If only he'd let me, I would give him everything.

CHAPTER
TWENTY-SIX

ANGEL

After we finish breakfast, I collect our empty plates and stash them in the sink for later. Then Rhys drags me back to his room and onto the bed.

"Have you ever thought about moving away?" he asks after we're snuggled under the covers together. Our faces are inches apart and our limbs are all tangled together.

The question takes me aback. I've thought about moving away about as much as I've thought about jumping out of a plane. "Where would I go?"

"Anywhere!" He gives me a gentle poke in the side.

Anywhere sounds terrifying. *Anywhere* might as well be *nowhere*, some nameless place with faceless people. It might as well be a haunted town with ghosts and zombies and monsters.

I scrunch up my nose. "I can count on my hands the number of times I've left the tri-state area."

Rhys's jaw drops, and my ears tingle with heat. I'm a homebody—everyone knows that. What reason would I have to go somewhere else when everyone I've ever known is right here?

"Seriously? What's the farthest you've been?"

I think for a second. I went up north of the city once for a football game in high school. And out to Long Island for a job once. I've done weekend trips out to the Jersey Shore with the guys… "Atlantic City?"

"Huh, Nico had his bachelor party there."

My ears heat even more. "Yeah, that's when I went."

Rhys leans in and gives me a kiss on the lips. A single, hard press as he wiggles himself deeper into my arms. He wraps himself around me like an octopus and I never want him to let go.

"Where would you want to go? If you could go anywhere? Not permanently, just for a vacation," he asks, barely whispering, brushing his nose back and forth across mine.

I don't know how to answer that question. I've thought about it about as much as I've thought about moving out of the neighborhood. So I say the first thing that pops into my mind. "Um… Disney World?"

Rhys doesn't react for a second. Then he giggles, bubbly and bright, wriggling against me until I'm giggling too.

"Disney World? Of all the places on the entire planet, you want to go to Disney World?"

I shrug, still laughing. "I don't know? Isn't that where everyone wants to go?"

"I mean, sure? But what about Venice? Rome? Barcelona? Madrid? Paris? Marseille?"

Now my jaw drops. I recognize the names of those cities, of course. But they're on the other side of the world.

We'd have to get on a plane to get there. I've never even been on a plane. I've never even left America. I don't even have a passport! "Europe? But that's so far!"

Rhys runs his fingers through my hair, through my beard. His expression grows so soft and tender that it makes my heart somersault in my chest.

"It doesn't have to be."

"You've been to those places?" I ask, hearing the awe in my own voice. I knew Rhys was much more worldly than I am. I guess I never really understood what that meant.

"Not all of them. But Noel took us on a Mediterranean cruise for his birthday a few years ago. We stopped at a bunch of cities along the way."

I blink, not entirely sure I understand what he's saying. How did Noel take them on a cruise? Does he mean Noel has his own boat? How is that possible?

"Noel's filthy rich," Rhys adds when I don't respond.

"Oh."

"Would you want to see those places? If you could?" Rhys asks.

The question is so far outside what I'm familiar with, it almost doesn't make sense. How would I see them? How would I get there? Where would I stay? Would I have to go alone? I don't think I could do that.

But if I went with someone… someone like Rhys. The images materialize in my mind like photographs. The two of us holding each other with the Eiffel Tower in the background. Us sharing a meal of freshly made pasta. Getting lost together while wandering around a super-old castle.

"Maybe? If we went together?"

Rhys smiles, but not too wide, almost like he's trying to fight it back. His eyes get a little glassy. He snuggles right into me, face tucked into the crook of my neck. "I would love that."

Warmth fills me. Heat and desire, but also something more. Something that's so powerful, it takes my breath away. It rocks me to the core, threatening to rip me right apart.

I cling to Rhys as he clings to me, so tightly it's like we're trying to merge into one person. Like we never want to let each other go.

"Teddy bear?" Rhys murmurs, lips moving against the skin of my neck.

"Hmm?"

"How come you don't have a girlfriend?"

The question sends a sharp pain spiking through me. The reminder that I've been alone for so long, that no one ever sees me or takes the time to get to know me. No one until Rhys, that is. I hold him closer, nuzzling my nose into his hair. "Girls don't like me."

He scoffs. "What? That's ridiculous. You're perfect. What's not to love?"

"It's true. I had a girlfriend in high school, but that's it. And even then..." I trail off, realizing only then that I've never told Rhys this before.

"Even then?" He prompts.

I swallow down the flurry of emotions inside me. Some of the lingering pain, some embarrassment and shame. But also the warmth that Rhys brings out in me. I have nothing to be self-conscious about. I can tell Rhys anything.

"Even then... we never..." I can't say the actual words. "You know."

Rhys doesn't respond right away, then he pulls back to look at my face. "Never had sex?"

My ears should be burning, but they're not. The flush should be spreading to my cheeks, but there's no heat. There's a strange peacefulness when I speak. "No. We fooled around a little bit. But it was mostly kissing and awkward groping. And it wasn't very good."

"So, you are, or you were, a virgin?"

I nod with a sheepish smile.

"So, the video we filmed was…"

"My first time?"

Rhys's eyes go wide just before he makes a hiccupping sound. "Teddy bear," he says, hand coming up to cup my cheek. "I didn't know. Why didn't you say something?"

"I don't know?" It hadn't seemed like a big deal at the time. Although, now that I think about it, I guess first times are supposed to be important, right? At least, that's what everyone says.

"I would've made it… god, I don't even know, better for you? Special somehow?"

"It was special. It was with you."

"Ngh, teddy bear!" Then he slams his mouth against mine.

The nickname he's given me makes my chest swell with that same warmth. It presses against my ribs, pushing and pushing until it feels like I'm going to burst.

"Rhys." His name comes out as a whine, desperate and needy, echoing with all the feelings I don't understand.

"Shh, I've got you."

Rhys tugs at the hem of my t-shirt, and we disentangle ourselves just long enough to strip our clothes off. Then we're right back in each other's arms. His smooth, toned body, rubbing up against my big, hairy one. His hard erection pressing into my belly. Mine poking him between the legs.

"I want you on top of me," Rhys whispers into my ear. "Like yesterday, pinning me to the bed, rocking into me."

Worry sprouts at the back of my mind, even as my dick pulses at the memory of how good it felt. "Are you sure?"

He nods. "One thousand percent."

He scrambles for the bottle of lube that fell onto the floor last night. Before I can react, he's slicked up his fingers and shoved two inside his body. With his free hand, he's tugging me into position.

"I can't wait, teddy bear. I need you to fill me up. All the way. Come here."

Rhys manhandles me, which sounds ridiculous given our size difference, but I shudder at how strong he is, at how easily he puts me right where he wants me. I feel big and small at the same time, tough and soft in the same exact moment. In control and yet utterly defenseless.

Rhys guides me to him, bringing the tip of my dick right up to his hole. Then he feeds me into his body, his muscles sucking me right inside. Before I know it, I'm bottomed out, every inch of me encased in the tight heat of Rhys's bum. The feeling is overwhelming, coursing through every cell, every nerve, touching me where I've never been touched before, changing me forever.

I tremble. With a yearning so potent it scares me. I want. So. Much. So. Hard. To the point where I'll give just about anything to satisfy the craving clawing at my insides.

"Rhys," I cry, dragging his name out into multiple syllables.

"I've got you." He kisses me, tongue pushing into my

mouth, swirling around mine. Forceful and demanding. He bites down on my bottom lip, tugging firmly enough that I whimper at the dull pain.

His fingers scrape over my scalp, over my back, leaving trails of fire everywhere they go. His legs are locked around my waist, heels planted firmly on my behind, keeping me buried to the hilt.

"Oh god, teddy bear, you feel so good."

I hum in agreement, my brain not able to gather letters into words.

"I love how thick you are, how much I have to stretch around you. So full. So stuffed."

I tilt my hips forward, giving him even more and Rhys moans.

"I love how heavy you are. I love your weight on top of me, holding me down, trapping me. I love how hairy you are, all this beautiful, soft fur."

I bury my face into the space between Rhys's shoulder and neck as he showers these words on me. These words that are as painful as they are soothing. They penetrate through all my layers, through all the things I thought I knew about myself, into the core of who I am. They break me open. They lay me bare.

"I love that I'm your first, that you haven't had anyone else but me. I love making you feel good, making you come, making you lose your mind."

I love that too. I love all the things Rhys has introduced me to, all the ways he's helped me step outside my comfort zone. I love the new things I've learned about myself, the way I've changed because of him. I love how he feels in my arms. I love how he makes me feel.

A choked sound escapes my throat as I thrust into his body, into his tight, welcoming heat.

"Yes, teddy bear, that's it. Just like that. Fuck me."

A protest rises up inside me. No. I'm not fucking Rhys. Nothing so crude. I'm making love to Rhys. I'm giving back to him all the things he's given to me. I'm pouring myself into him like he's poured himself into me.

I move slowly but steadily, maintaining that excruciating pace that's just enough to make my head spin. Rhys writhes under me, arching and stretching, urging me on.

"I've never felt this good, teddy bear. I've never felt like this before. You do things to me..." His voice breaks and he bites down on my shoulder with a sob. "Fuck, the things you do to me."

"What?" I ask, suddenly overcome with the need to know. "What do I do to you?" Are they anything like the things he does to me?

"You... you... you make me want things I shouldn't want."

A full-body shudder races through me, making me drive deeper into him. He makes me want things I shouldn't want either. Things like going to a gay nightclub, doing gay porn, visiting faraway places, leaving everything and everyone I know behind. "What do you want?"

Rhys shakes his head as his body clenches around my dick.

"What do you want, Rhys?" I ask again, hips snapping forward a little harder.

He cries out, a choked, broken sound. "You, Angel. I want you."

Rhys's admission trips something inside me. Like a

switch that's been flipped. I go wild. Almost feral. Rhys wants me? Then he has me. All of me. Forever.

With my arms snaked under his body, holding him secure, I pound into him. Again and again, like my hips are a jackhammer trying to break through concrete. The bed bangs against the wall. Sweat pours off me, creating a wet squelching sound as skin slaps against skin.

Rhys screams in my ear. "Yes! Yes! Right there! Harder! Ngh!"

I try to go harder, drawing on every ounce of strength, desire, and love I have to give Rhys the best orgasm of his life. My balls draw up. The base of my spine tingles. But I can't come before he does. I can't come until he says I can.

"Rhys, please!"

"Yes! Yes! Fuck! Fuck!" He clenches like a vise around me. "Now, Angel! Now!"

I let go just as molten lava explodes between us, coating my stomach and his. My orgasm erupts from me, twisting me around and chewing me up. Wave after wave crashes over me as I pump myself deep into Rhys's hole.

"Yes, that's it! Fill me with your cum, Angel! Drown me in it!"

I do my best, chasing every last drop of pleasure, leaving nothing in the tank. I collapse onto Rhys. Mind short-circuited. Body drifting in bliss. From somewhere in the distance comes a reminder that I'm heavy and I should roll off him, but my muscles have been liquified and I can't move.

Rhys doesn't seem to mind, from the way he's still clinging to me, peppering light kisses along my cheek, my neck, my shoulder.

That warmth from before, the one that has the power to

destroy me, it's love, I realize. Love for Rhys. And yeah, it can destroy me. But it can also make me whole.

CHAPTER
TWENTY-SEVEN

RHYS

The next couple weeks go by in a blur. Angel and I text back and forth every single day. We've even talked on the phone a few times in the evenings. But we haven't been able to see each other face to face since he spent the night at my place.

I miss him. God, I miss him so damn much.

I filmed the two scenes I was assigned for Sebastian's *12 Toys of Christmas* project, feeling weirdly lonely after both. They were solo scenes, just me and the toys, but I couldn't stop thinking about Angel the entire time. The roughness of his hands, the furriness of his body, the scent of fresh sawdust that I now associate with the best sex I've ever had. I wish he could've been there with me, to touch me, kiss me, hold me.

But he'll be here today, at The Bronzed Rail, which we've rented out to film our second video. I've choreographed the pole routine to "Dragon" by Miriam Bryant. It's a moody and haunting song, not exactly Christmassy, but whatever. It's what I'm feeling these days, so Sebastian can deal.

I'm pacing back and forth by the club's bar while Sebastian and Christian set up the lights and cameras around the stage. I've got my phone in hand, obsessively checking my messages to make sure Angel's still on his way.

I've never felt this way before, so anxious to see someone, to be in the same room as them. It's making me antsy and irritable and a bitch to be around. Just ask Hayden—he's been hiding in his room for days to avoid me.

Where is Angel? He's supposed to be here already. What if he doesn't make it in time? What if he doesn't show up? My heart aches with how much I miss him. It's making me want to crawl out of my skin.

"Hey, Rhys, you okay?" Sebastian's standing a few feet away, watching me with worry in his eyes.

"Yeah! I'm fine! Why do you ask?!" My voice is too high and slightly hysterical. I clear my throat and take a breath. "I'm fine."

Sebastian gives me a disbelieving look, but he doesn't argue. Instead, he holds up his iPad. "You forgot to sign the forms for the video."

I roll my eyes and drop my head back at Sebastian's love for paperwork. In all my years in the industry, I've never had to sign more waivers and consent forms than I have with Sebastian. "I've already signed those forms a million times."

"But not for this video." He taps the screen a couple times and holds out the tablet for me. "You really should read it before you sign."

I pin Sebastian with an annoyed look. "Have you made any changes to them?"

"No."

"Then I've already read them." I swipe my finger randomly across the screen and hit the save button. "There. Signed."

Sebastian sighs again. "Are you sure—"

The door opens and I spin around at the sound. My heart is racing, trying to beat its way out of my chest, and I hold my breath as I wait to see who comes through.

The nightclub is dark, backlighting the person stepping through the door. His face is cast in shadow, but I don't need to see his face to know it's Angel. I can feel him in the marrow of my bones, in the very depths of my soul.

My feet move of their own accord, catapulting me across the room and into Angel's embrace. He catches me with a small *oomph* and I latch onto him, arms tight around his body, face burrowed into the crook of his neck.

Neither of us speak. We just hold on, soaking in each other's presence after too many days apart. The press of his body against mine, the rasp of his beard against my skin, the scent of him. I want these things all the time. Not every two weeks. Not even every few days. I want Angel by my side every morning when I wake up and every night when I fall asleep.

When my heart stops racing and I can finally draw in a slow, steady breath, I pull back to peek up at Angel.

"Hey," I say, feeling a little sheepish about how I tackled him.

"Hey." His cheeks bunch with a smile.

They're rosy from the chilly fall weather outside, and when I pull him down for a kiss, his lips are cool and a little chapped. But they feel so good, that perfect softness molding to mine.

A throat clears next to us, but I ignore Sebastian. Can't he see we're busy? Apparently not, because he starts speaking, and Angel—way too polite—breaks the kiss and turns to him.

"We're on a tight timeline today, since we only have the club for a few hours." Sebastian waves us toward the stage where he and Christian are all set to go. "Rhys, you want to change into your costume?"

I sigh, loud and annoyed. I haven't had nearly enough of Angel yet. I don't want to let him go. But Sebastian gives me a look that says he wasn't really asking.

"Be right back, teddy bear." I lean up and plant a quick kiss on Angel's cheek before sprinting to the dressing room backstage.

It takes me one minute flat to strip down to nothing, then another couple minutes to lube up the metal dragon and slide it onto my semi-hard cock. A quick application of shimmering body spray and one last check of my hair and makeup, and I'm good to go.

Angel's sitting by the stage when I get back out there, on a chair next to a small table that holds a glass of apple juice that's been frothed up to look like beer. His gaze lifts when I step through the stage door and it locks onto mine. The rest of the nightclub falls away—Sebastian and Christian, the lights and cameras, even the bar along the far wall and the sound booth in the corner.

All that exists in this space is me and Angel.

Somewhere in the background, the opening strains of "Dragon" by Miriam Bryant filter through my awareness, and I tug on the belt holding my dressing gown in place. I let the fabric fall to the floor and step up to the pole.

Angel's eyes roam over my body, twin lasers that heat me up. My nipples stand at attention, goose bumps prickle my skin. My cock grows painfully hard in its metal confines, and my toes curl as desire courses through me.

With the weight of his gaze on me, I dance. My body moves through the choreographed movements, but my mind is focused on the man sitting mere feet away. On the way his lips part and his breathing quickens. On the way he shifts to the edge of his seat like he's about to bound onto the stage and grab me. I dance, using every ounce of seduction I possess to accentuate each position, to make him want me as much as I want him. And fuck, do I *want* him.

The song ends with me on my knees, body folded backward so my shoulders are on the floor and my dragon cock is standing straight up in the air. Slowly, I straighten, rising up onto my knees. Angel's half out of his seat and he's gripping the edge of the table like that's the only thing keeping him from rushing the stage.

"Cut! Okay, let's move things around for the next bit," Sebastian calls out, but I'm not paying attention. My entire focus is on Angel, on how he's practically vibrating with need.

Without thinking, I move toward him, crawling on my hands and knees across the stage. His chest expands with a quick inhale, then stills, like he's holding his breath. His eyes are wide and unblinking, as if he doesn't want to miss a single second.

"Goddamn it, Rhys, you need to wait for me to call action!"

At the edge of the stage, I spin around and slip down onto the floor. The soles of my platform heels hit the hard surface with a quiet *thud,* and I push away from the stage. I saunter toward Angel. He gulps. I stop a foot away from him, and his gaze travels up my body, inch by inch, stomach, chest, neck, chin, nose, eyes.

Our gazes collide, knocking the air right out of my lungs. Fuck. The heat in those dark brown eyes, the barely contained fire, the raging want. I've never felt so powerful before, so strong and so invincible. I feel like I could take down a building with my hands. I feel like I could fly.

I lift one foot and set it on Angel's chest. He immediately slides into his seat until he's pressed against the back of his chair.

"Haven't I seen you before?" I ask, voice way huskier than I intended.

Angel nods.

"You're that contractor, aren't you? You worked on my kitchen and I paid you with a blowjob."

He nods again.

Putting more pressure on his chest with my foot, I lean forward an inch. "Back for more?"

Angel drops his gaze from my face down to my shoe. When he looks back up again, his eyes are hazy with lust. "Y-yes. P-please."

They're just lines that Sebastian made up for us. Words that Angel's agreed to say for the camera. He doesn't necessarily mean them, but they still echo through me, shaking my foundation.

Fuck.

I drag my foot down the front of Angel's body, then

nudge his thighs farther apart so I can step on the edge of his seat, pressing against the bulge in his jeans.

"Did you miss my hole? Did you miss how hot and tight it was? I bet you haven't fucked a hole like that before, have you?"

Angel's lips part and he blinks those thick long lashes like he's fighting to stay conscious. I lean in, putting more pressure on his erection with the front of my boot. He shudders, hands gripping the edge of his seat as his hips buck against my boot. A quiet whine escapes his throat.

Does he… is he… from my boot?

I increase the pressure and Angel gasps as another shudder—harder this time—rushes through him, making him jerk and convulse. His head falls back. His eyes squeeze tightly shut. His hips tilt so he's grinding on my boot.

Jesus motherfucking Christ. He's getting turned on by my pole-dancing boots. Insanely tall platforms with spiky heels. This pair is black with dozens of straps across the top of my feet, leaving my red-tipped toes peeking through. The straps continue up my ankles and calves, stopping just below my knees. Aside from the dragon-cock sleeve, they're the only thing I'm wearing.

And if this is how Angel reacts to them, I'll wear them every fucking day for the rest of my life.

"Hold there for a sec," Sebastian directs, stepping in close with his camera to capture my boot against Angel's crotch.

I keep my gaze trained on Angel's face, on the expression of pure, unadulterated lust. I don't need the reminder that we're not alone here, that this moment, this discovery, is being captured for thousands of fans to witness. I want to pretend it's just the two of us, exploring Angel's apparent boot fetish.

My dick swells painfully against the dragon sleeve. Why is that so hot? Sweet, innocent Angel—who's so wholesome he doesn't understand eggplant and peach emojis—apparently gets turned on by sexy boots. Jesus, that's so kinky and unexpected that my balls tingle at the thought.

I wonder if he'd want to lick my boot.

Jesus. No. I can't let my mind wander in that direction or I'm going to come prematurely and entirely hands-free. Any boot-licking will have to wait until after the cameras are off.

"Got it. Keep going," Sebastian says, backing away to give us room to work.

I lift my foot from the chair, but instead of dropping it to the floor, I swing it over Angel's leg so I'm straddling his thigh.

I lean in to whisper my next words into his ear. "How about a lap dance, big boy? Then I'll give you another shot at my hole."

CHAPTER
TWENTY-EIGHT

ANGEL

Rhys says something about a lap dance and in some faraway part of my mind, I remember that's from the script Sebastian gave us. But really, all I can think about is that boot of his. The way it pressed into my chest, heavy and rough. The sharp point of the heel digging into me. The way his foot arched in the shoe, the black straps and shiny red toes. So elegant and vulnerable and dangerous at the same time.

I don't have a foot fetish. At least, I don't think I have a foot fetish. But sitting there with Rhys's booted foot in my face, a switch flipped inside me. I want to press the sole of his foot to my cheek. I want to suck each one of those perfectly pedicured toes into my mouth. I want to lick his arch and see if he's ticklish there. I want to come all over his feet and then clean them up with my tongue.

Dear lord, what's wrong with me? That's not a normal thing to want, is it? But maybe that's why it's got me so wound up. It's so far outside my comfort zone, so different from anything I could ever have imagined wanting. It's bad and forbidden, and I think that makes me want it more. Oh heavens, I'm so screwed.

I'm frozen in the chair as Rhys dances on top of me. I don't dare move. Not a single muscle. I don't trust myself not to tackle him to the ground and... I don't know, rub my dick all over his feet or something.

Dang it. Now I'm imagining myself rubbing my dick all over his feet.

Rhys rolls his body, sticking his dragon-decorated erection right into my face. It almost pokes me in the cheek, and I can smell the musky scent of his arousal wafting around me. The tip of his dick peeks out through the metal jewelry and is wet with pre-cum. The dragon looks like it's salivating, hungry enough to gobble me up.

Slowly, he drags his dick along my cheek. The metal is hard but warm, a strange contrast to the spongy softness of the head of his dick. He brings the tip down toward the corner of my mouth. My lips are parted as I pant through the desire churning in me. He nudges them wide enough to slip his dick between them.

I let out a muffled cry as the dragon's head enters my mouth, slowly, gently, like it's curious about what's inside. My jaw hangs open as Rhys carefully thrusts in and out. My tongue brushes against him, the taste of metal mixing with the salty bitterness of his pre-cum. I want to close my lips around him and suck. I want to draw out more of his delicious essence and drink it down.

Rhys stills, his dick still between my lips. "Go ahead. Suck my dragon."

I don't hesitate. I barely have time to think. My body simply reacts to his commands. I catch the head of his dick between my lips and suck as if my life depends on it. My mouth fills with that metallic bitterness, the odd combination sending my head spinning.

Rhys hisses and lets out a shaky, shuddering breath. "That's it, Angelo. Suck on my dragon-cock."

Strong fingers rake through my hair, sending tingles along my scalp and down my spine. The hand moves to my shoulder, clamping tight as Rhys shifts his weight. Then something heavy loops over my opposite shoulder— his boot-covered calf. His foot is braced against the back of the chair and his knee is bent right near my head.

I whine around the dick still in my mouth as the scent of the boot's plastic material joins the mix. I can't help leaning against Rhys's leg, feeling the synthetic straps against my shoulder, the side of my head. Without thinking, I let his dick slip from my mouth and I turn to run my tongue over his calf instead. Plastic straps alternating with salty skin. I lick up and down his calf, over every inch I can reach.

"Fuck, Angelo."

I can't help myself. My hand comes up to hold him in place as I mouth at the swell of his calf, then work my way down to his ankle. Rhys lifts his foot so I can bring it around to my front. Then I lick along the top of his foot, from his painted toes all the way up to his knee.

I'm lost. Hopelessly, utterly lost. My brain has short-circuited and my body is functioning on pure instinct now, chasing every pleasurable sensation, anything to feed the ravenous desire clawing at my insides.

My tongue glides over the slick polish on his toes. It slips between the small space between his arch and the shoe. I latch onto the knob of his ankle and suck.

"Fuck, Angelo, fuck!"

I find every patch of bare skin and bathe it with my tongue before moving onto the next. I work my way up his leg, to the soft skin of his inner thigh, and finally back to his dragon-dick, which I take into my mouth again.

He doesn't let me stay there long though, pulling back before I've had my fill.

"I'm gonna fall over if we keep doing that," he explains. Then he grabs the front of my shirt with both fists and hauls me onto my feet.

Rhys hops up onto the edge of the stage and leans back onto his elbows, bringing his legs up so his feet stick up in the air. His legs are spread wide, leaving his dragon-dick, round balls and cute little hole on display.

Rhys is a feast laid out before a starving man. I descend upon him, licking and sucking at anything I can reach. That tender strip of skin at his hip. That sensitive spot where the backs of his thighs meet his butt. The dusky patch between his balls and his hole.

I lick upward and take both balls into my mouth. My nose is buried in his groin. A moan erupts from me at the feeling of being stuffed like this, of being smothered in Rhys.

I move down, past his taint and to his hole. I don't stop —no hesitation, no second-guessing. I swipe my tongue over the wrinkled skin and I'm instantly addicted to the taste of him. Dark, musky, intoxicating. I lick and lick, digging into the center to gather up even more of his succulent flavor. I seal my lips around the bud and suck. I rub the wiry hairs of my beard over the sensitive skin, then do it all again.

"Jesus Christ. Fucking hell. Angelo!" Rhys's legs are

over my shoulders now, the weight of his boots heavy on my back. His hands are in my hair, holding me in place as I eat him out. It's the most delicious meal I've ever had.

I shove my tongue into his body, wriggling it around inside. He rocks against me as the ring of muscle tries to suck me deeper.

I can't believe what I'm doing. I can't believe how much I love this. It's satisfying a deep craving I had no idea I had. It's filling a pit in me that I didn't know existed. This is what I need. This is who I am now. A man who needs Rhys like I need air and water and food.

It's a heady feeling, but then the whole day has been heady.

Watching Rhys wrap himself around the pole, his body bending in unimaginable ways. His hair whipping through the air, the bright red strands catching the light. The way he looked at me like I'm the most important person in the world. Like I mean more to him than anyone else he's ever met.

Ever since his dad's birthday party, my life has been so spun around that I can't tell left from right or up from down. Everything I thought I knew about myself and my life has been called into question, and I don't know what's real or true anymore. Have I been living the life I want? Or have I merely been living the life that was handed to me?

The one sure thing, the one thing I have absolutely no doubt about, is Rhys and my feelings for him. I love him. It's bewildering, staggering, terrifying. But spending the last two weeks away from him has only confirmed that I don't want to live another day without him.

"Okay, let's get you both on the pole."

I don't stop eating Rhys's butt until he physically

pushes me away. I grab onto the edge of the stage to keep myself from stumbling. I'm drunk on Rhys. I'm dizzy with him.

I think I'm supposed to do something now. I'm pretty sure Sebastian was speaking to me, but my brain is in no condition to understand it.

Instead, Rhys tugs me forward and I clumsily climb onto the stage. His nimble fingers make quick work of the buttons on my shirt, and the two sides part to reveal my chest and stomach. Then he tackles my jeans, pushing them down along with my briefs, so they're trapped around the tops of my thighs.

Lube appears from somewhere and Rhys slicks me up before reaching back to spread the rest on his hole. With a quick wipe of his hands on a towel, he spins around, grabs the pole with both hands, and sticks his bum out toward me.

"Come here, big boy. Give me that monster cock of yours."

I stumble close enough for Rhys to grab my dick and guide me toward him. I love how he does this, how he takes my dick and feeds it into his hole. He's the one in control. He's the one impaling himself on me.

My eyes flutter shut as I sink into his wonderfully tight heat. Encasing me. Consuming me. Warmth spreads from my dick out to the rest of my body, burning me up from the inside out.

Rhys gasps as I bottom out. My hands go to his hips to squeeze us firmly together.

"Go at him, Angel. Fuck him nice and hard." Sebastian's directions come from some far-off place.

I grip his thighs and piston my hips back and forth.

The friction along my dick sends waves of pleasure running through me, but it pales in comparison to the sight of Rhys on display.

He grips the pole with both hands stretched high above. His back is arched, a long, elegant curve from his pert, round bum all the way up to his well-defined shoulders. His long hair—red to match his nails—covers the top part of his back in a shimmering waterfall.

I reach for it, tangling my fingers in the silky waves, mesmerized by the way the red strands wrap around my hand.

"Oh god!" Rhys cries out, head falling back. "Yes! Yes!"

He shouts every time my hips hit his butt cheeks. The sound rings through the air, through my ears, driving me forward. Harder. Faster. My hips working until I'm drenched with sweat and my clothes are plastered uncomfortably to my skin.

I need them off. I need to feel Rhys's body against my naked flesh. I need that closeness, the skin-on-skin contact. "Rhys," I whine.

He doesn't need me to explain. He just knows somehow, like he can read all the thoughts that flit through my mind.

He pushes himself away from the pole and the change in angle makes my dick slip out of his hole. He turns and helps me strip the rest of my clothes off. I tear at my unbuttoned shirt while he drops to his knees to untie my boots. They're gone in a minute and my jeans and underwear a second later.

He doesn't stand though. He holds me still with both hands on my thighs, then leans in to take my dick into his mouth.

"Ah!" I practically scream. My dick was just inside his butt a moment ago. And now he's sucking on it with his mouth. It's dirty. It's filthy. And I think I might come just from how wrong it feels.

Rhys gurgles and chokes, spit running down his chin and tears running down his cheeks. I stand there, staring. This beautiful, talented, strong man on his knees in front of me, greedily sucking me down.

"Rhys! Rhys!"

He pulls backs, smirking up at me with a knowing smile. Then he plants a quick kiss right on the tip of my dick and a fresh spurt of pre-cum comes gushing out.

"We're not done just yet, big guy." He stands and spins to face the pole again, but this time, he doesn't just grip it with both hands. He hauls himself up on it, pinching the pole between his thighs and crossing one calf over the other.

He glances over his shoulder, eyes dark and enticing, lips puffy from the blowjob. "Come here, fuck me."

I stumble forward until I'm pressed against that gorgeous back. I nuzzle his hair, then brush it out of the way so I can get to his neck. He tilts his head to give me more access and I lick a stripe from his shoulder to his ear. Salty. Delicious.

Somehow, Rhys has managed to position himself at the exact right height for my dick to slip inside him. It's awkward with him suspended on the pole, but we manage. Then he leans back, letting me take all his weight, resting his head on my shoulder.

He reaches up to grip the back of my neck, and my arms wrap around him, hands covering as much of his skin as I can. The smooth softness is a thin layer over hard muscles. I flick his nipples, grazing my thumb over the tiny, stiff nubs. Rhys trembles, caught precariously between me and the pole. He's got nowhere to go, no leverage to move. He's completely at my mercy.

The rush of power is no match for the sense of humility that floors me. Not for the first time, I have to marvel at how lucky, how *blessed* I am to have met Rhys, to have him in my life. I bury my face into his neck as gratitude almost brings me to my knees.

We don't stay in this position for more than a couple minutes, just enough time for Sebastian to get shots of Rhys's dragon-dick sticking up into the air. My movements are restricted when I'm holding so much of Rhys's weight and he can only grip the pole with his thighs for so long.

I hold him gingerly until he gets his feet back on the floor, but the next position seems just as precarious as the last.

Rhys rests his back against the pole and reaches up to grip it above his head. He lifts his legs into a V, boot-encased feet and calves in the air, pointing down to his dragon-dick and his glistening hole.

I step forward, fit myself back into his body, only to go a little berserk when he rests his legs on my shoulders. My vision goes a little blurry and my hips snap forward. His feet, his boots. They're within licking distance. Within biting distance. I turn my head to rub my cheek against the straps encircling his calf, and a violent shudder runs through me.

"Oh, fuck," Rhys mutters.

With my hands on his bum to help support his weight, I let my hips fly.

"I'm not going to last long," Rhys warns.

I'm not going to either. Rhys's tight heat around my dick. The heady sensation of his booted feet on either side of my head. The sight of him bent in half, pinned helplessly between me and the pole. It all feels too good. Too much. I'm strung out. Right on the brink.

I sink my teeth into the plastic leather of Rhys's boot, and breathe in the scent of it as it mingles with the smell of sex around us. My balls swing freely through the air, so heavy and full of the cum that I want to pump into Rhys's body.

"Fuck! Fuck! Right there! Yes, just like that. Just like that!"

I hammer away at Rhys's button as hard as I can, his body twitching every time I hit it. Then suddenly he's coming. His hole clamps impossibly tight around my dick, his body goes taut, and creamy white cum shoots out of the dragon's mouth, decorating Rhys's beautifully tanned and sweaty skin.

I don't dare stop, maintaining my rhythm and waiting for Rhys to give me permission to come too. "Rhys..." I whine, nuzzling his calf for comfort as the rest of my body is bursting at the seams.

"Yes, come for me, Angelo. Fill me up."

With a roar, I slam into him, emptying my cum into his hole until I'm completely drained. The room spins around me and my vision goes white. I don't know how I'm still on my feet.

Fingers touch my lips and I automatically open to let them in. The taste of Rhys's cum explodes on my tongue. I swallow down every drop he feeds to me, sucking every finger clean before I let it go.

When I finally soften enough to slip out of Rhys's bum, I drop to my knees and turn him around by his hips. I pull his cheeks apart and dive in, licking up the cum leaking out of him. Every trickle. Every spurt he pushes out. I go digging into his hole with my tongue to make sure I haven't missed a single drop.

Somehow I end up flat on my back, staring up into the bright lights around the stage. A warm body drapes itself over me and a soft, pliant mouth molds itself to my lips.

Rhys kisses me, soft and tender. The contrast to what we just did makes me shudder with an aftershock. I moan into the kiss, silently repeating the words that I don't have the courage to say out loud just yet.

I love you. I love you. I love you.

CHAPTER
TWENTY-NINE

RHYS

This might be the best and worst shoot I've ever done. It was really fucking hot and from the expression on Sebastian's face, it's clear that he's pleased with the results. But I'm wrecked by the time Sebastian yells cut.

Physically, it was demanding. I've never been fucked on the pole quite like that. Pro tip: don't try this at home.

But really, it's my emotions I'm worried about. They're so jumbled up and twisted into knots that I feel like laughing hysterically and crying just as hard at the same time.

The look on Angel's face at the end… oh my god. So dazed and cum-drunk. He was so pliable and soft that I wished we were in bed, snuggled together under the covers.

And Christ, the way he licked my boot, his tongue running over the straps and skin. How he rubbed his face against my leg, then sank his teeth into my calf.

He's so innocently erotic, unintentionally kinky. There's no pretense, no exaggeration. He's discovering all these new things about himself and he just… accepts them. There's no freaking out, no denying his reactions. He simply takes it all in his stride. Pure and unencumbered.

How could I not have fallen in love with him? I was a lost cause the moment he sat down next to me on my childhood bed.

Sebastian lets us lie on the stage for a bit while he and Christian work around us. Angel's breathing gradually slows to a point where he might be asleep and I reluctantly lift my head from his shoulder.

His lashes flutter and he blinks lazily at me for a second before a smile spreads across his face.

My heart stops at the sight, then swells impossibly large. It presses against the inside of my ribs until I think I'm going to burst. Goddamn it. I love him so fucking much.

And I have to believe that he feels something for me too. Maybe not the way I feel for him. Maybe not love. But *something,* right? People don't smile like that at people they don't care about. People don't say ridiculously sweet things to randos.

I cling to the idea, sink my manicured nails into it. It's the only thing keeping me afloat. It's the only thing preventing me from sinking into the depths of despair.

"Hey, you guys good?" Sebastian asks, squatting down next to us.

I watch Angel for his answer, scouring his face for any signs of discomfort, of regret. I don't find any.

"Yeah," he says, sitting up.

I follow him, keeping myself tucked into his side.

"That foot thing?" Sebastian shakes his head. "Whew, that was hot."

Angel's ears go red. "We didn't plan to do that. Is that okay?"

"Are you kidding me?" Sebastian laughs. "It's way more than okay. It's fantastic. We haven't had a foot video before. Fans are going to eat this up!"

Angel ducks his chin shyly, but his smile broadens. Fuck. I can't wait to get him alone so we can fully explore this foot fetish. I bet I could come just from Angel sucking on my toes.

"Great job, guys. You go get cleaned up. We'll put the rest of the equipment away."

I take Angel back to the dressing room. A pregnant silence settles over us as we wipe down and put our street clothes back on. There's so much I want to say to Angel, so much I want to tell him. And yet, I don't dare.

It's cowardly, I know. Especially since he's been so brave this whole time. Stepping outside his comfort zone, exploring all these new parts of himself. The least I could do is be honest with him about how I feel.

But I can't. Not today, at least. I don't want to ruin this buzz we're floating in. I'm greedy and selfish. I want to drag this out for as long as I can.

All dressed—Angel in his standard jeans and casual button down, me in mustard-yellow corduroy bell-bottoms and an oversized cream sweater—and with our coats on, we head back out to join Sebastian and Christian. I pull my phone out of my bag to check it quickly for notifications. There's a message from Hayden wishing me luck on the video. A few from social media, comments on posts about our first video. And a voicemail from Mom.

Argh.

Dread fills me and I stuff my phone back into my bag. Nothing good ever comes from a call from Mom. Who even leaves voicemails these days? Ugh.

"What's wrong?" Angel asks.

I wipe my annoyance from my expression. "Oh, nothing. My mom just called."

His eyes widen in concern. "Is everything okay?"

I shrug. "I'm sure everything's fine. I'll listen to the voicemail later."

"Are you sure? What if something happened?"

My heart does that stop-and-swell thing again at Angel's worry. He cares so much. Even for people he barely knows. Even for people I should care a lot more about.

Pouting, I pull my phone out again and tap the button to play the message.

"Ricky, this is your mother. I'm calling to remind you about cousin Barry's wedding in a couple weeks. You're expected to be there. Call me back."

I groan and roll my eyes. "It's about my cousin Barry's wedding. He's not even really my cousin. We're like, fifth or sixth cousins or something like that."

Angel nods, growing reserved. And when he speaks, he's suddenly quiet. "Yeah, I know him."

I freeze, realization dawning on me. "Are you going to the wedding?" *Say no, say no, say no.*

"Probably?"

That means yes.

Angel will be at the wedding filled with people from the old neighborhood. Apparently, I have to be there too. How... what...

We blink at each other for a moment, neither of us wanting to state the obvious. What are we going to do?

"Mario hasn't told anyone," Angel says finally. "He hasn't asked me about it again, either. It's almost like he forgot."

I nod. My throat feels like it's closing in on itself and I'm struggling to swallow around the mess of emotions getting trapped there.

Does this mean Angel doesn't want anyone else in the old neighborhood to know? Will I have to pretend that this thing between us doesn't exist? The thought of it feels like stepping back into a closet that I was never really in.

"You guys ready?" Christian calls out from across the club. "The car's all packed up, so we're going to head out. Rhys, you want a ride?"

I take a step forward, then hesitate. I don't know what I want. I don't know what I'm allowed to have.

"I can drive you," Angel jumps in.

When I glance back at him, there's more than a hint of fear in his eyes. It's the same fear sitting in the pit of my stomach.

He holds out his hand, and weak as I am, I take it. As his strong fingers close around mine, I have to fight back the tears prickling my eyes.

"We're good, Christian. Thanks for the offer!" I call out, surprised by how steady my voice sounds when I'm so torn up inside.

"Cool. See you later!" Christian ducks out, leaving us alone again.

"My place? Hayden might be there."

Angel squeezes my hand, then takes a deep breath, like

he's bracing himself for something. "How about my place?"

The world stutters to a stop as my brain processes his question. Then runs through it again.

"Your place?" I squeak. "But… your mom?"

He gulps, his Adam's apple working in his throat. "We'll be upstairs. You won't have to see her."

Hayden's warnings come flooding through my mind. About Angel being deep in the closet, about being in a relationship with someone who isn't out, someone who hasn't even acknowledged that they're gay. The world of hurt that I've most likely got waiting for me.

I don't know what to say. I don't know how to feel. Should I be excited that he wants to bring me home? Or should I be upset that he wants to hide me from his mom? Do I even want to meet his mom? Do I want to be anywhere near the old neighborhood if I can avoid it?

I don't fucking know! Why does life have to be so hard? So confusing? Why did I have to fall in love with someone from the life I left behind?

"You don't have to, if you don't want to. We can go to your place. Or I can just drop you off, if you'd rather be alone."

I stop Angel's rambling with my fingers on his lips. He immediately purses them to give my fingers a kiss. My heart aches at the tenderness.

Ngh.

Fuck it.

I'm too far in already. There's no hope for me, no way to protect myself from getting hurt anymore. Maybe I'll get lucky, a miracle will happen, and this will somehow turn into a romantic fairy tale. Or more likely, my heart will get trampled and I'll drag myself back to Brooklyn to nurse my wounds.

Either way, there's no turning back now.

I rise up onto my tippy-toes and replace my fingers with my lips. Just a simple, sweet press.

"Take me home, teddy bear."

CHAPTER
THIRTY

ANGEL

My heart pounds heavily against the inside of my ribs the entire ride back to Staten Island. But as terrified as I am, there's also a sense of rightness that I've never experienced before.

The past several months have been a series of firsts for me. First kiss with a man, first time having sex, first porn video, first gay nightclub. But this first feels more important. It feels weightier.

It's like I've been waiting my entire life for this moment. Like my whole reason for existing boils down to this one thing: taking Rhys home. Bringing his brightness into the blandness of my world. Demolishing the last wall in the box I've been living in.

And then I'll be free. Free to fly. Free to soar. Free to be myself and be with Rhys.

We don't speak much in the truck. Our hands are clasped across the center console, both of Rhys's sandwiching mine. His thumb rubs absentmindedly over my skin, a steady back and forth that ticks down the seconds until we get home.

Rhys takes a deep breath when we turn onto the street of the neighborhood where we both grew up. When I sneak a glance in his direction, he's staring resolutely out the window, determination in his eyes.

Doubt trickles through me, followed closely by guilt. Maybe I shouldn't have brought him back here? To a place he's worked so hard to escape? Maybe we should have gone to his place instead, even if Hayden would've been there.

But when Rhys turns to me, his gaze softens and his lips curl into the most tender smile I've ever seen. I squeeze his hand and he squeezes back.

We'll be okay. I have to trust in that. Whatever happens, we'll find a way through.

I pull into the driveway in front of the duplex I share with Mama. The curtains on the front windows of the house are open, but there's no movement inside. The weather is just chilly enough that the neighbors aren't sitting out on their front porches anymore. There isn't anyone around to see us arrive.

"Wait here," I say as I turn the engine off and hop out of the truck.

Rhys's brow furrows in confusion, but I just hurry around to the passenger-side door. I open it and hold out my hand to him.

He stares at it for a moment before he sniffles and gives me a watery-eyed smile. He slips his hand into mine and I help him down, carefully shutting the door behind him.

Opening the car door for a date is kind of an outdated thing. It's probably even a bit silly these days, but joy bubbles up inside me at this small gesture. I want to show Rhys how much I care. I want him to know how precious and important he is to me.

I lead him to the side door. It opens onto the stairs that take us up to my apartment. Once we're inside, Rhys stands in the small foyer, examining the space. I try to see it through his eyes, try to imagine what he would notice.

The kitchen and dining room is right in front of us and beyond it is the living room. The bathroom is tucked in behind the kitchen, and the bedroom branches off from the living room. It's simple. Basic. But it's all I've ever needed.

Rhys glides forward, running his hands along the butcher-block countertop, then across the backs of the wooden dining chairs. He peeks into the bathroom with its clawfoot bathtub and pedestal sink. I follow after him as he moves into the living room. He squeezes the plush leather upholstery of the oversized couch, then ventures into the bedroom and smooths his hands up and down a beam of my four-poster bed.

"This place is amazing," he says in a hushed voice.

I blink. Of all the reactions I thought he would have, this isn't one of them. "You think so?"

"Yeah." He chuckles and turns to me with a cocked eyebrow. "How much of this stuff did you do yourself?"

I look around. At the hardwood flooring and paneled accent wall behind the bed. At the built-in shelving unit that houses the TV in the living room. At the custom-fit cabinets in the kitchen and the mosaic tiles in the bathroom.

"Um, pretty much all of it?" My ears warm at the admission. I don't know why. It shouldn't be surprising. I'm a construction worker, so I know how to gut reno an apartment unit. Why wouldn't I do the work myself? "I mean, Mario and a couple other guys helped sometimes."

Rhys steps up to me and slips his arms around my waist. I gather him to me.

"Of course you did all of it. And of course you wouldn't take any of the credit." Rhys shakes his head. "Angel, you're incredibly talented."

I scratch my jaw. "I'm okay. This stuff isn't that hard."

Rhys rolls his eyes, but he's still wearing a teasing smile. "Okay, fine, it isn't that hard—for a trained and experienced professional."

I duck my chin as my ears grow hotter. "Do you, um, would you like something to drink? Beer? Water? I don't have anything fancy like margaritas or anything. But I can go get some if you want!"

"I don't need anything else." He takes my hand and leads me back to the living room. He pushes me down onto the couch, then deposits himself into my lap. "I've got everything I want right here."

I sigh into the kiss he gives me. Nothing rushed or urgent. We have all the time in the world to explore each other's mouths, draw our tongues into a dance, nibble on each other's lips. My dick plumps in my jeans, even though I came my brains out earlier in the day. But it's impossible not to react when I've got Rhys all flexible and pliant in my arms.

He's wearing a pair of yellow flared pants that hug his bum and his thighs, soft and fuzzy as he grinds himself down on me. My hands slip under his big sweater, and the skin at the small of his back is hot against my palms.

We make out for long minutes that stretch on and on. Licking and tasting and losing ourselves in one another.

I'm dizzy from lack of oxygen, drunk on Rhys's mouth, floating high and never wanting to come back down.

"Teddy bear," Rhys murmurs, resting his forehead against mine when we finally pause for a breath.

"Hmm."

He pulls back just an inch, just enough to run his thumbs over my brows, my cheeks, down the line of my nose. I turn my head and press a kiss into his palm.

Rhys sighs, a distinct note of resignation, hands falling to land gently on my chest.

"What's wrong?" I ask, not liking the hint of sadness in his eyes.

He smiles and I can tell he's trying to pretend that everything's okay, that everything's fine.

"You can tell me," I say, pouring every ounce of sincerity I possess into my expression. "I'm a good listener."

"I know you are." Rhys's gaze drops as he fiddles with the buttons of my shirt. "You're such a good person."

I don't know where he's going with this, but a warning light goes off in the back of my mind. "You're a good person too."

He chuckles softly. "Yeah, I'm not bad. But you... you're a *good* person." He lifts his gaze and looks directly into my eyes. "You're the *best* person."

I take his hands in mine and hold them to my chest. My heart is beating hard now, a heavy *thump* that reverberates through me. He must be able to feel the steady rhythm under our clasped hands.

"*You're* the best person," I repeat back to him. "You're the best person I know. You're so kind and patient with me. You've never laughed at me or thought I was dumb. You listen to me like the things I say are important."

Rhys sniffles and his fingers clutch at the fabric of my shirt.

"You're so brave. Look at the life you've built for yourself. It's so much more than anything anyone from around here has done. You know who you are and what you want, and you don't let anyone stand in your way. I wish I was brave like you."

"You are. You are brave." A single tear escapes Rhys's lashes and lands on my shirt.

"Not like you. You were so young when you left home. I could never have done that."

A second tear escapes, leaving another round wet spot on my shirt.

I don't know where these words are coming from, or how I'm able to string them all together into sentences that actually make sense. They're thoughts I've had for a long time now, but I never imagined I would have the courage to say them out loud. But now that they're spilling out of my mouth, I can't stop them.

"You're basically famous."

A choked laugh bursts from Rhys.

"Your online fans love you. They're always copying your fashion style, asking you for makeup tips. People go to The Bronzed Rail every week just to watch you dance. You're the star of the show."

Rhys shakes his head with a self-deprecating smile.

"You know that day? Your dad's birthday party? When I found you upstairs?"

He gives me a small nod.

"I kinda felt like a creep for following you up there."

"You followed me?"

"Yeah," I admit sheepishly. "I was out front with the guys when you arrived. That was the first time I'd seen you in years and you… you took my breath away. I went inside to look for you and saw you go upstairs. I couldn't stop myself from following you."

That same feeling wells up inside me again. The fascination, the draw. The sense that my destiny lies in this direction, with this man. The need to be near him, to be in his presence, to see him and be seen by him. I couldn't deny it back then, and I can't deny it now.

"I love you, Rhys."

He gasps, fingers tightening on my shirt, eyes going wide with shock.

"I know I'm a nobody and I don't have anything to offer you. I'm not cool or sexy or charming. I'm just…" I shrug. "A simple guy with a simple life. I'm not glamorous or fashionable or…"

I try to keep breathing as my heart tries to beat its way out of my chest. "You don't have to return the feelings or anything. I'd never expect you to love me back the same way. I just… I just wanted you to know. You've changed me. You've made me a better man. I was just going through life before, but not really living. I didn't know how much I was missing out on until you showed me. I—"

Rhys stops me with his fingers on my lips and my stomach twists into knots. Ugh, shoot, I've been rambling like an idiot. He's probably stopping me so I don't dig myself even deeper into a hole. I've embarrassed myself enough.

"Teddy bear." Rhys's voice cracks, it's so thick with

emotion. Tears trickle steadily down his cheeks. "I love you too."

I blink for a second, my brain not at all trusting my ears. He couldn't have said what I think he said. Why in the world would he? There's no reason for him to love me, of all people. He could have anyone he wanted—someone smarter, hotter, funnier, more interesting, more exciting, more full of life. I'd only weigh him down and drag him back to a world he wants nothing to do with.

"I love you," Rhys says again. Slower this time so there's no way for me to mistake it. "Because you are braver and more courageous than you give yourself credit for. Because you don't try to be someone you're not. You are unapologetically yourself, even if you're just discovering who that person is. You're thoughtful and caring and you give so much of yourself to people who don't always deserve it. You're good, Angel. And I want to be someone who deserves you."

"You are!" I insist, speaking through the fingers still on my lips. "You deserve more than me!"

"No, teddy bear, *you* deserve more than *me*. You deserve everything."

"I don't want everything. I just want you."

A choked sob escapes Rhys's throat right before he smashes his lips against mine. It's not really a kiss. More just us breathing each other in. He clings to me and I hold him tight, both of us trying to get closer, trying to squeeze out every offending molecule of air between us.

I want to be inside him. I want to be one with him. I want to bury myself so deep inside Rhys that I will never be able to leave.

Bang! Bang! Bang!

We jump at the loud knocking on my door.

"Angel! Why is the door locked? I know you're in there! It's time to make dinner! Do you have that girl in there?"

Rhys and I stare at each other in horror. He doesn't need me to tell him who it is, but I do anyway.

"Mama."

RHYS

Shit. Shit. Shit. Angel's mom is knocking on his door while I'm sitting in his lap—correction, grinding my ass onto his hard dick.

He stares at me, in just as much shock, neither of us moving.

She knocks again. "Angel!"

We both jump into action. I scramble off Angel, smoothing my clothes down, as if that will do anything to mask the way my lips still burn from our kisses.

Angel's got his hand on his cock, like he's trying to squeeze it back down to a normal size.

"Don't make me go get my keys!"

"No!" Angel shouts. "I'm coming, Mama! Just one sec!"

He takes a step toward the door, but I stop him with a hissed, "Wait! What about me?"

He blinks at me, dumbfounded.

"Should I hide or something?" I gesture toward the bedroom, imagining myself crawling under the bed.

Angel turns to face me and the expression on his face rocks me to the core. It's sincere and determined, concerned and a tad bit angry. But most of all, there's so much love shining through his eyes that I'm stunned into stillness.

Meanwhile, the commotion at the door has died down, which is probably not a good sign.

"No, Rhys. You were made to shine. You should never hide how bright and beautiful you are."

Oh god, I'm going to burst into tears again.

Angel closes the distance between us and takes my hands in his. "I'll never let anyone hide you away or cover you up or make you less than you truly are. I don't care who it is, not Mario and the guys, not your parents, not even Mama. Even if we need to leave and never come back. I'll always stand up for you."

I throw myself at him, burying my face in the middle of his chest, arms squeezing tight around his waist. He envelops me, strong arms holding me close, lips pressed against the top of my head.

How is it possible for one man to be so perfect? To check every single box I've ever had, and plenty more I didn't even know I wanted? God, I fucking love this man so much it feels like my chest is going to burst.

Angel brushes my hair back from my face. I gaze up at his warm brown eyes, at his oh-so kissable pink lips. He cups my cheek.

"Ready to meet Mama?"

No, I don't think I'll ever be ready to meet someone like Angel's mom. I've never given a second thought to reestablishing connections with anyone in the old neighborhood. But for Angel? For Angel, I'll go to the ends of the fucking earth.

I nod. "Yeah, let's go."

His hand engulfs mine when he takes it, and I cling to him like a child hiding behind his father. My stomach churns with nerves even as my heart douses me with a flood of love. I brace myself.

Angel pulls the door open, and on the other side is his mom, key in hand, poised to slide it into the lock.

She smirks knowingly, then glances past him to me. At first, there's curiosity in her eyes, an eagerness that eases my anxiety. It only lasts for a split second before she blinks and realizes who I am.

"You." Her brows slam together into a frown.

I gulp and tuck myself slightly behind Angel's arm. He squeezes my hand.

"You're not a girl. You're… you're Dina's boy."

"Hi, Mrs. Russo." I hate how small I sound. I hate how much I feel like teenage Ricky Gallo right now.

"What are you—" Her gaze drops to our clasped hands, to where I'm gripping Angel's arm with my free hand. Her lips flatten into a hard line and she stares for what feels like ages.

But before I can think of anything to say, before Angel can jump in, her gaze shoots back up to his face.

"It's time to make Sunday dinner." Then she spins on her heel and marches back downstairs.

Oh shitty, shit, shit. I forgot today was Sunday. I wouldn't have agreed to come out here if I'd realized I'd be intruding on Sunday dinner with Angel's family.

Angel steps forward, but I tug him back.

"Are you sure about this?" I ask, resigning myself to a

long subway ride back to Brooklyn. "Sunday dinner is a big deal. I'd understand if this is too much, too soon."

Angel's eyes blaze with a fierceness I've never seen in him before. "What do you want to do?"

I gape, trying to sort through the feelings tumbling around inside me. "I honestly don't know."

I don't want to run. I don't want to hide. But I also left this neighborhood for a reason. I've had enough of their silent judgment to last me several lifetimes. Why would I willingly subject myself to that again?

For Angel.

I'd do it for Angel.

He's stepped so far outside of his comfort zone for me. Done so many things that must've been terrifying for him. He had plenty of opportunities to turn around and walk away, but he never let fear dictate his actions. He never said no because he was scared.

He's been so brave—he's *being* so brave. Bringing me to meet his mom at Sunday dinner is exactly the opposite of what Hayden was afraid he would do. It's the least I can do to be brave in return. It's only one meal, after all. A few hours, tops. I've lived through worse. I can survive this. Then we'll escape back upstairs, or maybe even go to my place. It's not the end of the world.

I take a deep breath. Yeah. Okay. Sunday dinner with Angel's mom isn't what I thought I'd be doing after shooting a porn video today. But lemons and lemonade. I can do this.

I nod and Angel leads us downstairs.

The downstairs apartment is laid out almost exactly the same way my parents' house is. We go through the living room to the kitchen where Mrs. Russo is chopping vegetables. Very aggressively.

We stop in the doorway. "Hey, Mama."

She doesn't look up. "Roll out the gnocchi."

Angel and I exchange a silent look. She's obviously talking to him, since I have no idea how to roll out gnocchi and should never be allowed to try. He nods to the kitchen table, and as quietly as possible, I slide onto a chair.

Angel starts opening drawers and pulling out kitchen utensils I wouldn't have a clue what to do with.

"Where's Sabrina?" he asks.

"Out."

"Did she take Jonah with her?"

"Yes."

Angel shoots a tense glance in my direction. "Is she coming home for dinner?"

"I don't know, Angel. If you want to know so badly, why don't you call her yourself? It's not like I know anything that's happening with my children."

I shift awkwardly in my seat. I certainly hope she doesn't know everything her children do. If she was aware of all of Angel's extracurricular activities, I doubt I'd be allowed to sit in her kitchen like this.

Angel's ears go red, but Mrs. Russo is so focused on murdering innocent veggies that she doesn't notice. Thank fucking god.

Silence descends on the kitchen as the two of them work side by side. It's actually fascinating, watching them move around each other as if they've been doing this their whole lives. Mrs. Russo hands Angel utensils and he immediately knows what she wants him to do next. He grabs things from the tops of cabinets before she asks for them. There's a comfort between them that I've never had with either of my parents.

Is this what's at stake here? Angel's so close to his mom. They depend on each other so much. Is my relationship with him going to put this in jeopardy? Could I live with myself if I came between them?

Gradually, the scent of home cooking fills the kitchen and my stomach grumbles in anticipation. Dishes of gnocchi with fresh tomato sauce, roasted vegetables, caprese salad, and cheesy garlic bread fill the table. I offer to help set the table and Angel hands me forks and knives and napkins.

Mrs. Russo is the last to sit down and the second her butt hits the chair, she launches into saying grace. "Bless us, O Lord, and these, Thy gifts, which we are about to receive from Thy bounty. Through Christ, our Lord. Amen."

I hurry to make the sign of the cross, which I haven't done since... god, I don't even remember. My family is more of a Christmas-and-Easter type, so even though Mom has some crucifixes hanging up at home, we never said grace before meals.

"How is Dina?" Mrs. Russo asks, and it takes me a moment to realize she's speaking to me.

"Oh, uh, my mom? Yeah, she's good." I think. Other than the voicemail she left me today, I haven't spoken to her in weeks.

"You don't have Sunday dinner at home?"

I shoot a panicked look in Angel's direction, but all he can do is shrug.

"Uh, I don't really go to those."

Mrs. Russo's eyes flit to me, hard and fast and a thou-

sand percent disapproving. "Sunday dinners are important. Family is important."

"Uh… yeah." Explaining the concept of found family
probably isn't going to win me any points with her.

"Angel's a good boy. He always takes care of his
family."

"Mama—"

She turns her glare onto him before he can get any
further. He gulps, looking like he wants to crawl into a
deep dark hole. I don't blame him. I kind of do too. But
instead of backing down, Angel sets his fork on the table
and sits up a little straighter.

"Mama," he says, wincing when she stabs a piece of
gnocchi especially violently. "Rhys and I—I mean, Ricky?
And I?"

She scowls at him. "What are you talking about?"

I laugh nervously. "Oh, it's nothing. My friends like
calling me Rhys. It's just a nickname." I definitely don't
want to explain why I need a stage name.

"Right. Uh, so, Ricky and I…" Angel takes a breath and
looks straight into my eyes. "We're in love."

Mrs. Russo pauses with her fork halfway to her mouth.
We all sit stock-still, Angel and I holding our breaths as we
wait for her reaction.

Except she doesn't react. She just lifts her fork the rest
of the way and takes a bite of gnocchi. She chews. Slowly.
Then takes a sip of her wine. By the time she sets the glass
down, it feels like it's been hours.

"But you're a boy."

Angel and I exchange a look. Who is she talking about?
Me? Him? Both of us?

"Yes," Angel replies.

"You can't be in love."

I watch as emotions flit across Angel's face. His ears redden with embarrassment. His expression blanches from fear. Then a look of indignation as he works himself up to argue with his mom. We've never spoken about this before, but if I had to guess, I'd say that Angel's never talked back to her before. Ever.

"Mrs. Russo," I jump in. I don't know how tonight will change Angel's relationship with his mom. From the way things are progressing, it doesn't look good. But if there's anything I can do, anything I can say to help salvage it, then I owe it to Angel to try. "I do love your son."

Mrs. Russo wipes her lips with her napkin, looking like she's about to excuse herself from the table. But then, she sets her napkin down, folds her hands into her lap, and waits.

"You're right. Angel is good," I continue. My words are directed at Mrs. Russo, but I'm looking at Angel as I speak. His eyes are wide with a mix of worry and adoration and the love in my heart wins out over the anxiety eating away at my stomach.

"He's honest and hardworking. He's caring and protective. He would do anything for his family. But would you do anything for him?"

Her gaze snaps to me, eyes burning with outrage. "What kind of question is that?"

I can't help but shrink back in my chair a bit, but I dig deep for the courage to continue. "It's a legitimate one, Mrs. Russo. I love Angel. And if that means I need to cut my hair, change what I wear, and move back to the neighborhood, then..."

I never in a million years would've been willing to do

any of that—not until this very second. Not even earlier this evening, when we were upstairs confessing our love to each other. But sitting at this table with Mrs. Russo, asking her what she's willing to do for a son she claims to love, I realize that I'm willing to do anything—everything —to show Angel I love him. It wouldn't be easy, and maybe a part of me would die in the process, but I would gain so much more by being at Angel's side.

"I would never!" Angel's chair scrapes against the floor as he shifts, lunging across the table to reach for me. He grabs my hand and his gaze bores into me. "I would never ask you to do any of that! I would move out first. I'd leave and never come back. I love your hair. I love your clothes. I love you exactly the way you are."

I grip his hand as hard as he's gripping mine, and tears well up in my eyes. "I know you do. And I know you would never ask me to change. Which is why I'm willing to."

Bang! Mrs. Russo slams her hand down on the table, making the dishes and cutlery rattle. Angel and I tense, bracing ourselves for what comes next.

She glowers at me, then Angel, then me again, before pushing to her feet so forcefully, her chair almost tumbles backward. Without a word, she stalks out of the kitchen, and a second later, a door shuts with a loud, firm *thud*.

I blink as the last few minutes fully sink in. I just told off Angel's mom, basically accused her of not loving her son. If I was trying to impress her, trying to win her over, I have epically and spectacularly failed. Now she hates me and maybe she'll end up hating Angel, and I think I've just ruined their relationship forever.

"I'm sorry." I slap a hand over my face. "Oh god, what the hell was I thinking?"

Angel stands and comes around the table. He pulls me to my feet so he can take my seat, and I settle back down on his lap.

Burying my face against his shoulder, I groan. "I'm such an idiot. Why did I say those things?"

Angel nudges my chin to get me to look up at him. His lips are curled into a small, shy smile that makes me feel all melty and gooey inside.

"I liked the things you said," he whispers to me. "Thank you for defending me."

"Always," I say, putting a hand on his chest, right above the steady beat of his heart. "I love you."

His smile widens into a grin and the tips of his ears turn pink. He puts his hand over mine. "I don't care what Mama thinks. I don't care what the neighborhood says. I love you and that's never going to change."

CHAPTER
THIRTY-TWO

ANGEL

Rhys helps me put the leftovers away and clear up the kitchen before we head back upstairs to my apartment. Mama doesn't come out of her bedroom, and I don't bother knocking to see if she's okay. It's best to let her calm down on her own when she gets upset.

"I'm sorry about Mama," I say, shutting the door to my apartment behind me.

I lean back against it as Rhys presses into me. "It's not your fault."

"It kinda is. I forgot it was Sunday." Guilt threads through me, making me feel all twisted up inside.

"Well, we had a lot going on today." Rhys smiles suggestively at me, hands sliding up my shoulders and fingers playing with the hair at nape of my neck.

It's hard to believe that we shot our second porn video this morning, and then I had Sunday dinner with Mama. Those two thoughts in the same sentence should have me burning up. But for some reason, it doesn't.

I'm not ashamed of the porn videos. I mean, I'm not going to tell Mama about it, obviously. But there's no embarrassment making my ears flush. There's no regret eating away at me. I'm glad I did gay for pay, because it brought me to Rhys.

Although… now that we're together, I guess I'm not really straight anymore? And the for-pay thing… well.

"Um, I, uh, think I need to tell you something." Now my ears heat.

Rhys's gaze shifts to my left ear, then my right. His eyes twinkle with amusement. "I would be worried, but judging by the color of your ears, it might not be so bad?"

I reach up to scratch my jaw. "Maybe we should sit down?"

Rhys's eyes dim a fraction, then he takes my hand and leads me into the living room. Like earlier, he pushes me down onto the couch, then sits himself down in my lap.

"Okay, we're sitting. What do you need to tell me?" He's still wearing a teasing expression, but there's a hint of wariness underneath it.

I take a quick steadying breath, then spit it out. "You know how I'm supposed to be gay for pay? Well, I'm not. Gay for pay, I mean."

The concern in Rhys's eyes morphs into confusion. "The gay part or the pay part?"

"Either. Both."

He looks more confused.

I scrunch up my face. I'm not explaining this right. I'm only making things worse.

"Hey." Rhys brackets my face with both hands. "Let's start from the beginning. You were supposed to be gay for pay, but…?"

"I was supposed to be straight, but doing gay porn for money."

Rhys gives me a decisive nod. "Right, yes, I'm following."

"But I'm not straight." That's the first time I've said it out loud and just as the words leave my mouth, a light, bubbly feeling floats up in my chest. "I'm not straight!" I exclaim.

"I figured as much." Rhys laughs out loud, throwing his head back, exposing his long, elegant neck. His hair swishes through the air and all I want is to nuzzle my nose to where his pulse beats the strongest.

I have to clear my throat before continuing, and I reluctantly drag my gaze away from Rhys's neck. "If I'm not straight, then what does that make me?"

He gives me a one-shouldered shrug. "Bi? Pan? Maybe you are gay? Doesn't matter. You don't have to figure that out right away."

I nod, though I don't really know what he means by "pan". I have pans in the kitchen?

"What's the pay part?"

"Uh…" This is more embarrassing to admit. "Well, the thing is, I didn't really need the money? I mean, the money's great. We have a second mortgage on the house because of my pop, so the money'll help pay it off. But like, I was managing with just my construction paycheck, so we weren't about to lose the house or anything."

Rhys hesitates before responding, his brows drawing together a fraction, like he's trying to process what I said.

"So you don't need the money," he clarifies.

"No."

"And you didn't need it before we started either."

"No."

"And you knew you didn't need the money."

"Yes."

"So the whole money thing was an excuse."

"Yes."

Rhys's eyes narrow in suspicion. "If money was an excuse, why did you really want to shoot porn with me?"

The answer is so obvious, I don't even know how to explain it. "Because... Because I..."

Rhys's suspicion fades as he watches all the emotions that must be flying across my face. "Teddy bear?"

"Because I couldn't stop thinking about you."

His lips part in a silent gasp, and for a second he looks like he might start crying. But then his face breaks out into a wide grin. "I couldn't stop thinking about you either."

I close the distance between us, catching Rhys's lips in a desperate kiss. He tastes like the marinara sauce Mama makes from scratch, tangy with a kick of spice. Exactly how Rhys should always taste.

"Stay the night?" I ask, keeping my lips against his.

He smiles without pulling away. "Don't you have to work tomorrow morning? At like, the ass-crack of dawn?"

"Yeah, but you can sleep in." My hands slip under the hem of his sweater. "You can stay here for as long as you'd like. I'll give you the spare key so you can come and go whenever you want."

He giggles, and his hair shimmers in a curtain around us. "Then I can snoop around your apartment all day."

"I've got nothing to hide." And I really don't. Not anymore. Everything I have, everything I am is laid out in the open for Rhys. He can have all of me.

Rhys's smile widens. "No, you don't. That's why I love you so much. Now take me to bed."

I shift forward, then scoop my hands under Rhys's bum. He clings me to me as I pick him up and carry him to the bedroom.

I fall backward onto the bed and Rhys climbs up to straddle my hips. I fill my hands with Rhys's muscled thighs, that perfect curve at the crease of his hip, the swell of his bum. Rhys arches, pushing back into my palms, even as he rubs himself all over my front.

I moan as he plunges his tongue into my mouth, licking deep and nibbling at my lips until my head spins from lack of oxygen.

"I love you, teddy bear."

"I love you, too, sweetheart." The endearment just slips out.

Rhys pauses, gazing down at me, surprised.

A burst of panic makes my stomach clench. "Is it okay if I call you that? I don't have a nickname for you, and 'baby' feels… I don't know, weird. You're not a baby. You're a man."

I can feel my ears heat a bit at the explanation. I've never had anyone I could use a term of endearment with, and I want to make sure it's something Rhys will like.

Rhys's smile breaks wide across his face. "'Sweetheart'. I love it. It feels very you. You're definitely not a 'baby' type of guy."

"Sweetheart." I try it out again and Rhys's breath hitches in response. I like it too. It feels right. It feels like us. "Sweetheart."

Rhys attacks my mouth, tangling his tongue with mine as his fingers fumble with the buttons of my shirt. I drag my hands up Rhys's back, taking his sweater with them. We break apart just long enough to pull Rhys's sweater off, then he's back, feeding me his tongue.

It takes us ages to undress, neither of us willing to stop kissing to remove our clothes. But eventually, we're naked and I've got Rhys's lithe body sliding against mine.

"Please, Rhys, I want to suck you," I plead with him.

"Hmm, well, when you ask so nicely, how can I say no?" He plants one more kiss on my lips before righting himself.

But instead of shuffling forward so I can get my mouth around his dick, he turns around so he's facing my feet, knees on either side of my head.

"Wha—"

Rhys tilts his hips so his erection pokes me in the chin, and at the same time, he takes my dick in hand.

Oh. I get it. I guess this is what they call a sixty-nine. I can get on board with that.

I lift my head and take Rhys's dick into my mouth. It's a bit awkward since he's so much smaller than me, and I have to hold my head above the bed or else he'll slip out. But at this angle, Rhys can slide his dick right into my throat without triggering my gag reflex. I grab a pillow to stuff under my head, then tug on his hips to encourage him.

"Fuck, teddy bear." Rhys nuzzles his face into my crotch, his breath hot against my balls as he keeps stroking me with his hand.

"Mmm," I hum, unable to respond when my mouth is full of his dick.

"Oh god." Rhys is gentle with his thrusts, his hips moving slowly as he pushes his dick into my throat.

His balls rest heavily across my face. I suck in a quick breath every time he pulls out. And every breath is full of Rhys's sweet, flowery scent.

I'm drowning in him. Saturated in him. I didn't know life could be this good.

I jerk when Rhys's lips seal around the head of my dick. I'm still a little sensitive from shooting the video earlier today, but Rhys is careful as he suckles me. His tongue swirls around the crown of my dick and the way he works me with his hands and his mouth feels like the most erotic massage.

I drift in that blissful place between awake and unconscious. My brain checks out and all I'm left with is sensation after sensation.

The scent of Rhys's arousal. My throat full to bursting. The heat of his mouth on me. His talented hands wringing pleasure from me in ways I could never have before imagined.

He takes me all the way in, swallowing around me as his lips reach the base of my dick. The pressure of his throat is incredible, and when he hums the vibrations make me groan.

My arms snake around his narrow waist, and the slimness of his body, how small he is compared to me, makes me shiver with delight. I hold him to me, content to be stuffed full of him just as he's stuffed full of me.

"Fucking hell, teddy bear." Rhys's voice is hoarse. "You keep moaning and it feels so goddamn good."

His hips lose their graceful rhythm, growing jerky as he nears his orgasm. He tries to pull away, but I keep him captive. I want him to come in my mouth. I want him to come down my throat.

"Christ on a stick, I'm going to come," Rhys murmurs into my groin, and I moan extra long and extra loud.

I wriggle my tongue against his length and swallow experimentally around the obstruction in my throat.

"Oh! Fuck!" Rhys throws his head back and his body arches.

I fill my palms with his bubble butt and my fingers graze his hole.

"I'm coming!" he warns a split second before his hot seed floods me.

I swallow as fast as I can, drinking down the bitter, salty cum that has become my favorite beverage of all time.

Rhys is still spurting when he takes me back into his mouth. He sucks and strokes, drawing that low hum of pleasure higher and higher. I'm buzzing. Vibrating. Stretched taut and ready to snap.

"Rhys! Sweetheart! Please!"

He hums around my dick and that's all the permission I need to empty myself into him. Rhys strokes me through every wave of my climax, not stopping until I'm wrung out and dry.

Then he flips around again and presses his lips to mine. I open for him, letting him feed my own cum back to me. The perfect dessert to a lovely dinner.

I'm still floating, limbs loose and languid, when Rhys tucks us into bed. He pulls the covers over us and snuggles down in my arms. We're both lying on our sides, his back molded against my front. My dick is nestled between his bum cheeks, and his hair tickles my nose.

I have never been happier in my entire life. I feel like I've finally become the man I was always meant to be. And none of this would ever have happened if it wasn't for Rhys.

Only one thing could make me even happier, and honestly, I can probably live without it. But in an absolutely ideal world, Mama would welcome Rhys into our lives with open arms. I'd be able to parade around proudly with Rhys on my arm, showing off our love the same way everyone else in the neighborhood does.

Would it be too much to ask of him? Should I be happy with what I have? It's already so much more than I could ever have dreamed of. I shouldn't be greedy by wanting even more.

"Teddy bear?" Rhys turns and whispers to me over his shoulder.

"Hmm?"

"What's bothering you?"

I hesitate. I shouldn't say anything. Especially not after making love together. Today has already been a lot. This can wait for another day.

Rhys shifts, turning in my arms so he's facing me. He hikes one leg up over my hip and wiggles until we're snug again.

"You can tell me anything. You know that, right?"

"I know."

"So tell me." He cups my cheek with his hand.

Somehow, that touch gives me the courage to speak. "You know how your cousin Barry is getting married?"

Rhys's eyebrows shoot up at the unexpected question. I don't blame him. I didn't even realize I was going to ask it myself.

"What about it?"

"Are you going to go?"

He rolls his eyes. "I guess? I'm not sure Mom would forgive me if I didn't."

"Would…" I gulp and steel myself. I'm pretty sure I know what his answer will be. But that doesn't make me feel any less like a high-school kid asking someone to homecoming. "Would you like to be my date for the wedding?" I spit it out as quickly as I can and then hold my breath.

Rhys blinks and his lips curl into a slow smile. "You're asking me to be your date? In front of everyone in the neighborhood?"

"Yes. And you can wear whatever you want. Like, a big ball gown or something. Don't feel like you have to wear a suit or a tux or anything. I don't care what any of them think. I want you to be exactly who—"

Rhys cuts me off with a hard kiss that quickly softens into something tender and sweet. "Yes, teddy bear. I'll be your date to the wedding. And I'm going to wear something spectacular."

CHAPTER
THIRTY-THREE

RHYS

"Grr, this curl!" I shout at the bathroom mirror, attacking an errant strand of honey-blond hair with the can of hairspray.

"If you use any more of that stuff, you're going to pass out from the fumes." Hayden leans against the doorframe, waving his hand in front of his face.

"Shut. Up. Everything has to be perfect!"

Hayden shoots me a sympathetic look through the mirror. "You positive you don't want me at the wedding? I have a suit I can wear. I'll just, you know, hang around the edges in case you need backup."

I sigh and drop the hairspray onto the counter with a defeated clatter. The hair will just have to do. Ugh.

"No, it's okay. I wouldn't wish the old neighborhood on my worst enemy, never mind my best friend."

Hayden winces. "If it's that bad, are you sure you want to go?"

I turn to Hayden, letting my insecurities show. "I don't

know. I mean, yes, I'm definitely going because Angel asked me to and I'm not about to let him down. But honestly?"

"You wouldn't wish it on your worst enemy," Hayden repeats back to me. "Yeah, I get it."

I take a deep breath, just like I do to calm my nerves before getting up on stage. "It's fine. Everything is fine. It's just for a few hours. I've been through worse."

"Well, one thing's for certain, you'll be the best-dressed person. Hell, you'll probably upstage the bride," Hayden says with a grin.

I glance down quickly at my 'fit. Angel said I could wear a ball gown. My dress isn't quite a ball gown, but it's close.

The floor-length blue and gold dress is made out of a shimmery satin material with long, tight sleeves that go all the way to my wrists. The front is modest, cutting across my collarbones in a wide boatneck collar. The back of the dress is another story, plunging all the way down to my lower back. The slit up the side is subtly cut, but if I stick my leg out just right, the fabric parts at the top of my thigh. The dress is stunning, but I don't think I'll upstage the bride. The colors are just muted enough to avoid being too loud.

Frankly? I look fucking amazing. I can't wait to see Angel's face when he comes to pick me up.

I told him it wasn't a problem for me to call for a rideshare. But he was insistent about driving to Brooklyn, even though it means we have to turn around and go right back to Staten Island for the wedding.

But he enjoys doing chivalrous things like that. Running around to open car doors. Escorting me with his hand on my lower back. Pulling out my chair for me. I could argue that the gestures are old-fashioned and maybe even a little chauvinistic, but it makes him so happy, I can't bring myself to stop him.

And if I'm honest, I kind of like being treated like a princess.

"I do look good, don't I?" I let myself preen a little bit, shoring up my defenses for whatever Angel and I will encounter when we get to the wedding.

The intercom buzzes and I frown at the little box on the wall. "Is that Angel? I told him he didn't need to come up."

Hayden gives me a skeptical look. "Did you really think he would just wait in the car? After driving all the way here?" He hits the button on the intercom. "Hello?"

"Hey, hi, uh, it's me. Uh, Angel."

I put a hand over my heart as it tumbles over itself at how adorable Angel is. He's been here at least a dozen times now, and every time he buzzes up, he stammers like he doesn't know what to say.

Hayden chuckles. "Come on up." He goes to unlock the door to our apartment, and when he gets back to the living room, he holds out his hand. "Your phone?"

"Why do you need my phone?" I ask, placing it on his palm.

"So I can take pictures."

I roll my eyes. "We're not in high school, and we're not going to prom."

Hayden tilts his head, eyes narrowed in suspicion. "*Did* you go to prom?"

I huff. "No, I didn't. But that's beside the point."

"This can be your prom do-over. Complete with your own Prince Charming."

"Hello?" Angel's voice echoes down the long hallway that leads to the front door.

"In here!" Hayden calls.

I stop breathing as I wait for Angel to appear. And when he does, I'm not at all disappointed. He's fucking gorgeous in a cream-colored suit that complements the gold in my dress. It fits him perfectly across his broad shoulders and follows the line of his body close enough to show off his bulk. The white shirt underneath is open at the collar, showing off his thick neck, that delicious dip at the base, and his signature gold chain. There's a royal blue silk handkerchief tucked into his breast pocket, and his hair and beard are freshly trimmed.

He looks sophisticated and poised, like he just stepped off the pages of a fashion magazine. I love him, no matter what he's wearing, but a part of me can't help being proud that my rough-and-tumble construction worker cleans up really damn nice.

"You're beautiful," Angel says in a hushed tone. His gaze had wandered slowly down my body and now it makes its way slowly back up. When his eyes meet mine, the love shining in those warm browns steals my breath away.

Before I met Angel, I never really gave relationships much thought. I'm young and I figured I would find someone eventually. But Angel exceeds all my wildest dreams and craziest fantasies. And the fact that he's from the old neighborhood feels like poetic justice somehow. I've snatched him from their clutches. He's mine now and they can't have him back.

He holds out his arms and I rush into them, not caring whether the hug will wrinkle our clothes. It's more important that I touch him, hold him, kiss him. Thank god for smudge-proof lipstick.

"You're so fucking hot," I murmur against his lips, and they stretch into a wide grin.

His hands slide up from my lower back and a shiver runs through me when his rough palms meet skin. He kisses the corner of my mouth, up my jaw and down my neck. Heat pools low in my stomach.

"If you keep kissing me like that, we might not make it to the wedding."

"I'm okay with that," Angel mumbles, tightening his hold on me.

"Ngh." I give him a half-hearted push. "But… but…" Why was it so important we go to this thing? There was something we wanted to do there… oh yeah. "But, the people."

I couldn't have been vaguer, but Angel knows what I mean. He sighs, breath hot against my neck, then straightens. His pupils are blown wide and his lips a rosy pink. "Right."

I tug on his lapels and fluff up the handkerchief that got a little flattened. Only then do I notice Hayden hovering a few feet away, holding up my phone, camera pointed in our direction.

"Have you been recording this?"

He smirks, not taking his eyes off the phone screen. "Yup."

Angel's ears go pink and I spin toward Hayden, tucking Angel behind me.

"Denny!"

"We need to document this for posterity." He taps the screen, then lowers the phone. "Now for some stills. Sebastian's going to love these. Go stand by the wall."

I put on my annoyed face, but deep down, a part of me is thrilled that Hayden's making such a big deal out of this. I've never felt like I missed out on prom, not until Hayden decided to turn this into a production. And now I feel like a teenager again, giddy and a little nervous about the big night.

Angel snakes an arm around my waist and pulls me in close, his hand resting on my opposite hip. He stands straight and tall, smiling joyfully into the camera.

I drape myself over him, cocking my hip out so the dress falls away and reveals my inner thigh. I turn away from Hayden to show off my back, then look over my shoulder at the camera. I lay my arm over Angel's shoulder, then lean in to press a kiss to his cheek.

The photoshoot lasts a full five minutes before Hayden is satisfied.

He hands my phone back to me, along with my glittering gold clutch, and hands Angel the faux fur mini-cape I'm wearing over my dress.

While Angel slips it over my shoulders, Hayden pins him with a stern glare.

"What time will you have him home?"

Angel's eyes go wide and his jaw hangs open in surprise. "Uh, I, um…"

"Gurl, seriously? Don't wait up." I give Angel a smoldering look. "I'm not coming home tonight."

Hayden chuckles as I drag Angel toward the door. "Beware of the spiked punch!"

"I can bring you back after the wedding," Angel says as he helps me down the stairs in my sexy-as-hell stilettos.

"We can come back here if you want, but I intend on sleeping in the same bed as you tonight, teddy bear."

He shoots me a shy, but pleased, smile, then tucks my hand into the crook of his elbow to lead me out to his truck. He managed to find a spot not too far away, and gentleman that he is, he opens my door and lifts me up into the cab. Then he waits for me to finish arranging myself before shutting the door and racing around to the driver's side.

I keep up the chatter all the way back to Staten Island —how the *12 Toys of Christmas* project is going, how our second video is doing after it dropped a few days ago, some drama among the drag queens at The Bronzed Rail. But even with all that, I can't help the nervousness that grows the closer we get to the wedding.

It's one thing to say "fuck them" when we're tucked safely away in bed. It's another thing entirely to show up as a couple, dressed like this, and feel the weight of all those stares. It's not something I'd ever voluntarily put myself through, but I'm not worried about myself. I'm worried about Angel.

Obviously, I'll draw a lot more attention than he will, but I've got years of experience with being in the spotlight —whether I wanted to or not.

Angel doesn't have the same armor I have. He's always been accepted as one of the guys. He's been a member of their fiercely protective community since the day he was born. He's never stepped outside their circle, never challenged who they thought he was.

Neither of us knows how they'll react. Stares and whispers would be the least-bad outcome. Things could get so much worse than that.

Am I doing the right thing? Dragging him into the spotlight with me? Wouldn't he be better off blending into the background like he always has? It would be safer and easier for him to quietly slip away, leave the neighborhood without making an announcement.

But it wouldn't be honest. And if nothing else, Angel is honest. My respect for him, my love for him, is that much stronger because of it.

Whatever happens, I'll be there to protect him. I'll be there to pick up the pieces and bandage up any wounds.

We pull into the parking lot of the local Catholic church. It's the same one everyone in the neighborhood goes to, including my family on Christmas and Easter. We've arrived at the same time as everyone else, and the truck creeps forward as guests dart around us.

I recognize a lot of the faces. Neighbors. Classmates. Cousin's uncle's third wife. Most of these people knew me as Dina's boy, the queer one. And back then, they didn't use that term the way I use it now.

Angel parks the truck and I force myself to take a deep breath. My heart is beating way faster than normal and my stomach is all tied up in knots. I wasn't this anxious when I went to Dad's birthday party at the end of the summer. This is basically the same crowd. So why am I all twisted up and panicky now?

Angel shuts off the engine and turns to face me. "Sweetheart?" The alarm is evident in his voice.

"I'm fine," I squeak. I've done this before. I can totally do this. I'm *fine*.

Angel takes both of my hands in his. "We don't have to

go in. We can go back to my place. Or back to yours. Wherever you want."

I shake my head. "No. No running away. Not anymore."

I meet Angel's gaze and let myself take comfort in all the emotions I see flitting across his face. Concern, understanding, fear, and love. So much love.

"I left when I was eighteen—"

"Because this wasn't a welcoming place for you," Angel interjects on my behalf.

"It wasn't, you're right. And that was the right thing for me to do at the time. But now, I don't need to run anymore. And I don't want to make you feel like *you* need to run. We should be able to be ourselves, no matter what anyone else thinks."

Angel gives me a decisive nod. His lips tighten into a firm line and his eyes take on a steel glint. "I'll protect you."

A laugh bubbles up in me, a mix of joy and self-pity. He wants to protect me, and here I am, thinking I'm going to protect him.

"We'll protect each other."

He lifts my hands and plants a kiss on the back of each. "We'll protect each other."

ANGEL

I jump out of my truck and use the two seconds it takes me to walk around the cab to gather myself. My palms are sweaty, my stomach is practically cramping. I think I might throw up.

But I won't. Because Rhys needs me to be strong for him.

I asked him to come to the wedding with me. I told him to dress however he wants. I need to protect him against whatever fallout might follow.

Holding the door handle, I take a deep breath, then pull it open. Rhys gazes down at me, looking like a queen sitting on her throne. His dress is dazzling, but it pales in comparison to his own beauty. Dark, smoldering eyes and glistening, pouty lips. His hair is blond today and it falls in perfect curls around his face.

When I first laid eyes on him in his apartment, I thought I'd died and gone to heaven. Because no human could look like that, right? He has to be an angel.

I take Rhys's hand and hold him steady as he steps down. I close the door behind him and we stand there, shielded by my truck, and gaze into each other's eyes.

Rhys is my life now. He is my future. I don't care what happens today, I will do whatever it takes to be with him forever.

"Ready?" he finally asks.

I nod and hold out my elbow. He slips his hand inside and I place mine on top of it.

Then we walk.

The entire neighborhood has shown up for this wedding. Every single person I've known since I was a baby. And the second we round the bed of my truck, all eyes zero in on us—or rather, on Rhys.

I don't blame them. He's a vision. Stunning. How could you not stare? But not all the gazes are as appreciative as mine.

Beside me, Rhys holds his head up high. His posture is ramrod straight, and he struts like he's on a catwalk. Part of it is a defense mechanism, a shield. I can tell now that I know him so well. But I'm still proud of him for showing up, for being unapologetic, for being bold.

I love him. I couldn't be more honored to have him on my arm.

I see Nico's wife, Ariana, wrangling their two kids across the parking lot. She stops in her tracks, an expression of shock on her face when she sees us. Then she hurries the kids into the church like they're trying to flee the boogeyman.

I grit my teeth. Of all the people at this wedding, I was sure Nico and Ariana would be safe. Rhys's hand tightens on my elbow when he notices her reaction. I hate that he saw it.

But then, before we manage more than a few yards, Nico appears in the open doorway of the church. He scans the parking lot and the instant he sets eyes on us, he breaks into a smile. Ariana must have rushed inside to send him out.

"Ricky! Angel!" He marches toward us, arms held wide like he's welcoming old friends back home.

Rhys lets out a shaky breath, releasing some of his tightly coiled tension.

"Holy shit, baby bro! You look like you're going to the Met Gala. You know you're in Staten Island, right?" Nico teases as he pulls Rhys into a hug.

"Yeah, I know. That's why I dressed up. If I don't bring the fabulous, who will?" Rhys is all sass and confidence. There's no hint of anxiety and I can't help puffing up my chest in response. He's an amazing performer. He's gonna nail this.

"Angel, my man." Nico gives me a bro hug and we slap each other on the back. But when I pull away, Nico doesn't let go. "You treating him right?" He growls at me in full big-brother mode.

I smile with a joy so deep and uncontainable, it just shoots out of me. "Yeah. For sure."

"Good. Glad to hear it."

When Nico releases me, Rhys isn't where I left him. He's been enveloped by a group of women about our age. They're all gushing over his dress and his hair and his makeup, and he's holding court like the queen he is.

Nico and I stand back, letting Rhys have his moment.

All around us, guests are still making their way from

their cars to the church. Most of them stare, but I'm almost glad they do. Let them see how many people we've got on our side.

Mama and Sabrina pause on the sidewalk, halfway between our group and the church's entrance. Sabrina turns to say something to Mama, but Mama shakes her head and turns toward the church.

Pain stabs straight through my heart at the sight. Things have been tense between us. I don't like it, but I also don't know what to do about it. Sunday dinners have been awkward with Sabrina trying to fill the silences. And when I tried to talk to Mama about it one time, she shut herself in her bedroom again. She isn't happy about me dating Rhys, but I'm still holding out hope that she'll come around.

Sabrina beams as she approaches us. "I should've known. It's always the quiet ones you need to watch out for."

My ears heat at her teasing, but I hide it by taking Jonah from her arms. She's got my nephew dressed in a mini-suit, complete with a mini-bowtie, that is utterly adorable.

"Hi Jo-Jo!" I say in that silly voice people use with babies.

"'ncle 'ngel!" He grabs my face with spit-covered hands, and I grimace but bear it.

Jonah is a good distraction, but not quite enough to keep me from monitoring the parking lot. Mario shows up with a girl I don't recognize. She looks curious, but his face is shut down in a frown. We've only had minimal exchanges at work since I came out to him. It sucks losing one of my only friends, but I don't regret doing what I did.

Rhys and Nico's parents arrive and it takes them a few moments to realize it's their son in the center of all the excitement. Mr. Gallo tries to go into the church, but Mrs. Gallo drags him toward us instead.

My heart races as the women around Rhys part as if they're the Red Sea and Mrs. Gallo is Moses. Rhys's posture stiffens when she stops in front of him. Mr. Gallo stands behind his wife, arms crossed, glowering. The parking lot descends into silence as Rhys's mom gives him a thorough once-over.

Rhys stays perfectly still during her examination. I'm this close to stepping between them when Nico stops me with a hand on my arm.

"Just wait," he whispers.

"Hi, Mom," Rhys says, his intonation not giving anything away.

"That's some outfit," she replies.

"You like it?" He strikes a pose.

She sighs like she's giving up on a naughty child and shakes her head with a resigned expression. "You look good," she finally concedes.

Then she turns her gaze to the people standing around him. The women all look terrified. Nico and Sabrina both stare her down. When she finally gets to me, it takes every ounce of courage I have not to look away.

I love her son. I'll protect him. Even from her, if I have to.

She breaks first, heaving another heavy sigh. Then, with one last glance at Rhys, she says, "I'll see you inside," before walking away. Rhys's dad doesn't even look at us before following his wife inside.

Air rushes back into the little bubble that formed

around the group. Sounds of traffic in the distance filter through again. We all breathe a sigh of relief.

"Guess we should all find our seats," Nico says, leading the way.

I hand Jonah back to Sabrina and hold out my arm to Rhys. He takes it and presses himself into me. "You okay?"

He nods with a bittersweet smile. "Yeah, I think so."

I hold Rhys's hand through the ceremony. The priest drones on about love and respect and devotion, and all I can think about is how much I want to repeat those same words to Rhys.

I can already imagine it. Rhys in a spectacular wedding gown with flowers in his hair. The sunlight would make his skin glow and his eyes sparkle. He would be radiant as we dedicate our lives to each other.

I want that. I want to marry him, to be his husband. I want to build a house for him and create a life together. Maybe we'll even have kids? I don't know how he feels about kids. But I can see him braiding their hair and putting on home fashion shows.

It's all very domestic and I know Rhys isn't a domestic kind of guy. But maybe…?

Clutching my hand, Rhys gazes toward the front of the sanctuary where the bride and groom are exchanging rings. His eyes are wet with unshed tears and there's a longing in his expression that makes me wonder.

After the ceremony, the guests linger in the sanctuary as the photographer calls up various groups of friends and family for pictures. Rhys and I find a dark corner and I draw him to me, his back against my front. I slip my arms around his waist, and with his heels on, he's tall enough for me to dip down and rest my chin on his shoulder.

He sighs and melts back into me. "Would you ever want to do that?" he asks in a quiet voice that travels the short distance between us.

I breathe in his floral scent, letting my eyes drift shut as I bask in his presence. "Hmm? Do what?"

"That." He nods toward the front of the sanctuary. "Get married."

I still, then open my eyes and straighten. Rhys turns to look at me over his shoulder. My stomach is doing that fluttering thing I've only ever felt around Rhys. It's nervousness and excitement. It's anticipation for something I know will be scary but also amazing.

"Do you?" It's a cop-out question, but I need to know.

Marriage always seemed inevitable for me, even though finding a girlfriend felt impossible for such a long time. I don't need marriage to be happy with Rhys, but if that's something he's open to, then I would jump at the chance to put a ring on his finger.

"No," he says with a softness in his eyes, and my stomach drops. "Not before. I never understood the point. But now…"

I gulp. "Now?"

He turns fully in my arms, sliding his hands up my chest and around to the back of my neck. My heart thumps like a drum in my chest, so hard and loud I'm sure he can feel it.

"Now that I've found the right person? It makes all the sense in the world."

CHAPTER
THIRTY-FIVE

RHYS

The wedding isn't a total disaster. In fact, if I ignore anyone over the age of sixty-five who keeps glaring in our direction, I'd even say the wedding is fun.

The reception is in the church's community hall. It's basically a gym that they've managed to disguise as a reception space with white fabric strung up across the ceiling and fabric curtains lining the walls. Round paper lanterns and fairy lights cast a warm glow, making the large echoey room feel inviting and cozy. The round tables are covered in white tablecloths and the chairs have big, pale pink bows on the back. White and pink flowers make up the centerpieces on each table, and more flowers sit on pedestals dotted around the room.

The buffet was catered by another obscure relation of mine who owns a restaurant, and the dessert bar came from a fancy bakery in Manhattan that the bride is obsessed with.

Angel and I sit at the same table as Sabrina and Nico

and his wife, Ariana. The three of them have been a human shield around us the entire time. No one talks to us unless they've been vetted, no one even gets close to our table without an approving nod from one of our siblings.

When I left the old neighborhood, I left Nico, Ariana, and the kids behind too. I didn't give it too much thought at the time. I was so completely focused on escaping the judging looks, the snide remarks, the overwhelming feeling of oppression. But seeing their unquestioning support for me and Angel today, I think I was too hasty in condemning anything that had to do with my childhood.

Not everything from the old neighborhood is bad. Not everyone thinks I'm that weird Gallo kid who likes to pretend he's a girl. There are good people here. People who love me. People who I love.

Like Angel.

All evening, when he wasn't busy making sure I was okay, he was playing with the kids and keeping them entertained. He's so good with them, and there's such obvious joy in his eyes when he laughs with them. He would make such a good father.

He could teach them how to throw a ball and how to work with their hands. He could give them rides on his back and hoist them up on his shoulders. My throat grows a little tight at the thought of Angel with a little boy with big brown eyes and floppy brown hair.

I'm not a kid person. I'm not really even a marriage person. Those aren't things I've ever envisioned for my life. But those are things Angel definitely deserves. They're things I want him to have.

Can I give him that kind of life? Marriage, house, white picket fence and two-point-five kids? In a neighborhood that looks alarmingly like this one. All the things I worked so hard to get away from.

Six months ago, I would have revolted at the idea. Absolutely no fucking way. But now…

Like I told Angel earlier, with the right person—with him—the idea doesn't sound all that bad.

After the giant wedding cake is cut and the happy couple have their first dance, the DJ cranks up the music.

I catch Angel watching the dance floor apprehensively and I take pity on him. "It's okay, teddy bear. We don't have to dance."

"But you love to dance," he says, full of concern.

"I can dance whenever I want. I don't need a wedding to shake my ass."

For a moment, it seems like Angel will take me up on the offer to stay at our table, but then he sets his jaw and shoots to his feet.

"No, I want to dance. Will you dance with me, sweetheart?"

I would never say no to dancing, but when he calls me sweetheart, I'm putty in his hands. He leads me to the edge of the dance floor and hesitates like he's standing on the edge of a cliff.

I take a step over the invisible line and turn to show him that I haven't fallen through to the basement or spontaneously burst into flames. He joins me cautiously, then starts to dance.

At least, I think that's what he's trying to do. A giggle escapes me as I watch Angel bob up and down, completely out of time with the music. He's so awkward and eager and unbelievably adorable, I could die.

I can't stop the massive grin spreading across my face. I

can't stop myself from laughing out loud. I don't care if anyone is watching. I love this man and I'm not going to hide the way he makes me feel.

The music changes, switching from a fast, upbeat song to something slow and sweet and romantic. We step into each other's arms and stare into each other's eyes. Angel's ears are lobster red, but his cheeks are bunched up into a delighted smile. The browns of his irises draw me in until I'm drowning in their rich, comforting depths.

It's hypnotizing. And I never want to wake up.

The party is still in full swing when we slip out. It's been a long day for both of us, and all I want is to crawl into bed for cuddles with my teddy bear. Angel takes us to his house and I pad up the stairs after him in my bare feet, heels in my hands.

When we're finally alone in his apartment, Angel pauses and glances down at my shoes.

"Can you, um, can you…" His ears flush red frighteningly fast and his wide chest hitches as he tries to catch his breath.

I slowly lift the golden stiletto pumps with the dangerously pointed toes, and Angel tracks their progress, his gaze never wavering. Lust slams into me at the reminder of Angel's unexpected shoe and foot kink. My cock fills and my balls tingle. My hole clenches desperately.

"Do you want me to put these back on?" I ask. My voice is husky without any effort.

His Adam's apple works in his throat and he nods jerkily.

"Then, follow me, teddy bear." I sling the shoes over my shoulder and lead the way into the bedroom. Angel follows after me, practically panting after the treat I hold in my hands.

I sit on the edge of the bed, heels dangling from my fingers. Angel immediately drops to his knees in front of me. My dick throbs at the sight of him down there, my big teddy bear, looking so debonair, kneeling in front of me, eagerly waiting for what comes next.

I hold out the heels. "Put them on me." I lift a foot, toes pointed.

Angel's hands shake as he carefully takes my foot, an expression of awe on his face. He kisses each toe, his breath hot against my skin, his lips impossibly soft, and his beard ticklish and scratchy. He moves to the sole of my foot, trailing kisses over the arch and toward the heel, then up and around to my ankle. His lips latch onto the bony nub on the inside of my ankle and he sucks.

I gasp at the weird sensation that feels so much like he's sucking on a nipple. I grip the bedcovers behind me as my hips tilt forward, looking for friction. "Oh my god, why does that feel so good?"

Angel doesn't answer me, though. He's too consumed with worshiping my foot. He licks along the inside, back toward my toes, before taking my big toe all the way into his mouth.

"Oh, fuck." I grab my dick, squeezing hard enough to stave off the orgasm rushing at me out of nowhere.

His tongue swirls around the toe, the way he likes to do to my cock, and I'm about *this close* to coming. It only gets worse when he moves on to the next toe and does the same thing. Then the next. Then the next. His tongue slides between them, wet and wiggly, and Jesus Christ, I'm going to come just from Angel sucking on my foot.

"Wait!" I shout, pulling my foot away.

Angel glances up at me with alarm. "Was that okay? Did I hurt you? Was it bad?"

I'm hovering right on the edge, so close that I can't even speak. I press my foot against Angel's chest, as if I can physically kick the orgasm back. Gradually, the need to come eases enough for me to talk.

"That was… too good…" I pant.

A pleased smile graces Angel's lips as he takes the shoes I've dropped to the floor and reverently slips one of them onto my foot. He runs his hand over the top, cups the back of my ankle, smooths his palm up my calf. With one last kiss to my foot, he gingerly sets it down on the floor.

Then picks up the other.

Jesus Christ. I'm definitely going to come if he does that again.

I push my dress apart at the slit, revealing the gold-colored thong I'm wearing underneath. The fabric is already soaked through with pre-cum and my dick is poking out the side. I pull the thong out of the way and clamp my hand around the base of my dick.

Angel's gaze grows even hungrier as he stares at my cock. He doesn't break his stare as he licks and sucks on my other foot. He bites gently on the inside of my foot, right at the high point of my arch, and a gush of pre-cum oozes out of my cock.

I stroke myself. I can't help it. There's no way I'll be able to hold off an orgasm, so I might as well give in.

Angel rubs his beard against the underside of my foot, and the tingles that shoot up my leg go straight to my cock. "Fucking hell, do that again."

He does, and pleasure ripples from the sole of my foot right to my dick. I tighten my hand, speed up my strokes. My balls draw up tight. And when Angel takes my toes between his lips again, I come.

"Fuck! Oh my god, fuck!" Cum shoots out of me in an orgasm like nothing I've ever experienced before. The pleasure is sharper, clearer, piercing through me rather than crashing down on me. There isn't the typical haze that dulls the sensations. Instead, I feel every single fucking thing.

The wet suction of Angel's mouth. His tongue as it runs across the base of my toes. The grip of his hand on my heel. The contrast between his soft lips and wiry beard. The pleasure is fucking acute, which is not something I ever thought I'd say.

"Rhys!" Angel's cry breaks through the roar of blood in my ears.

At some point, he's gotten his pants undone and pulled out his own gorgeous cock. He's stroking himself, concentrating the friction right below the red, engorged glans. He's close too. Just from worshiping my feet. From watching me come while he worships my feet.

An orgasmic aftershock stabs me again, and more cum spurts from my dick.

"Do you need to come, teddy bear?" I ask, rubbing my bare foot against his cheek.

He turns his face into it and nods.

"Do you want to come all over my shoe?" I hold up my other leg, the one that's wearing the golden heel again, holding it so my foot is poised directly in front of Angel's cock.

He nods and whines at the same time.

"Go ahead then, my sweet teddy bear. Shoot your cum all over my shoe."

He lets out a strangled cry and does exactly as I tell him. His cum lands hot on the top of my foot, on my ankle, on the pointed toe of the stiletto. Angel watches at first, but then he squeezes his eyes shut and presses his face into the sole of my other foot.

God in heaven, it should be illegal for someone to be so fucking adorable and sexy at the same time. How the hell did I get so lucky?

When Angel's shudders soften, I lift my cum-covered foot.

"You've made a big mess, teddy bear. Clean it up."

He doesn't hesitate, immediately switching his attention to my other foot. His tongue comes out, licking every inch of the shoe, the top of my foot, my ankle, until not a single drop of cum remains.

"And my mess too."

He lurches forward, headfirst into my crotch. I lean back, giving him access as he searches for all the cum I splattered over myself. He licks my hand clean, then laves my dick with his tongue. He roots around the base of my cock and under my balls too.

"Come up here, big guy." I tug on his shoulder and he quickly climbs onto the bed with me.

I drag him down for a kiss, licking between his lips to snag a taste of our combined essence. It's delicious. Angel's delicious. I'm hooked and I'll never get enough.

"Well," I murmur as we gradually come back to ourselves. "That wasn't quite what I had planned."

"Was it okay?" Angel asks, again with that hint of concern.

"More than okay, teddy bear. I loved it."

The tips of his ears turn pink. "I liked it too."

Eventually, we undress and climb into bed, pulling the covers up around us.

"Thanks for coming to the wedding with me," Angel murmurs into my ear as he tucks me securely into the curve of his body.

"Thanks for being with me through the whole thing."

"Always."

And I agree. With Angel… "Always."

CHAPTER
THIRTY-SIX

ANGEL

It took us a while to find a Saturday that worked for everyone. Rhys had his brunch with the boys one week. Then Nico and Ariana had to take their kids to Jersey to visit her side of the family. But eventually, we found a day that everyone was free.

And now I'm on my hands and knees in Nico and Ariana's living room, pretending to be a horse. The two Gallo kids have put Jonah on my back and I'm currently "galloping" across the Wild West.

"He's really good with them, isn't he?" I overhear Rhys saying from his spot on the couch next to Ariana.

"Yeah, he is. Would you…?" Ariana trails off.

"Want kids?" Rhys finishes the question for her. He sighs. "I don't know. I mean, I kinda just assumed I never would. But… I do want to see Angel be a dad."

"Gurl, you can have my kids whenever you want."

Rhys laughs softly. "I'm sure Angel will be thrilled."

"Drinks!" Sabrina announces as she comes in from the

kitchen. "Bloody Marys, sangria, and lemonade for the little humans. Nico says brunch will be ready in ten."

The kids abandon Jonah on my back to grab their lemonades and Sabrina plucks him off me.

"Thanks, sis." I straighten, rolling my shoulders and bending side to side to work out the kinks.

It's nice seeing Rhys with our siblings like this. He's not quite as flamboyant as he is when he's with his boys or at The Bronzed Rail, but he isn't tense either. He doesn't have his guard up, isn't eyeing everyone with suspicion.

Since the wedding, Nico and Ariana have made a point of reaching out to Rhys. He went to their place for dinner once, then he stayed with me that night. There's been discussions about them visiting The Bronzed Rail to see him perform, but I'm not sure anyone is ready for Nico to watch his kid brother on stage, practically naked, humping a pole.

Sabrina got a job at a nail salon, so she's been leaving Jonah with me more often. It means I can't get out to Brooklyn as much as I'd like, but Rhys has been great about coming down so we can babysit together.

I join Rhys on the couch, taking the sangria he holds out to me, and he snuggles right into my arms. Sabrina asks him about some new foundation that's gone viral on social media and Rhys immediately gives her the rundown on whether it's worth buying.

"Time to eat!" Nico calls out from the kitchen.

The kids race out of the living room while the adults follow a little more slowly. They've got their own kiddie table that Nico has set up for them, while the rest of us take seats around the kitchen table.

Brunch is waffles with all the fixings, including bacon

and fruit. Rhys is quick to pile my plate high before grabbing a couple things for himself. He's still not much of a breakfast person, even though I try to feed him as much as I can when we're together in the mornings.

"How's work going, Angel?" Nico asks.

I shrug. "It's fine. Maybe another month before this project wraps up."

"Mario still being an asshole?"

I grimace. "He's not that bad."

"Don't defend him!" Rhys jumps in. "Yes, Mario is still being an asshole."

The truth is, we try to avoid each other on the jobsite. He's never said anything rude or offensive, and as far as I know, he hasn't been talking about me behind my back. But we don't eat lunch together anymore or carpool to and from work. I'm sad about losing the friendship, but having Rhys more than makes up for it.

"Screw Mario," Sabrina says as she bounces Jonah on her knee. "He can go suck it."

"Sabrina!" I hiss, looking pointedly at my nephew.

"What? He's too young to understand."

"But the other kids aren't." I nod toward the kiddie table.

"Don't worry about it." Ariana waves away my concern. "They've heard so much worse."

Under the table, Rhys squeezes my thigh. "You don't need Mario. You've got us."

I gaze into his eyes, lightly lined today, with shimmering pink makeup on the lids. "Yeah, I do."

After brunch, Sabrina stays a bit longer to do mom stuff with Ariana while Rhys and I drive back to my place.

It's not a long drive and Rhys takes the few minutes to check the notifications on his phone.

"Oh my god." Rhys shakes his head with a laugh. "Sebastian's trying to get a sponsorship deal with the shoe brand. You know, the boots I wore for our second video? Apparently, fans have been tagging the brand when posting about the video and now they want to discuss things with us."

I only understood about half of that, but from the way Rhys is smiling, I assume it's good news. "That's great!"

"Sebastian's always doing these business-y things." Rhys rolls his eyes.

"He's good at them." I would know, considering the money he keeps sending me from the two videos we've done. Sebastian wants to make more with me and Rhys. I haven't decided yet, but if I do, I'll have the second mortgage paid off in no time.

I pull into the driveway and shut off the engine. "Hold on."

I jump out of the truck and rush around to open Rhys's door for him.

"You know you don't have to do that every time, right?" he says, turning to face me.

"I know."

He smiles at me, eyes dancing in the bright winter sun, then leans in to give me a kiss. He tastes like tomatoes and honey, and a whimper escapes me as our tongues tangle together.

Behind me, a door opens and we both jump apart. Mama's standing there, glaring at us. Rhys and I freeze.

Even though he's been coming over a lot, Rhys has managed to avoid Mama when coming and going. He hasn't been to another Sunday dinner yet—I don't want to put him through that again. This is the first time they're seeing each other since the wedding.

"What are you doing standing out in the cold?" she snaps at us. "At least go inside before you start taking off your clothes." Then she slams the door shut.

Rhys and I exchange a look.

"Was that… did she just…?"

I glance back at the door, but it doesn't have any answers. "I've got no clue. But I think she's right."

I help Rhys out of the truck and we rush upstairs, giggling like kids. We don't stop until we're tumbling onto the bed, leaving a trail of clothes behind us.

"If you get a sponsorship deal with the shoe company, does that mean you'll get all the shoes you want?" I ask breathlessly between kisses.

Rhys pulls back with a questioning look in his eyes. His hands are on either side of my face and I'm sure he can feel the heat in my ears.

"Probably," he answers, voice husky with a note of teasing. "Why do you ask?"

I feign innocence. "They have cool shoes."

His elegant eyebrow arches. "That's it? No other reason?"

"Nope." I press my lips together, trying to hold back my grin. But I'm awful at lying, even when it's just for fun, and finally break out in giggles.

Rhys flips us over so I'm on my back and he's straddling me. Our favorite position. He leans down and whispers in my ear. "I'm going to make sure this sponsorship happens."

My dick hardens against Rhys's bum.

"And I'll get them to send me every style they have. I'll wear a different pair every day."

I grip his thighs and whine.

"You get to test them out, of course. We'll need to know which ones look the best with your cum smeared all over them."

My hips come off the bed and Rhys grinds down on me.

"You're gonna have to build me a separate shoe closet."

I nod frantically. "Yes, yes, I can do that. A really big one."

He gasps, hips tilting forward to rub his erection against my stomach. Then he lets out a breathy laugh. "Jesus Christ, why is it so hot when you say things like that?"

"Things like what?"

Rhys braces himself above me with elbows on either side of my face. His gaze grows soft and his lips curl into a gentle smile. The love pouring out of him fills me with warmth.

"Teddy bear, you're amazing."

"No, *you're* amazing."

Rhys's smile widens and he plants a hard kiss on my mouth. "We're both amazing."

EPILOGUE

RHYS

I lean in to whisper into Angel's ear. "This is for the shoe closet."

I can feel the sudden spike of heat against my lips as Angel flushes bright red. I fucking love that he has a shoe fetish and I especially adore how he reacts every time I remind him of it.

"I'll make sure it's secure in the truck." He takes the box and gives me a quick kiss before carrying it out of my bedroom.

We're moving me from the apartment I've shared with Hayden to Angel's place in Staten Island. It only makes sense, I've been spending more time there than he's been spending here. Which I never, in a million years, would've guessed.

Angel has always offered to stay in Brooklyn with me, but it never felt quite right for some reason. Maybe because having Hayden around was weird?

Not because Hayden disapproves. He's gotten over his

protective, suspicious thing against Angel. I think the wedding we went to solidified it. If Angel's willing to parade me around on his arm in front of everyone in the old neighborhood, then he's probably not going to dump me like a hot potato the next day

Honestly, Hayden's been great, and I'm going to miss him loads. But there's just something about having our own space.

Plus, with Angel's early mornings and random babysitting duties with Jonah, it's easier for him to be closer to home.

Being in the old neighborhood so much hasn't been as bad as I expected. Sabrina's cool, and I've gotten to hang out with Nico and Ariana more. It's been nice to reconnect, and I hadn't realized how much I missed my big brother until I started seeing more of him.

When Mom found out that I was hanging out with Nico, she coerced him into bringing me to Sunday dinner. I one-upped her by bringing Angel with me. It was an awkward evening, but no one said anything offensive and we made it through. Things with Mom and Dad still aren't great, but maybe there's hope.

Things with Angel's mom, however, have been… surprisingly okay? She's never apologized for that first dinner we had together, never said anything to clear the air between us. She just started treating me like I had always been there. Like her son had always been attracted to men and having Dina's boy over at the house all the time was perfectly normal. It's weird, but honestly, I'll take it. It could've been so much worse.

"Okay, what's next?" Hayden appears in my doorway, ready to carry the next box down to Angel's truck.

Bellamy and Noel are right behind him—Bellamy with his sleeves rolled up, Noel examining his fingernails. He's been following Bellamy up and down the stairs like a puppy without actually carrying anything. He's such a grumpy marshmallow.

"You can take this one and this one." I point to two boxes stacked against the wall. "And then, I think that's it!"

I don't actually have that much stuff to move, since I'm not bringing any furniture. It's mostly my shoes and clothes and toiletries. I swing a large makeup bag over my shoulder and follow the guys out.

They head down to the truck, but I pause in the living room.

I'll be back here all the time. Hayden's still my best friend and we're still going to hang out. But it'll be different now and a part of me feels guilty about leaving him on his own.

He's a happy guy, always positive and joyful. Recently, though, there's been something off with him. I've tried talking to him about it, but he brushes me off and changes the topic. I have a feeling that my moving out is only going to make things worse. I hate it, but… Angel.

I say a silent goodbye to the apartment and make a promise to be back often.

Down on the sidewalk, Angel's got the truck all packed up, a bright blue tarp covering all my precious belongings.

The guys are all standing in a circle, waiting for me.

"What are you going to do with the extra room?" Bellamy asks.

Hayden shrugs and there's a tightness at the corners of his mouth that I'm not sure anyone else sees. "I don't know. Find a roommate, I guess? I'll be okay on my own for a couple months, but then…" He shrugs again.

Angel's brows draw together in concern. I was wrong, Angel definitely sees what I see.

"What about Santino?" Noel's tone makes it sound like he doesn't like the dude, but then, Noel always sounds a little annoyed.

"Who's Santino?" I ask.

"My old roommate from San Francisco," Bellamy answers. "He's spending the summer here, but I don't know if he's figured out where he's staying yet."

Hayden brightens and I'm suddenly desperate for Santino to move in. If Bellamy lived with him, he must be a good guy, right? Hayden needs someone cool in the apartment.

"If he hasn't, he can totally have Rhys's room," Hayden offers.

Rhys's room. The guilt grows a little more and I throw myself at Hayden.

"I'm going to miss you," I say, hugging him tight.

He chuckles as he returns the hug. "I'll miss you too. But I'm happy for you. You deserve this."

With one last squeeze, he gently pushes me away, but I don't let go of him that easily. "You sure you'll be okay?" I study his face for any signs of distress.

He does a pretty good job of schooling his expression, but there's still a hint of sadness in his eyes. "Yes, I'll be fine. Go."

I debate staying for a little longer, putting off the inevitable. But at the end of the day, I have to make a decision, and I've already made a commitment to always choose Angel.

"I'll be back all the time. I'm just a text message away."

Hayden smiles, genuine this time. "I know."

I pull him back into one more hug. "Love you lots, Denny."

"Love you too, babe."

Then I plant a kiss on his cheek and let him pass me into Angel's arms.

Angel opens the truck door for me and gives me a hand up into the seat. He waves goodbye to the guys and goes around to the driver's side.

He looks over at me once the door is shut. His concern is obvious, and that's how I know I've made the right decision. Angel is too good for words. Even though I'm leaving Hayden behind, I know Angel will help me take care of him.

"You good?"

I reach for Angel's hand and intertwine our fingers. "With you, I'm always good. Let's go home."

BONUS SCENE

I don't know how Rhys wears leather pants. I feel like I've been attacked by saran wrap. It's tight. It doesn't breathe. It squeaks when I move.

The leather harness I'm wearing on top has the opposite problem. The thick black straps wind around my shoulders and connect across the upper part of my chest, leaving everything else exposed—most of my chest, my nipples, my belly.

With heavy boots on my feet, studded cuffs on my wrists, and brimmed cap on my head, I barely recognize myself in the mirror. My thighs look huge. The outline of my dick is clearly visible between my legs. My shoulders look wider than normal. I can't stop staring at my tummy.

I rub my hands over it. I'm not usually shy about taking my shirt off, but there's something about wearing the harness that makes my stomach all fluttery and unsettled. I feel more exposed like this than I do without the harness, as if it's a neon sign drawing attention to the fact that my chest and belly are on display.

The rings of the dressing room curtains rattle behind me, and Rhys pokes his head around the fabric. His hair is electric blue this week. "Holy shit."

To read the rest of the bonus scene, sign up for Linden Bell's Very Important Reader newsletter here: bit.ly/angel bonusscene.

SANTINO

Hayden is the golden retriever of his friend group, but his new roommate, Santino, just rubs him the wrong way. Watch sunshine-y Hayden get grumpy as he faces off with his new enemy in the fourth and final The Camboy Network book, *Santino*, bit.ly/santinobm.

THANK YOU

If you've enjoyed *Angel*, please consider recommending it to your friends. Leave a review on social media, your own blog, Amazon, Goodreads, or Bookbub so other MM romance lovers can get to know Angel and Rhys too.

If you would like to stay up to date on future Linden Bell books, join the Very Important Reader mailing list and also receive the exclusive bonus scene! bit.ly/angelbonusscene

You can also follow me on:
Instagram - instagram.com/authorlindenbell
Facebook - facebook.com/authorlindenbell
Amazon - amazon.com/author/lindenbell
Goodreads - goodreads.com/authorlindenbell
Bookbub - bookbub.com/authors/linden-bell

ABOUT LINDEN BELL

Linden Bell writes romances that heat you up and make you smile. Her books are low angst, feel good reads with no third act breakup!

- instagram.com/authorlindenbell
- facebook.com/authorlindenbell
- amazon.com/author/lindenbell
- goodreads.com/authorlindenbell
- bookbub.com/authors/linden-bell

ALSO BY LINDEN BELL

Mars Fitness Series

Where the jocks of Mars Fitness meet the nerds of their dreams.

The Camboy Network Series

When sex on camera turns into love behind the scenes.